A SORT OF TRAITORS

A SORT
OF TRAITORS

NIGEL BALCHIN

COLLINS
ST. JAMES'S PLACE, LONDON
1949

ANYTUS, the accuser of Socrates, laid it as an article of charge and accusation against him that he did withdraw young men from due reverence to the laws and customs of their country ; and that he did profess a dangerous and pernicious Science.

The Advancement of Learning

"MINE eyes are full of tears, I cannot see ;
    And yet salt water blinds them not so much
But they can see a sort of traitors here.
Nay, if I turn mine eyes upon myself,
I find myself a traitor with the rest ;
For I have given here my soul's consent."

King Richard II

I

ABOUT an inch and a half in the middle of the glass tube was now bright orange in the blow-pipe flame. Arthur blew gently into the end of the tube and a perfectly symmetrical bulb expanded. It looked easy and inevitable. Arthur had been blowing glass in the Haughton Laboratory for forty-five years. It was his favourite little joke when demonstrating to students. " Professor Sewell and me came to the Haughton about the same time, him as an undergraduate and me as a lab. boy. Professor Sewell went on and studied physiology and zoology and bio-chemistry and I went on and studied glass. We both learnt a lot since then, gentlemen." Arthur could remember Sir Phillip Lowes and the early work on synthetic amino-acids, and he had made a gas analysis line for Chubb in 1909. He was always rather short with Professor Sewell. In private, he thought him a great man, though not, perhaps, as great a man as Lowes or Chubb.

Pearce came in, carrying a broom, and said, " That monkey's took my cap." Arthur cut off the air so that the blow-pipe flame became long and yellow and smoky. He flicked his dark glasses up on his forehead and slowly twirled his bulb in the cooler flame. " Well, don't let him eat it," he said, without looking up. " He's on a diet."

" Took it clean off as I was sweeping," said Pearce indignantly.

Arthur carefully put down his bulb, sighed, and slid off his stool. He said, " I don't see what you want to wear a cap for in here. Afraid you'll catch cold ? "

They went into the long, rather narrow animal room. There was only one big cage. The rest of the place was occupied by hutches containing rabbits, rats and guinea pigs. Arthur went up to the big cage and said, " Phillips, what you doing with that ? Give it back." The young chimpanzee was sitting at the back of the cage holding the cap in its hand and biting tentatively at its peak. It looked up for a moment and then turned its back, hunched its shoulders and clutched the cap to its chest. Pearce said, " Took it clean off my head. Reached out see Arthur."

Arthur said, " I'd better get Miss Byrne to him."

Lucy Byrne was a dark girl of about twenty-five who looked as though she hadn't slept for a week. She went up to the cage and said, " Oh, *Phillips* ! " very reproachfully.

The chimpanzee turned its head and then, closing its eyes firmly, huddled over the cap again. Lucy said, " All right. It's bribery but . . ." She put her hand in the pocket of the white overall, produced half a biscuit and clicked her tongue. Phillips ambled eagerly over to the bars and put out a hand. Lucy said, " Oh, no. Fair does. Give Pearce his cap first." Phillips looked at the cap and then dropped it disinterestedly on the floor of the cage near the bars. Pearce made a quick grab and seized it. Lucy put the biscuit in the chimpanzee's hand. She said, " He hasn't hurt it, has he ? He never does hurt things."

Marriott looked up as Lucy came in and said, " Get it ? " Lucy said, " Oh, yes. I think he was glad to get rid of it. He always has a conscience when he steals things." Marriott said, " As chimpanzees go, Phillips is a white elephant. What's the point of keeping him if he's too valuable to use ? This is a lab., not a zoo."

" Phillips is all right," said Lucy. " The silly part is keeping him in a cage and having old Pearce free. Phillips is much more intelligent than Pearce. And he's got a nicer nature." She climbed on to her stool. " We'd got to eighty-nine."

A Sort of Traitors

Marriott bent over the Petrie dishes.

"Ninety," he said. "Slight growth. Ninety-one, slight growth. Ninety-two, slight growth. Ninety-three, slight . . . no, half a mo'." He studied it for a few moments. "Ninety-three," he said carefully, "slight growth."

Lucy gave a deep sigh. "I wish you wouldn't do that," she said. "It's so disappointing."

Marriott said, "Ninety-four, slight growth. What's disappointing?"

"When you hesitate like that. It makes me think something exciting's coming like 'no growth' or 'strong growth.'"

"Ninety-five, slight growth. Ninety-six, slight growth. Ninety-seven, slight growth. The trouble with you is that you've got a craving for excitement. Ninety-eight, slight growth. Anything for a change, that's your motto. You had a 'no growth' only two days ago. You want to live in a whirl. Ninety-nine, slight growth. One hundred, slight growth." He straightened up. "And that's the end of batch two."

Lucy said, "How many batches to-day?"

"Five."

"Just be time to get them through and wash up and go?"

"That's about the size of it."

Marriott took his glasses off and looked at her thoughtfully. Without his glasses he suddenly became surprisingly handsome in a fair, pale, transparent-skinned way. He said, "Do you think it's quicker like that than when we both examine and both write?"

"I don't know," said Lucy vaguely.

"The snag is that if we both examine we may use different standards."

Lucy said, "When I say I don't know I really mean I don't care."

Marriott put his glasses on again and said, "Like that, is it?"

9

" Yes. Just like that." She went and looked out of the window with her back to him. She had a habit of crossing her arms and pulling her shoulders forward as if she were cold. " How many does Prof. want done altogether ? "

" Twenty thousand, he said."

" Why twenty thousand ? He'll get all it can possibly tell him out of five."

" Twenty thousand sounds a nice lot. He'd probably like to do a million. If there's nothing showing at five thousand we might see if he'll chuck it. But you can bet something'll turn up in the last couple of hundred and . . ."

" Call it twenty thousand then. We can do about two thousand a month. Reckon a couple of lots going wrong. It makes just about a year."

" That's right."

Lucy said, " There's a tree out there just beginning to bud. It'll put out leaves, and then it'll be spring, and then the leaves will get dusty and it'll be summer, and then they'll fall and it will be autumn, and then it will stay bare and it'll be winter. And then it will begin to bud again, and about then, if we're lucky, we shall finish this."

Marriott said, " Well, what about it ? "

" You don't mind that ? "

" If you mean this is a bloody dull job, of course it is. Particularly since we know the answer's a lemon. But it's only once a week and it's got to be done, hasn't it ? "

" Has it ? "

" Look," said Marriot gently, " you don't want me to do one of Prof.'s lectures on validity, do you ? "

" I do not," said Lucy rather huskily, still looking out of the window. " In fact, at the moment I don't want any part of Prof. at all."

" Well, for God's sake," said Marriott rather irritably, " what's wrong with Prof. ? Maybe he does waste a hell of a lot of time. But it's worth more to you later on to have spent a couple of years here, even messing about like this, than to have spent five with anybody else."

Lucy turned away from the window and began gathering up the Petrie dishes in silence. Marriott sat watching her, making no move to help. After a while he took off his glasses, swallowed, and said, " What you want is more— more fun in your spare time."

She turned and looked at him in silence for a moment. He smiled uncertainly, but she did not smile back.

" What sort of fun ? " she said. " Having my hand held in the back seats at the pictures ? "

Marriott flushed. " Well, why not ? " he said bravely. " What's wrong with having your hand held ? "

" I didn't say there was anything wrong with it."

Dr. Shole came in as they finished collecting the Petrie dishes and said, " How's it going ? "

Marriott said, " Just the same. All slight growths, except about one in every batch. It's a damned slow business."

Shole picked up one of the Petrie dishes and looked at it. He said, " I don't like this ' slight growth ' and ' strong growth ' business. It doesn't really mean anything. I wish we could *measure* something." He peered at the dish with his small, deep-set brown eyes. The gelatine in it showed three small, round, pink patches. Shole said, " You see, I'm not sure that you're justified in calling that *slight* growth. I mean—there's quite an area of it. Would you still call it ' slight ' if there were only one patch ? "

" Yes."

Shole said, " I think I'd better have a word with Prof. about it. There ought to be some way of getting it more accurate than that."

Marriott said, " That's how we agreed to do it."

" Oh, sure. It's not your fault. It's mine. But I'd like to get Prof.'s reaction."

He took a couple of the dishes and went out. Lucy said, " You know what'll happen now ? "

Marriott said, " Yes. Prof.'ll scrap the whole thing and begin again. He always begins again if there's the slightest excuse for it. How many have we done ? "

" About four thousand." Lucy picked up a Petrie dish, poised it, and dropped it carefully on the concrete floor. Surprisingly, it only broke in half.

Marriott said, " Here, steady, Lucy."

She said, " It was only one. I'm entitled to one."

Marriott said, " You're very jumpy, aren't you ? I think you need some leave."

" Leave ? " said Lucy. " Nonsense. When am I being taken to the pictures ? "

Marriott blushed and said, " Anywhen you like. Sooner the better."

Sewell was in his most off-hand mood. Sometimes he would come striding in, looking like a venerable film star, flashing his brilliant, boyish smile at everybody, patting Lucy, prodding Shole in the ribs, throwing out suggestions at a rate of one a minute and good ones at about two an hour. On these occasions one had no doubt that he had slid down the banisters on the way to an enormous breakfast. To-day he came in, nodded curtly to Marriott, didn't look at Lucy, picked up a dish, looked at it for a moment and then said sulkily, " Well ? "

Shole planted himself squarely on his short legs and said, " I don't like it."

There was a rabbit in a cage in the corner. Sewell went over and poked his fingers through the wire at the rabbit and said, " Then why do it ? "

" At present," said Shole calmly, " we're only dividing them into three categories—strong growth, slight growth and no growth."

" Meaning what ? "

" That's the point. Slight growth covers too wide an area."

" Well, what do you want me to do about it ? "

" Do you think it matters ? "

Sewell raised his eyebrows and stroked the top of the rabbit's head with his finger.

" Presumably if the job's worth doing at all it's worth doing properly."

Lucy said, " Isn't the point of the experiment to confirm that there's been no change in infectivity ? "

Sewell turned and looked at Lucy as though noticing her for the first time. He said, " The point of the experiment is to get accurate information. Never mind what you want the answer to be."

Marriott said, " But we already know that the chances are all against . . ."

Sewell said, " If you know all about it, why the hell waste your time on it ? Go to a football match or something."

" The question is," said Shole gently, " whether we can't get some positive measurement."

Sewell sighed. Snatching up a piece of paper, he drew a rough circle. " Look," he said, " this is a Petrie dish. Instead of prodding about all over the gelatine, put your bugs in the middle. If it takes, it'll spread out in a circle. Get a bit of glass with concentric circles. Call the smallest slight growth, the next medium growth, the next strong growth or whatever. All you've got to do is pop it over each dish and read off."

He threw the pencil down and turned away. Shole said, " That's an idea."

Marriott said, " I'm not sure the growth will be regular enough. And of course . . ."

" Of course what ? "

" . . . it'd mean scrapping all we've done because they won't be comparable."

Sewell said, " Well, if they're no good, you've got to scrap them anyhow."

Lucy said bravely, " I'm not sure they are no good. We've spent two months on them and there isn't a sign of anything signficant coming out of it."

Sewell turned away from the rabbit and looked at her with interest. " Two months ? " he said. " Only two months to learn not to start too soon ? It's cheap." He turned to Shole. " You'd better scrap and start again, hadn't you ? "

Shole nodded silently. Sewell was looking at Lucy. " After all," he said gently, " Bill Rocker spent two years on the start of this stuff and at the end of it we threw it all away and started again."

Lucy had turned away and was fiddling with the lid of a Petrie dish. Sewell walked round and stood in front of her. The sulky expression had gone and his eyes were twinkling.

" Don't want to start again ? " he said softly.

" It's not that," she said, not looking up. " It's just that . . ."

Sewell took her by the arm and turned her round towards the door. " Go home," he said, giving her a gentle slap behind. " Go home and come back when you don't feel like murder."

" I don't *want* to go home, Professor Sewell," she said quietly. " I only want to—to get on with whatever we're going to do."

Sewell hesitated and then shrugged his shoulders. " All right." He turned to Shole. " I'd try that central infection idea. It may not work but it's worth having a go."

Sewell sat down in his chair and lit his pipe. His hands were very beautiful and they moved with a sort of self-conscious grace. Everything he did—even the little things —could have been photographed and it would have come out perfectly posed. Sometimes he was a big, handsome, silver-haired old man with the fires still burning brightly ; sometimes, nowadays, he looked haggard and ashy and cold. But he never looked unintentional. He was in a better temper now. He had made a suggestion. He had followed one of his principles—that time wasn't important and that accuracy was. He had touched an attractive woman. Mr. Can't had disappeared and Mr. Can had arrived.

Sewell ran his hand over the beautifully kept silver hair and said, " How much good is that girl ? "

Shole said, " Lucy ? Oh, she's all right. Good kid."

" Not very impressive over that. She didn't give a damn whether what they were doing was any good or not. All she wanted was not to start again."

Shole said, " Well, it is a dull job."

" About ninety-nine per cent. of lab. work is—if you don't relate it to what you're trying to do."

Shole said quietly, " I think she has rather a tough private life."

" Women always have," said Sewell. The idea pleased him. He went and stood by the window, looking at Shole with his brilliant, wide-eyed, youthful grin. " Women are always either in love or not in love. In either case it makes a complicated private life and interferes with their work. She's not in love with young Marriott, is she ? "

" I shouldn't think so."

Sewell said, " And this feeling about time. Men haven't got it. But women are all clock-watchers. Only about thirty years, you see, to have their babies in. And anything which isn't to do with having babies is a waste of time. That's why they're no good to science."

Shole said, " I don't know. They have a certain sort of patience."

" Nonsense," said Sewell. " They're quite good at routine jobs where they don't have to think and can dream about their precious private life. Apart from that the only reasons for using them are that they've got small hands and they're cheap. They've no *real* patience at all. And no principles."

Shole waited a moment and then said, "Have you got through my revise of the paper?"

Sewell nodded.

"What d'you think of it?"

"It frightens me."

"Why?"

"Because I can't see anything wrong with it. And if there isn't anything wrong with it, then it opens up such tremendous possibilities. . . ."

"All of them rather a long way ahead."

"I dare say, but . . ." Sewell suddenly drew himself up to his full height. "In 1925," he said in a curious, formal, lecturer's voice, "I conceived certain ideas about the relationship between bacterial infectivity and virulence. Judd and then Parsons and then Rocker worked on the job for—let's see—ten years, at the end of which everything I had thought had proved to be wrong. Then Jackie and you and I dreamed up the idea of working backwards from the supervirulents. By the way, can you remember exactly how we got on to that?"

Shole shook his head. "I've an idea it all started from something you said to Jackie, but I don't remember what it was."

"Nor do I. Anyhow, Jackie went on. And then the war came, and Jackie died. And then in '44 you got the first immunisation stuff through. And now, unless I'm blind or mad or something, we're on the right track." He shook his head. "It doesn't seem like twenty-four years."

Shole said, "You think we should publish now?"

Sewell hesitated. "I'd like to think it over a bit more. But . . ." He broke off. "My only regret is that Jackie isn't alive."

"I don't quite get you," said Shole patiently. "You *do* intend to publish now?"

" I hate publishing things," said Sewell simply. " Once one publishes . . . Oh, you know how I feel."

" I do indeed," said Shole with mild bitterness.

" I've been criticised and criticised for hanging on to things too long. But it's better to do that than to speak before you're sure." He ran his hand over his hair. " You think we ought to publish now ? "

" Yes," said Shole briefly.

" You're probably right. Of course I can see that it's important to you. You'll walk into the Royal Society on it."

" I wasn't thinking so much of that," said Shole, un-offended. " But what this job wants now is a mass of field work all over the world. The war gave us a lot of stuff we shouldn't have got otherwise. But there's still a hell of a lot of work to do before anybody prevents an epidemic in China or Chile by using our stuff."

" Yes." Sewell suddenly smiled his most juvenile smile. " One gets old and over-cautious, you know, Freddy."

" I suggest," said Shole gently, " that we should spend another week working over that paper again and that then, unless we find some definite reason against it, we should publish."

Sewell said, " All right. Agreed." But he said it rather huffily. Shole had not smiled back when he made the joke about being old.

Arthur came in and said, " Mrs. Peach outside to see you."

Sewell said, " Mab ? What in the name of God does *she* want ? Bring her in, Arthur."

Mab was about as like her father as a woman of thirty-five can be to a man of sixty-odd. She, too, was big and handsome and grey-eyed and quick-moving. She said, " Hullo, Lucas," with a bright but slightly wary smile, and he said, " Why, hullo, Mab," with exactly the same intona-tion, the same smile and the same wariness. Mab thrust a small box into his hands, and said, " Many happy returns, darling."

Sewell said, " Good God—is it my birthday ? "

Mab said, " What's the origin of that, Lucas ? Pretending that you don't remember it's your birthday ? "

" To make it clear that if other people had forgotten you wouldn't be hurt," said Sewell at once. He looked at the parcel. " What is this ? "

" Pipe."

Sewell said, " What a lovely pipe. Just what I wanted," and put it down unopened on the bench.

" Rather caddish not to open it, Lucas."

" My dear," said Sewell, " I can open it, gloat over it, or even smoke it when you're gone. While you're here, I prefer to look at you. After all, it's not a pleasure that I get very often."

" I know, darling," said Mab. " Usually you manage to pretend you're out." She looked at him thoughtfully. " You're looking well for your age."

" So are you," said Sewell. " Just a trifle stouter, perhaps."

Mab closed her eyes. " In many ways, Lucas," she said, " you are, and always have been, the foulest of God's creatures. Why I should spend money buying you a rather good pipe I don't see."

Sewell chuckled. " It's really quite absurd that we don't see more of each other," he said. " I always enjoy your company, my dear."

" And I yours. But in small doses, Lucas. Just about once a year for an hour. Then I love you very much."

Sewell said, " How's your husband ? "

" Ralph ? Oh, he's very well."

" I didn't know he was ever very well. Last time I saw him he was suffering from nervous belly-aches."

" He still does. It's worry. Hadn't you better come and dine ? "

Sewell said, " Are you going to stay married to him indefinitely ? "

" Why not ? "

" It just seems an odd thing to do. For you."

Mab said, " You're a bad old man, Lucas, in some ways. A mischievous old man."

" My dear Mab," said Sewell, " I don't care a damn what you do as long as you're happy." He looked at her steadily with the fine grey eyes. She looked back for a moment in silence and then turned her head away with a slight frown and said, " Cut it out, Lucas."

" Cut what out, my dear ? "

" Worrying about my happiness. We both know whose happiness you worry about."

For a moment he was offended. Then, with a slight effort, he smiled. " All right, my dear. Have it your own way."

Mab was relieved. She said, " I'm sorry, darling, but you mustn't do that stuff on me. It spoils the game. How's work ? "

Sewell squinted at his pipe. " As the result of a life of mischievous selfishness," he said, " I am shortly going to publish something that should eventually save about half a million lives a year." He looked up and grinned the juvenile grin. " Always supposing it doesn't turn out to be nonsense next time I look at it."

*   *   *   *   *

Marriott said, " What *is* the point of messing about here if you feel rotten ? I can do it perfectly well."

Lucy shut the door of the sterilizer and said, " Stop being nice about it. I'm just in a thoroughly bitchy mood and the nicer everybody is to me the bitchier I shall be."

" I don't like you to look like that," said Marriott simply.

She turned and looked at him. Normally if she did that

he flushed, but this time he just gazed back steadily and calmly with a slight frown.

Lucy smiled. " All right. Then I'll stop."

" Good. And have a drink after, eh ? "

She hesitated. " Might do, if we get away early. Mustn't be long, though.

Shole came in and said, " Look, folks, I'm sorry about that stuff with the Prof., but I think it's the right thing. How do you feel about it ? "

" Furious," said Lucy brightly. " But so what ? "

" His glass gadget won't work," said Marriott. " But we might think of something better."

Shole said, " I've just been talking to him and I think he's going to publish the paper."

They both stopped short. Marriott said, " He *is* ? "

" Yes. Unless he gets cold feet again."

" When ? "

" As soon as he's looked it over again."

There was a moment's silence. " I thought you'd like to know," said Shole rather awkwardly and went out.

Marriott took off his glasses. " When that paper is published," he said casually, " I shall kiss you. As a celebration."

" By the time Prof. gets around to publishing we shall both be too old for that sort of thing," said Lucy without turning.

Marriott's face was bright pink. " I have long thought," he said even more casually, " that it would be nice to kiss you, but somehow I never have. Now I shall."

Lucy scraped some gelatine out of a Petrie dish and said, " Sex in the laboratory went out with H. G. Wells."

" It didn't," said Marriott, " it certainly didn't. You ought to have been in Poyning's lab. It was a hotbed. An absolute hotbed."

" I know. You've told me before." She looked at him thoughtfully. " I'm glad it *is* going to be published for Doc.

Shole's sake. He's so damned good and just because he doesn't tell everybody so, nobody realizes it."

Marriott put his glasses on and said, " I quite agree. Shole's all right. Not brilliant of course, but quite all right."

*   *   *   *   *

Mab sat on the high stool with her long legs crossed and her hands clasped round her knee. Sewell looked at her with approval, as a woman might look with approval at her own reflection in a mirror. He said, " Have you seen your mother lately ? "

Mab flicked the ash off her cigarette and looked at it thoughtfully. " Saw her about a month ago."

" How was she ? "

" Exactly as usual."

" Happy ? "

" I tell you—she was exactly as usual. She's got a new psychiatrist who's a genius. That was the main item. As a matter of fact, he does sound quite good. Anyhow, he's told her there's nothing the matter with her except that she's bored and hasn't got enough to do."

" Will she believe that ? "

" Oh, yes. She'd believe anything he told her at the moment. But it doesn't really make much difference. You see, before she used to have headaches and nervous prostration and so on and think she was ill and be pathetic, whereas now she still has it all and says it's purely psychological and is brave instead."

Sewell said, " Yes. That's very characteristic. Your mother always liked a good formula."

" You know, she's rather pathetic about you," said Mab reflectively. " Much less bitter than she used to be. I can remember when you were just Satan and that was the end of it. But she seems to have got past that. Nowadays she's often quite funny about it. And rather touchingly humble in a way. When she tells me stories about you, you're

21

always ' The Genius ' and she's ' The Duffer.' ' Of course, dear, the Duffer didn't realise that that was important, but when the Genius came home there was a holy row.' It's half satire, of course. But the other half isn't."

" Ought I to go and see her ? "

Mab looked at his earnest face with mild dislike. " Not if you're going to look like that," she said. " Why should you anyhow ? You don't want anything from her."

" With all humbleness," said Sewell sarcastically, " I was wondering if she wanted anything from me."

Mab crushed out her cigarette. " Of course she does, but it's nothing you'd be likely to give her. Or anybody else." After a moment she said quickly, " Why did you ever get married, Lucas ? "

Sewell said, " Why does anybody ever get married ? There's no case for it."

" And to Mummy, of all people, who's so soft that she's practically liquid ? " She shook her head. " I've never quite forgiven you that. If you'd chosen somebody who could fight back it would have been different. But Mummy was too easy. And you must have known it."

Sewell said, " My dear, when we were married I was twenty-six and your mother was a very attractive woman."

" And that was enough reason for—for taking candy from a kid ? "

Sewell got up and walked over to the window. Speaking over his shoulder he said, " I'm sorry to see a woman of your intelligence indulging in gross over-simplifications."

" Am I ? "

" Yes. You're trying to explain me as just straightforwardly and completely selfish. I hope I'm more complicated than that. Not *better*, you understand. Just a little less easily dismissible."

" I don't think you're selfish."

" No ? "

" No. I think it's the wrong word. All I think is that you

shouldn't have married Mummy or had children when you were already married to something else and had children by it every year." She leant forward. "You see, Lucas, if you'd just been a proper scientist and worn thick spectacles and forgotten to put on your trousers and been a dim, gallant, unambitious failure, obviously with no thought for anything but your work, nobody would have minded. Mummy would have loved it, for one. But you look like you look, and you go around being very personal and emotional and deliberately attractive and altogether human, and people believe there's something there for them. And when they find you haven't got it in the shop—or at least not for them—they're hurt and disappointed. You're not selfish. You're just completely irresponsible over your dealings with people."

Sewell waited a moment and then said, "Is that all?"

Mab said, "Yes, darling. Except that it's all very Freudian really, because I thought you were wonderful and couldn't get what I wanted from you. And I was cross with you about Mummy. The female freemasonry." She slid off the bench. "I must go now."

Sewell said slowly, "I think most of that is true. But there's a reason for it. Nobody's got more than a certain amount of sincerity or scruple, and so on. And I've always needed all mine on the job. I stayed married for fifteen years and then when I found it was interfering with my work I stopped, because I happen to think that my work's more important than your mother or you. Or me." He looked at her with a slight frown. "I *think* that's true, Mab," he said. "I *think* I've thought of it as being more important than me."

There was a moment's silence.

"I should like to know whether that's your impression," he said rather formally. "It's rather important."

"Darling, how should I know?"

"Of course you don't know," said Sewell angrily. "You

23

don't know anything. But you're prepared to talk fast enough about the other side of it. All I'm asking is whether you've ever known me cheat on my job? Or let it down? Or put myself or any other bloody thing in front of it?"

" No. And if it's any satisfaction to you, I've never heard of any one who has. You have been faithful, Cynara, after your fashion. Or if you haven't, the news hasn't got round to me."

" Thank you," said Sewell. " Now you can go away. Thank you for the pipe. Lovely pipe. Just what I wanted."

Mab said, " How about coming to dine?"

" That would be nice. Some evening, eh? When I've got this paper off my chest?"

Mab took his hand in hers and looked at it for a moment. Then she gave it a slight squeeze and released it.

" That's right, darling. Some evening. Just ring up."

II

IT was muggily warm in the downstairs bar and there
was a vacant table in the corner. The place smelt of
pine disinfectant.

Lucy said, " Can I have lemon-squash ? I mustn't be
long and I can't drink beer quickly."

Marriott said, " You can't come out to have a drink and
then drink lemon-squash. It's unco-operative." He went
away to the bar and came back with a pint tankard of beer
and a gin and lime. He put the drinks down on the table
and said, " Lend me threepence."

Lucy opened her handbag, rooted among the mass of
coppers and produced a two-shilling piece. She said, " I
haven't got threepence. You'll have to have this."

" All right," he said with relief. " Remind me about it
to-morrow." He went back to the bar.

Lucy glanced at her watch. It was just six o'clock. A
quarter of an hour would do it, and that would only mean
getting home at quarter to seven instead of at half-past six.

Marriott came back. As he sat down he said, " You won't
let me forget to pay that back, will you ? "

Lucy smiled at him and said, " No. You can give me
your watch as security if you like."

Marriott said, " That's an idea," and started to take it off.

" Don't be an ass," she said, raising her glass. " Cheers."

" Cheers." He filled his mouth with beer and swallowed
it, in two distinct movements. " Very good beer here. Is
yours all right ? "

" Fine," said Lucy. The gin and lime had an odd
background taste of Parrish's Food. There was a moment's
silence.

25

" Why don't you ever come to these Junior Research do's ? " said Marriott.

" Too busy. Are they any good ? "

" There's one this evening. Why not stop being busy and come along ? "

Lucy took another sip of Parrish's Food and said, " Can't. I'd like to, but it's not on. I must be home by quarter to." She put her glass down and noticed with relief that it was half-empty. " I've never been sure what the Junior Research does. Just coffee and buns and the Meaning of Science ? "

" It's a bit like that. But quite good. Some very good people come. Booth's giving a paper to-night."

" On what ? "

" It's one of a series on the scientist's position in the modern world. It ought to be rather good because Booth's a physicist to end all physicists, and he thinks science is a branch of physics."

" Most physicists do. Particularly since the atomic bomb."

" Oh, well," said Marriott a trifle too quickly, " I suppose it's their turn. The nineteenth century biologists had all the fun of thinking they'd finished off God, and now the physicists are busy finishing off civilisation and feeling hell's own chaps about it."

He drank some beer and reflected that it still wasn't right. The idea was there, but the words wanted polishing. Lucy was looking across the room and smiling to herself. He suddenly realised that at any moment she would say she must go, and he hadn't got anywhere.

" You know, what you said to-day about sex in the laboratory being out of date is bunkum. You speak, if I may say so, from the depths of your virgin experience."

" Probably," said Lucy.

" Practically all physicists have satyriasis or nymphomania and chemists are absolutely goat-like."

" That's because they're not dealing with the facts of life.

It'd be different if they spent half their time in our animal room."

Lucy finished her drink and said, " I must go."

" No," said Marriott quickly. " You said you needn't be back till quarter to seven and it'll only take you twenty minutes."

" Half an hour."

" Nonsense. Besides—I want to know when we're going to the pictures."

Lucy said, " Oh—sometime." She turned and smiled at him. He felt the dark eyes searching his face behind the smile and his hand went instinctively to his glasses. He took them off and blinked sharply to re-focus. He said, " I've always wondered what you do with yourself in the evenings. I suspect you of a double life."

" No," said Lucy rather bitterly. " Barely a single one, I assure you." She was still looking closely at his face, as though not realising that she was doing so. He found it embarrassing and looked away.

" Well," he said with dignity, " I don't want to be—to be importunate. But unless you have more interesting fish to fry I wish you *would* come sometime." He leaned towards her and said with mock solemnity, " Miss Byrne—is there Another ? "

" Of course there is," said Lucy. " Up to a point, anyhow."

" Oh," said Marriott, slightly disconcerted. " What point ? "

" It's all rather complicated. I'll tell you about it some- time. Anyhow, it takes up a lot of time and energy."

" Is it also the reason why you often look half-dead ? " said Marriott.

" Maybe," said Lucy indifferently. " Anyhow, I *must* go." She got up. " Don't you come. You haven't finished your drink."

" Doesn't matter. I don't want it. What I really like is

27

two thirds of a pint of beer. I wish they'd sell one two-thirds of a pint."

He followed her up the stairs. She was wearing a check-patterned tweed skirt and he was acutely and miserably conscious of the movement of the pattern as they climbed. When they reached the street Lucy said, " I want a Number 11 bus and I want it quickly." She shivered and hunched her shoulders forward. " It's damned cold."

Marriott swallowed and said, " Let me get this straight. The existence of Another doesn't wash out our going to the pictures ? "

" I don't see why it should," she said slowly. " If we can ever fit it in. It's very nice of you to ask me." She turned and smiled. " And thank you very much for the drink. You were quite right. It was a good thing."

As the bus drew away he saw her lurching forward towards the front of it and a vacant strap. There were no empty seats. He waved and she waved back. Marriott turned away, glancing at his watch. It was twenty past six and the meeting of the Junior Research Association was not until eight o'clock. He had an hour and a half to fill in, but that included having a meal. He reflected that it was lucky that Lucy hadn't had threepence, otherwise he wouldn't have had a bean. There was a perfectly good ten-shilling note in his digs, and he considered going home to get it. But that had to last the next day and he would have to repay Lucy's two shillings. He decided that the one and ninepence left in his pocket would have to do. The bus to and from the meeting would be fourpence and coffee would be another fourpence. It looked as though he would have to have supper for a bob.

*　　*　　*　　*　　*

The Number 11 bus became involved in one traffic jam in the Strand and another in Victoria Street. The clock at

Victoria said quarter to seven. There was no chance now that Ivor wouldn't notice that she was late, but Lucy decided calmly and quietly that it had been right to go and have a drink with Bob Marriott. If one was going to do a decent job for Ivor, then it was essential to stop doing it every now and again whatever it cost. Otherwise it was untrue—something that one didn't feel.

It was only five to seven after all when she let herself into the house and climbed up to the third floor. Ivor was sitting in his chair with the reading table across him. He greeted her with a bright smile and said, " Hallo, darling," in an almost caressing voice that made her heart sink. She went across and kissed him and said, " Hallo, I'm late. Sorry." As she kissed his forehead she realised that it was damp, and that told her all she wanted to know. But there was nothing to do but wait for it. She took the hankerchief out of his pocket and wiped his forehead. She said " Comb ?" " If you please," said Ivor very politely.

As she combed back the rather long, black, smooth hair she glanced down at Trevelyan's *Social History* which lay open before him. " How are you getting on with that ? "

Ivor said, " These two pages are admirable. But it would be nice to go on to another soon. I've been reading these for about an hour now."

She saw it coming but there was nothing to be done about it. She said, " But you can turn over, Ivor."

He smiled at her brightly and said, " No. I'm afraid I've lost both my arms. The left one is gone as you see, and if you look closely you will see that this one on the right is artificial."

" But you could turn over all right this morning, darling," said Lucy uselessly. " Have you lost the trick ? "

He said, " I expect that's it. I've lost the trick." He glanced at the tin alarm clock. " These people believe in getting their money's worth out of you."

Lucy answered the question without hesitation. " Oh, I

wasn't late at the lab. I went and had a drink with Bob Marriott. It was rather nice."

There was a moment's pause. With a movement that involved the whole side of his body, Ivor moved his artificial arm on to his knee. " Good," he said gently. " I wish you'd do that sort of thing more often, darling. It isn't good for you to come straight back after a day's work to this."

Lucy looked at the brilliant blue eyes staring at her out of the sunken face. He smiled at her, showing those lovely, white, even teeth. She took no notice of the smile. " It was a damned selfish thing to do," she said. " But I wanted to do it. You must try not to mind when I do these things." She turned away. " Now the next thing is food. Are you reasonably comfortable if I go and get it ? "

" Of course you wanted to do it," said Ivor in a low voice. " And in the name of God why shouldn't you go and have a drink ? "

Lucy said, " Would you like to go on reading or will you have the radio ? "

" Don't bother. I'll come and watch you cook. It gives me a chance to talk and I like to talk occasionally."

" All right," she said hopelessly. She moved the table aside and with a quick, practised heave Ivor rose to his feet.

He was only just over six feet, but his thinness and the empty left sleeve made him look fantastically tall. Lucy went into the tiny kitchenette and he came and leant against the door-post.

Lucy said, " It seems that we can have baked beans or baked beans. Sorry."

" You keep on saying you're sorry," said Ivor. There was only the faintest trace of the Irishman in his voice. " Why should you be sorry ? You can't help the country's food supply position." He shook his head. " You take your responsibilities too seriously, darling."

Lucy rooted in a drawer for a tin opener.

" Do I ? " she said. " Let's see, I heat these *before* I open them, don't I ? "

Ivor said, " Of course you do. It's like a breath of fresh air when you go and do something just because you want to—like stopping off to have a drink with what's-his-name."

" Bob Marriott," said Lucy. " Man in the lab. Boy in the lab. really. Actually age twenty-four. Mental age about seventeen. But quite nice." She lit the gas. Her hands were shaking. This was always the worst bit, when one knew it was coming but it wouldn't get started. Like wanting to be sick and not being able to.

Ivor said nothing. She turned and he was still standing leaning against the door-post with that very sweet smile. She smiled back and said desperately, " He suggested that we should go to the pictures and hold hands. That's the sort of person he is."

Ivor laughed and said, " That's the sort of person we all are, darling. I hope you accepted."

Lucy put the saucepan on the gas with the tin in it. " I said I thought that would be very nice."

Ivor was still chuckling. " Of course," he said happily. " And what a pleasant change for you to have a hand to hold." He waited for a moment and then said in an odd, brittle voice, " I said, ' What a pleasant change for you to have a hand to hold.' That was quite a good joke. When I make as good a joke as that you might laugh."

Always, at that stage, there was the wild desire to turn and say, " Ivor—don't do it—it isn't worth it—you'll hurt yourself." But she knew better than that now, and she began to cut slices of bread without even looking at him.

" Because after all," said Ivor rather breathlessly, " a man who's got hands—two real hands—can do a lot of things with them besides hold yours. Even in a comparatively public place like the back of a cinema, for example, he can . . ." He was breathing very hard now. " And of course you want these things, don't you, darling ?

It would be, as you say, very nice. Well, why the hell not ?
You're young and attractive. Why hang around here being
bored and disgusted ? What good do you think it's doing ?
I could go in somewhere and get every care and attention
—far better attention than I get now. And it won't be for
long anyhow. . . ." His voice cracked. Lucy waited, but the
tears didn't come. She took the toast out from under the
grill and said in a matter-of-fact voice, " When I want to
go I'll tell you so and go. Till then, why worry ? "

" That's right," said Ivor jerkily. " The day that you
think it would be nice to get rid of me you'll pack me up in
a parcel and put a label on it and post it somewhere. D'you
think I don't know that ? And until then you'll stay around
feeling noble and grand and self-sacrificing. Except when
it suits your book to do something else. . . ."

When the food was ready, she carried it to the table
and said, " Come on. Supper." Ivor was still standing
in the doorway. The tears had come now, and she went
over and wiped them off his cheeks and said, " Come on,"
again.

Ivor said childishly, " I don't want the bloody stuff."

But when she put an arm round him and guided him to
his chair he did not resist. Lucy cut up the toast and beans
into small pieces and put a forkful to his mouth. His lower
jaw was trembling violently. He took the food in and
chewed it miserably and feebly, but he took it, and she knew
that it would be all right now.

Suddenly Ivor said politely, " Do you mind wiping my
eyes again ? " She did so and he said, " I think what we
really need is a change of organisation. This business of
their bringing me back here from the Centre is a mistake.
It would be far better if I stayed there till you fetched
me."

Lucy took a big, rather shaky breath and said, " Well,
we can very easily do that. I've always told you we could."

" It would take you out of your way."

A Sort of Traitors

" Only ten minutes."

" There's no real reason why I shouldn't come home by myself. I could have a season ticket in a case sewn on my jacket or something."

Lucy said, " Bit tricky in the rush hour, darling. People barge one so. I'd rather fetch you."

" We could try it. You could come, but you could pretend you weren't with me and see how I got on."

" That'd be rather fun." It might slip back—there might be more to come before the evening was over. But it looked as though the gin and lime was paid for.

* * * * *

By half-past seven the waitress decided that Marriott had had quite enough space-time for a cup of coffee and two sandwiches and came and gave him his check pointedly. He folded up the copy of *Nature* which was stamped " Haughton Laboratory. Not to be taken away," and wandered out into the Strand. As he walked slowly into Aldwych he felt curiously detached from the people scurrying all around him. It was a pleasant, peaceful feeling. He suddenly remembered that the Molecular Theory came to Kekulé when riding on a bus. It was not difficult to see how, when you looked at people and the way they grouped themselves. A young man was coming along the pavement with a girl on each arm. Clearly a divalent male atom, forming a molecule with two monovalent female atoms. Formula MF_2. But was the female atom always monovalent ? There was this business of Lucy. From what she had said, it looked as though there might be a molecule with the formula M_2F.

He smiled at the pleasant possibilities of the scientific fancy—a smile that was carefully a little wry. The young scientist on his way to a meeting of research workers, considering his mistress in terms of valencies. The layman would find that a curious idea. He looked at the assorted laymen who filled the pavements outside the theatres and was profoundly glad not to be a layman.

The Junior Research Association had a pleasantly flexible membership. In theory it was for those who had not yet taken research degrees, but there was always a sprinkling of Lecturers and Readers, and occasionally even a Professor. They were not exactly members, but they came. Having come, they were found sitting modestly in the very back row, and were only persuaded with great difficulty to sit on the platform, and with even greater difficulty to speak in the discussion. But somebody always managed to persuade them.

It was a bigger audience than usual. By the time Marriott arrived about forty people were standing about in groups drinking coffee, and the room was blue with smoke. Marriott went and took a cup of coffee and dropped his threepence in the saucer. Root was just in front of him looking discontentedly at the saccharine. Marriott said, " Hullo, Root," and Root said, " Hullo. Why in the hell can't we have some sugar at these things ? " He took a tablet of saccharine and dropped it into his coffee, looking at Marriott as though it was all his fault. He was an enormously bulky young man with a shock of fair hair and very thick glasses.

Marriott said, " Your prof.'s got a good audience."

" The bastard," said Root moodily. He seemed to be in a very bad temper. " Why the hell should I have to come here and listen to Booth ? Don't I get enough of it every day ? "

" Is he going to say anything worth saying ? "

" He'll say he's wonderful, of course. He always does."

Marriott touched him warningly on the arm. Professor Booth was coming up behind him with an empty coffee cup. Booth said to no one in particular, " Do you think I could have another three penn'orth ? Very thirsty."

34

Root said cordially, " Here you are, sir," and turned and gave him a full cup.

Booth said, " Oh, hallo, Percy. I didn't know *you* were here. No, no—I'll pay. Here . . ."

Root said, " You're not allowed to. Against the rules."

The J.R.A. was a free and easy affair. Marriott gulped and said, " Are you going to flay the biologists to-night, sir ? "

Booth looked at him blankly for a moment and then remembered that the J.R.A. was a free and easy affair, and smiled and said, " I'm going to flay all of us. You a biologist ? "

" Yes. I'm in the Haughton."

" Oh, yes. How's Professor Sewell ? "

Marriott said, " He's in great form."

Booth turned away saying, " Well, give him my regards," over his shoulder.

Root looked moodily round the room and said, " I wish these old hacks like Pearson and Ives wouldn't come. What the hell's the use of a Junior show if they're going to push in ? Nobody dares open his mouth—at least, nobody from their departments. Do you remember that chap who said Ives was talking bunkum at a meeting last winter ? Well, he's gone from Ritter's lab. Ives worked him out."

Marriott said, " Thank God no one else from the Haughton ever comes." He had just been wishing that there were a few more people there whom he knew. But he did not want to seem less cynical than Root. At the J.R.A. one was always bitter and disillusioned over the coffee.

The Chairman led the way on to the small platform. He was a tall young man with a pale, frozen face. He had been made Chairman because, though he never spoke if he could possibly avoid it, he always appeared to be completely calm, and could stand silently drinking coffee beside any guest of the evening, however distinguished, without a trace of nervousness. Professor Booth sat at his right hand, darting quick, appraising glances at the audience. He was a distinguished younger-school physicist, and if he hadn't actually been involved in the Atomic Bomb project he had written several forceful and authoritative letters to the press about it. He was just in a transition stage between the well-groomed and ill-kempt schools of physics, and wore an excellently cut suit over an old sports shirt and a distressing knitted wool tie.

The remaining four seats on the platform were all occupied by protesting senior scientists, so the committee perched on the edge of the platform at the sides. It always did. As they took their seats Root whispered, " Yo-ho ! This'll start something. They've put Pearson on the platform and left Ives in the audience. I'll bet you a bob Ives will be gone in ten minutes."

The Chairman rose and said grudgingly, " Ladies and gentlemen. You all know the subject of this evening's paper. It is the third in our series on the Scientist's Place in the Modern World, and it is given by Professor Booth. Professor Booth." He sat down, aloof and pale.

The speaker rose. Three visitors clapped and stopped clapping quickly. Booth raised his long nose as though trying to smell his audience and said that he was honoured at being asked to address the J.R.A., but didn't look particularly overcome by the honour. The committee, sitting on the edge of the platform, alternated uncomfortably between screwing its necks round towards the speaker, and sitting with its backs to him.

*　　*　　*　　*　　*

" One becomes very tired of the statement that this is the Age of Science. Every age has been an Age of Science, and the intelligent ruler has always realised it. That brilliant scoundrel Cesare Borgia employed Leonardo da Vinci as a military engineer ; and Napoleon took on his expedition to Egypt a complete scientific establishment. Science is no more, and no less, than systematised knowledge. These men were intelligent enough to know, as were some of our military commanders in the last war, that if their plans were to succeed they must command the finest intelligences and the widest knowledge available."

A spectacled girl with straight black hair, sitting in the second row, was scribbling hard. Booth's eye fell on her and he paused for a few seconds till her head came up expectantly.

" But though men like Borgia and Buonaparte placed some value on men of science, that value, in practice, was not high. The scientist was regarded as a specialised craftsman—rather like a superior carpenter or stonemason—and infinitely inferior to both the politician and the soldier. Napoleon created plenty of Princes of This and Dukes of That. But one finds no savants amongst the Roll Call of the Empire. One has no doubt that Cesare Borgia regarded himself as a much greater man than the mere technical employee, Leonardo." Professor Booth leant forward and thrust out his chin until only the nostrils of the long nose were visible. " And this is the vital point—one also has no doubt that Leonardo agreed with him." He paused for a moment and stood looking at the back of the hall. Dr. Ives was tiptoeing silently towards the door with an apologetic smile. Root whispered, " That's a bob you owe me."

" Now that idea of the relative value and importance of Leonardo and Cesare Borgia seems funny to-day. But is the position really so different in our own world ? After all, in those days the idea that men were great by reason of birth was generally held. But we live, or are supposed to live in a democracy, where a man's worth should be estimated by what he contributes to society. In considering the proper place of Science in the world to-day, our first question must therefore be ' What is the value of its social contribution ? What place does it *earn* by its efforts ? ' "

37

Root muttered, " It's coming. Booth worked for six days and created the world. So he took Sunday off. That'll be it."

Marriott frowned slightly and shook his head to silence Root. His eyes were on the speaker.

" Let us therefore try looking around us at what we call ' progress '—at what distinguishes the world as we know it from the world of the past—and asking ourselves who brought about these changes ? Whose brains devised them and made them possible ? The politicians ? The soldiers ? Or the chairmen of boards and corporations and companies ? Hardly." He looked slowly round at his audience and said quietly, " Surely they were made possible, ladies and gentlemen, by your scientific predecessors ? And if so, surely you should consider the proper place of the scientist in the modern world from the standpoint that the modern world is largely his creation, and that its future progress is largely in his hands ? " He paused and stood for a moment in silence. Nobody coughed. " I need hardly point out to *this* audience," said the Professor with a sly smile, " that the material rewards offered to the scientist are hardly in keeping with this position. . . ." He waited for the laugh to subside and then went on with sudden fierce seriousness. " But that doesn't matter. I can safely say that if any man in this room had taken money or social position as his aim in life, he wouldn't be here. The point is rather that the scientist is not only still paid a mere craftsman's wages, but that he is still regarded *and regards himself* as a mere craftsman, whose knowledge and intelligence and trained habits of thought may not be employed outside a narrow specialist field. He is there to speak when he is spoken to—to advise some Solon, whose chief claim to power is that he could persuade an ignorant electorate to vote for him." He leant forward like an excited pointer. " Ladies and gentlemen, as young research workers, you have in your hands the making of blueprints for the future of civilisation. But realise that, unless there is a marked change in the position of the

38

scientist, no one will give you one atom of power or responsibility for carrying them out. They will apply the
products of your brains. But they will resist bitterly any
suggestion that you should have any say in the application.
Unless you people face the vastness of your responsibilities,
throw off the habit of silence and retirement which is the
scientist's curse, and insist that the scientist's influence in
the world shall be in proportion to his contribution, you will
continue to live in a world run by children for children.
Take the development of sub-atomic physics. . . ." With
a sigh that was just audible, half-pleasure, half-resignation,
the audience settled back in its seats to take the development of sub-atomic physics.

* * * * *

The clock at the back of the room chimed the half-hour
with sudden and startling sweetness. Booth's eyes flickered
up to it. He picked up his single small page of notes and
began to fold it carefully like a man folding a five-pound
note. " Don't think that anything I have said is urging you
to seek or court power for any personal reason. We are not
career politicians. And in particular, don't think that I am
urging that Cabinets should consist entirely of scientific
super-men. The scientist has his characteristic failings and
limitations, as has every other type of professional man. But
I submit that they are no greater than those of the lawyer,
the business man, the economist and all the other groups
from which our leaders are regularly drawn. Let us by all
means practise humility, and admit our own failings with
frankness and objectivity. But there comes a time when
men must, in all modesty and humbleness, face their
responsibilities towards humanity, and when not to do so is
false modesty and laziness. Science, by not insisting on its
rightful place in the social organisation, has denied civilisation the full and proper use of its gifts. Don't let us over-
estimate ourselves. But with the objectivity that our training

has given us, let us measure what we have to offer against the contribution of other men and calmly, firmly and with dignity assert our right to use our little wisdom to the full. To do more is conceit. To do less is a betrayal of our trust."

Booth sat down. Under cover of the applause Root said, " To-morrow I shall go calmly, firmly and with dignity and assert that what I've been doing for the last three months is a bloody waste of time."

" It was rather a good paper, though," said Marriott. " That wanted saying."

" Saying? It's been *said* often enough. What it wants now is *doing*. And that's another thing again."

* * * * *

As they were coming out of the hall they saw Fines. Fines was tall, slim, languid, and rather gigolo-like. Marriott said, " Good meeting, I thought." Fines looked down at him with his eyelids drooping and said, " Did you? I thought it was one of the most irresponsible papers I'd ever heard."

" Why? "

" Laddie," said Fines wearily, " did you look around you when Booth was burbling? Did you look at this bunch who make the blueprints of the future of civilisation—these people who're going to assert themselves and insist that they shall all be in the Cabinet? No? Then you should have done."

" I don't get you. He didn't say that. And anyhow, what have their faces got to do with it? "

Fines said, " I don't know if these men will frighten the enemy, but by God, sir, they frighten me." He took down his coat and looked at Root and Marriott under his drooping eyelids.

" I think you will find," he said in his delicate voice, " that men with an urge for power nearly always begin by recommending the stupid, the incapable and the ignorant to assert themselves and claim their rights. Move one of the born demagogue's gambit. Good night."

A Sort of Traitors

When he had gone Marriott said, " Booth would approve of Leslie Fines. There's no false modesty about *him*." The bitter thing came again and he added childishly, " Thank God I didn't go to Oxford or Cambridge. The old school tie gang can never see that science . . ."

" I shouldn't have said that modesty was the thing that was wrong with scientists, anyway," said Root. " A more conceited bunch than our staff you couldn't find."

" He didn't quite mean ' modest ' in that way. He was talking about accepting one's responsibilities. There's nothing conceited about doing that."

It was only just after ten, so Marriott walked home. Apart from Fines he had enjoyed the meeting, and Fines didn't matter. He nearly always enjoyed the J.R.A., though it was fashionable to pretend that it was a bore. A man and a girl came by, arm in arm, and Marriott remembered with a slight shock that before the meeting he had been thinking of the men and women on the pavements as molecules. That, of course, was the danger—the cool, cynical, amused, detached, scientific attitude with no sense of responsibility. He looked at the faces of the people he met. Most of them looked rather stupid, and it warmed him towards them. They were so very helpless. He had always been proud of being a scientist, ever since the day at school when he had first come top in chemistry. But it had never before been this serious, responsible, objective pride that half-frightened him. There was no doubt about it, Booth had said something that rang a bell.

A girl was walking slowly and with purposeful vagueness along the top of Southampton Row. Marriott saw her and crossed to the other side of the street in plenty of time. Something about the way she moved reminded him of Lucy, and he reflected that it was a great pity that Lucy hadn't been at the meeting to hear Booth talk about responsibility. She was rather inclined to think of her job as just a job.

III

SEWELL examined the U-tube carefully. It had two absorption bulbs on each leg and a T-piece fused into the bottom. Sewell said, "Looks all right. Probably won't work, but's worth trying."

"That's how I was told to make it," said Arthur rather huffily.

"Oh, yes. It's a beautiful job. But then you always do beautiful jobs, Arthur."

"Yes, and when I've done them they get smashed or thrown away and it's something different that's wanted. I know." Arthur sighed. "Well, it won't be long now, that's one thing," he said grimly. He took a length of glass rod, measured it carefully and cut it off to length with a file.

Sewell lit his pipe and perched himself on the bench. "What won't be long?"

"Before I'm out of it. Six months. That's all I've got to do."

"What d'you mean?" said Sewell, puzzled.

"Six months before I retire, sir. Forty-five years I shall have done, come next autumn."

"You mean—you're really thinking of going?"

"I don't have any option," said Arthur happily. "There's a retiring age fixed. After that you're too old."

Sewell frowned. "Yes, but . . . look here, you can't go off like that, Arthur. The place wouldn't be the same without you. I could probably fix an extension. . . ." He paused and then added almost roughly, "You don't want to retire. What the hell would you do with yourself anyway? You'd be miserable."

42

Arthur glanced up for a moment. " Miserable ? " he said.
" *Me ?* " He bent his head over the glass rod with a quiet
smile. " Don't you worry about that, sir. I've got plenty
to do."

" What ? "

" I'm going to have a rest, sir, for one thing. An' I'm
going to do my garden and—and have a bit of time to
myself. I been here forty-five years. That's enough for
me."

" You mean you *want* to go ? " said Sewell, startled.

" I don't know that I *want* to so special. But I reckon it's
time if I'm not going to die an' be buried here."

" Oh, well, if that's how you feel it's different," said
Sewell curtly. " Anyway, I suppose you've earned it. Let's
see, how old are you—ninety-two or ninety-three ? "

Arthur pursued his lips. " You can reckon out how old
I am, sir, by me being just under a year older than you."
He smiled quietly at the glowing glass.

Sewell looked at him sharply and then smiled with a
slight effort. " Well, what about it ? "

" Nothing about it, sir. You asked me how old I was an'
that's how old I am." Arthur frowned slightly. " You don't
have a garden, do you ? "

" No," said Sewell curtly. " I don't. I've got too much
work to do."

" Ought to have a garden. Get's you out of yourself."

" I don't want to get out of myself."

" No. But maybe you will some day. Gives you an
interest when you're getting on."

Sewell got down off the bench and picked up his file of
typescript. " I don't know whether to publish this." He
said curtly, " Shall I ? "

" Is it any good ? " said Arthur, not looking up.

" Yes. I think so."

" Well, then, it's no good just to keep it to look at, is it ? "
Arthur suddenly raised his head. " I remember hearing

43

Professor Chubb say to Dr. Blackburn—not young Dr. Blackburn, the old man—he said, ' You're a miser with your work, Blackburn. Like a miser with his gold. You want to keep it just to run your hands through it.' And Dr. Blackburn, he said, ' Yes, but I suspect that some of it may be brass.' He had a very high voice like a woman's. You remember him. That's what he said to Professor Chubb." He turned back to his tube and said irritably, " Now that's gone too far. Talking instead of thinking what I'm doing."

Shole was holding a guinea pig and looking carefully at its eyes. Marriott said, " See what I mean ? "

" Yes, I think so. In the corners ? "

" That's it."

Sewell came in and Shole said, " Let's see if the Professor can see it." He handed Sewell the guinea pig and said, " Can you see anything funny about the eyes ? "

Sewell held it rather a long way away and looked at it. " No," he said. " Looks all right to me."

Marriott said eagerly, " You haven't got your glasses on, sir. If you had . . ."

" Doesn't make the slightest difference," said Sewell sharply. " I can see well enough. What's supposed to be wrong ? "

" Marriott thinks that the corners are inflamed and I thought I could see it too. We may be wrong of course. . . ."

" No," said Marriott quickly. " I'm quite sure they're different."

" Well, what about it ? " said Sewell.

Shole said, " That's supposed to be an immune. All the immunes are like that. Of that batch at least."

" How about the controls ? "

" They're all right."

Marriott took his glasses off and said, " You see, if the immunes have this and the controls don't, it looks as though there might be a sort of sub-infection. I mean, instead of being clear they might be infected but resistant."

Sewell stared at him unseeingly for a few seconds. He said, " It might be that or it might be any one of about twenty other things. This was just one batch of ten ? "

" Yes, sir."

" Well, then, do it again. Do ten batches of ten and see what happens."

Marriott said, " We shan't have enough pigs for that."

" Then go and breed some more. Or buy some. Or steal some. Anyhow, get some facts and then we can talk. Remind me and I'll come and have a look at them." He smiled and added, " With my glasses on."

Marriott blushed and said, " I didn't mean you couldn't see, sir."

" Yes, you did," said Sewell, " and you're quite right. I can't see a damn' thing close to." He handed Marriott the guinea pig and said, " Go on, sweetheart. Increase and multiply."

When Marriott had gone Sewell said, " What a very silly young man that young man is, even as young men go."

" He's very keen," said Shole.

" Oh, yes. Those always are. And he'll probably do an excellent job, as long as he doesn't burn the place down with the best intentions in the world."

" He didn't strike me as being particularly silly then. I thought it was rather well spotted."

" But why did he have to remind me that I can't see ? "

" Oh, if you mean he's tactless, of course he is."

" The tact of the elephant and the nous of the mouse. What a lot of things education can't do. It's taught him a lot of biology but it hasn't taught him *sense*. Or how to tie his tie properly." Sewell tossed the typescript on the bench. " I've been through this and I've only one doubt on it. It's the same point that Marriott's raising about those pigs really. I'm not sure that you can say on what you've got here that 80-40 immunises and that there's no sign of a sub-infection."

" Well, I did that stuff myself three times and there was no sign. . . ."

" Yes, but the conditions were always the same. Might be different if you'd been exhausted."

" We can easily try it if you like."

" I'd feel happier. Tie it up with what Bob's going to do on the pigs."

" But with a human subject ? "

" That's it."

Shole nodded. " We can do that." He hesitated. " And apart from that you're satisfied ? "

" Yes. I've marked two places where I think you're being too positive and about a dozen where the sense needs clarifying. Otherwise it's all right." He turned and smiled at Shole. " In fact, it's a good deal more than all right."

Shole flushed with pleasure. " There's just one thing," he said rather awkwardly. " This has been a team job. I think we ought to say so and—and to mention all the people who've worked on it."

" You mean people like Jackie and Rocker ? "

" Yes—and these younger people—Marriott and Miss Byrne."

Sewell shrugged. " As you like. As long as you don't make it too like the start of a film, with about ten minutes of advertising for a lot of people. Bill Smith in association with Fred Jones by permission of Henry Robinson and so on. Put in anybody you like. Put in Arthur. Put in Phillips if it comes to that."

" Phillips hasn't made any contribution," said Shole, with his gentle smile. " Besides, it doesn't mean anything to him professionally."

" Phillips wastes a hell of a lot of time. That girl Byrne's always feeding him or cleaning his cage or something."

" She's good with animals."

" All right, all right ! " said Sewell hastily. " All your geese are swans. Did I tell you that we're to be honoured with a visit from Sir Guthrie ? "

" Guthrie Brewer ? What for ? "

" God knows. He just rang up and was very matey and asked if he could come and bring a man named Childs."

" The Childs who was at Cambridge ? "

" Don't know. I said, ' Isn't this place a bit out of your line ? ' and he said, ' Not as far as you may think and, anyhow, can we come ? ' What could I say ? "

" Just a friendly visit ? "

" I suppose so. Anyhow, he's coming this afternoon. I shall turn him on to you if he wants to see things. I can't abide the man myself."

" You don't mind what he sees ? " said Shole.

" Lord, no. Why should I ? There's nothing he can steal. It'd be different if we had any silver teaspoons about."

Shole picked up the typescript and said, " Well, if they're coming I suppose we'd better have a clear up."

" Bunkum ! " said Sewell sharply. " This lab.'s well enough kept for a . . . for him. Nobody's to waste a minute more on him than they can help. I certainly shan't."

" Just as you like," said Shole placidly. " What time's he coming ? "

" After lunch. Probably about three."

Shole watched Sewell go back to his office and then turned into the first door in the corridor. Parkin had a colorimeter apart and seemed to be rebuilding it from scratch.

Shole said, " Hallo, Charles." He looked thoughtfully round the room. Apart from the bits of the colorimeter, there were bits of several other unidentifiable things, two dirty teacups and an old pair of shoes on the bench. The floor was festooned with wire and there was a rusty biscuit tin containing a small amount of dirty water in the corner.

Shole said, " We're having a visit this afternoon from Sir Guthrie Brewer. The Professor doesn't want a special spit and polish. He just wants Sir Guthrie to see the place as it is." His eyes went to the shoes and from them to the biscuit tin. Parkin's followed. " Is that clear ? " said Shole, with his gentle smile.

" Sure," said Parkin, grinning back. " Right away." He rose, picked up the shoes, looked at them for a moment and then, losing interest in them, dropped them into the biscuit tin, opened a cupboard door and propelled the tin inside with a dexterous kick. He pointed to the colorimeter and said, " This is a wonderful gadget, Doc. It'll do in five minutes what used to take me two hours on the other. It always takes half a day to get it working. But think of the saving in labour."

Shole said, " Why d'you want so *much* wire ? I never saw such a chap for wire."

*   *   *   *   *

When they were sitting on a seat in the square after lunch Marriott said, " I don't want to pry into things that don't concern me, but you did say you'd tell me about—about how you spend your time. At home, I mean."

A pigeon with its head on one side was closely examining Lucy's toe. She moved it slightly and the pigeon hopped back a couple of feet.

Lucy said, " Yes, I did." She thought for a moment and then said, " Well—what do you want to know ? "

Marriott hesitated. "You're not married by any chance ? "
" No."
" Engaged ? "
" Not exactly."

48

He gulped and said, " You live down in Pimlico, don't you ? "

" Yes."

" By yourself ? "

" No. I live with a man."

There was a long pause. Marriott was looking at her still, but he didn't say anything.

Lucy stirred her foot and the pigeon hopped back again.

" I live," she said in a flat, rather passive voice, " with a man named Ivor Gates, to whom I was once engaged. But I'm not engaged to him any more."

" Then why do you live with him ? "

" Because he lost both arms in the war. I met him in 1943. I was nineteen and in my first year at Oxford reading science. My mother had just died and I was as lonely as hell. We got engaged. The idea was that I should go on and get my degree and then when the war was over and he came back we'd get married." She put her head a little on one side and frowned at the pigeon. " It all worked out beautifully except that they blew Ivor's arms off and then he wouldn't marry me. So there we are. He's completely helpless and somebody's got to look after him. There's no point in getting married because he's a complete mess physically, apart from his arms, and he can't live long. Not more than a few years anyhow." She turned and faced him. " That's how it is. So now you see why I can't come out and have to get home early and so on. During the day he goes to a centre where they teach him how to do some things for himself. I take him in the morning, and now I'm fetching him in the evening."

Marriott said, " I had no idea it was anything like that."

" No," she said indifferently. " It is a bit odd."

There was a long silence.

" It isn't possible for him to—to go somewhere where he'll be looked after ? I mean to say . . ."

" Yes. It's quite possible. But he'd hate it."

D

" But surely it'd be much better for—for you ? And for him, I should have thought."

" You may be right."

" Are you in love with him ? "

Lucy frowned. " It isn't as simple as that," she said rather irritably.

Marriot took off his glasses and blinked at her averted face. Suddenly he said, " You know, this is all wrong."

" Is it ? "

" Of course it is. I'm a—an interested party, but even if I weren't I should still say so."

Lucy glanced at him with a slight smile. He was looking very serious and very handsome. He said, " After all, you've had a scientific training. You know how to think straight. What you're doing may make you feel very grand and self-sacrificing. But socially it's inexcusable. One has no right to these emotional luxuries."

" Why is it inexcusable ? "

" Because it's sacrificing a fit, useful member of society for a—a person of no social value." He flushed uncomfortably. " I know that sounds pretty foul. Of course one's frightfully sorry for your—your friend. But one simply must put aside sentimentality and face these things. Society can never get anywhere if it wastes all its time and energy on . . ." His memory came to his rescue. " Carrying in the wounded under fire wins V.C.s but it never won a battle."

Lucy said nothing. Marriott put his glasses on again and said, " The truth is that you're being thoroughly self-indulgent. You don't realise it, of course, but you are. You scamp your work to get back to him. . . ."

" And I can't come to the pictures when I want to."

Marriott flushed and rose to his feet. " I'm sorry," he said stiffly. " I thought we knew one another better than that."

Lucy said, " Yes. That was very childish of me."

Marriott sat down again. " If I may say so," he said,

" that's the trouble with you. You're so—so *young* in the way you think about these things."

Lucy looked at him sharply, and then slowly turned back and poked a toe at the inquisitive pigeon.

" After all," said Marriott, " one must have some sense of —of responsibility. If we don't, who will ? It's our job as scientists to—to blueprint the future of civilisation."

* * * * *

As soon as Shole told them that he wanted to do the experiment Marriott knew he would have to be the subject. Everybody would volunteer of course. Everybody always did. And nobody else would mind, whereas the mere thought of it turned him sick. That was why he must do it. But even so, he let them go on and talk about it for as long as possible before he offered.

When they had argued it into shape, Shole said, " Right. I'll be the victim and Lucy can record, and you and Parkin can observe."

Lucy said, " How long will it mean being out of action ? "

" About four days. Five to be on the safe side."

" You can't be away from everything for as long as that, Doc. It's absurd. I could probably fix to be free if I could have a couple of days. . . ." She glanced at Marriott, and he realised that he had left it too long. He said, " No, you couldn't. Who'd look after—things at home ? Besides, there's no point in it. It'll make much less difference to me than to either of you. I'm a homeless waif. I might just as well be in the observation room as in my digs."

Shole said, " I think we'd better use me." He smiled at Marriott. " After all, there's no danger, Bob. If there were, I'd probably let you do it and win the George Cross or something. But it'll be less dangerous than crossing Oxford Street, and much duller. Besides, I did it last time, so it'll be strictly comparable."

" But it's silly for you to be tied up for five days," said

Marriott. " Who's going to run everything ? No. It's me. Wheel on the—wild beasts." He had meant to say " the flies," but somehow he couldn't say " flies."

Lucy said, " I think he's probably right, you know, Doc."

" Please let me," said Marriott simply. " I always rather enjoy these every-man-his-own-guinea-pig do's. And they *like* biting me. Bill Lewis wore a cage for two days once, and instead of biting him the little bastards just died."

Shole hesitated and then said, " All right, If you're willing, Bob. I suppose I'd better tell Prof."

" But we can start right away, Doc ? This afternoon ? " There must be no night to put in before it.

" I should think so. If Parkin can get everything ready."

Shole took out his pipe and slowly filled it. " The main idea is to see whether we get any trace of a sub-infection under 80-40 conditions with a subject who's pretty exhausted. We either didn't get it or didn't notice it when Seaton and I did the original 80-40 work, but then we were at rest. I thought I'd give Marriott a pretty good go on the stationary bicycle in the hot room and then put the flies on him."

" You don't think there's any chance of his getting a real packet ? "

" I shouldn't think so. The flies bit Seaton and me all right and nothing happened at all. Nothing's ever happened with the pigs except this very slight eye inflammation. The only chance is that exhaustion will help the sub-infection. But I should be very surprised if it made it virulent. We shall watch it, of course."

" You say Marriott wants to do it ? "

" Yes. I was going to, but he was very insistent so . . .'

" It'd be a waste of your time, anyhow." Sewell reflected " If there were a nice war on we could have used a pacifis volunteer." He looked up and said suddenly, " Marriott' rather like those boys in some ways, isn't he ? "

" Like the pacifists ? Why ? "

" Looks like them and—and has the same manner. I always think of them as being fair and looking very young and a bit over-serious."

" The ones I had were a very mixed bag," said Shole. " I shouldn't have said that they were very like anybody."

" No. Of course it's all nonsense to say they were all fair. But there was something that they'd all got. . . ."

" They'd all got guts," said Shole. " Maybe that was it. I always think some of the things they did were—were very gutful. Not the dangerous things. The bits like sleeping in blankets infected with scabies. Because they hated it, you know."

" Oh, yes, they'd got guts. But it wasn't that. It was that they were trying to—to prove something to themselves. You look at Marriott sometime. When he's being serious. There's the same air of—of——"

" If there were any justice," said Shole, " one ought to be allowed to use ardent militarists for experiments in peace-time, if one uses pacifists in war. But I suppose they wouldn't volunteer."

Marriott was wearing running shorts and a singlet. He said, " Hail, Cæsar. Those about to die salute thee." He was one of the people who look bigger without their clothes. In his white overall he was shapeless and scholarly. Stripped, he had a deep chest and a narrow waist.

Lucy said, " Take your glasses off. They spoil the Greek effect. We've got some absolutely ravenous flies for you."

She could say that and not mind. Nobody else minded, and it was ridiculous that he should.

Shole and Parkin were in the hot room. Parkin was messing about with the revolution counter on the stationary bicycle. He was still wearing all his clothes and his white overall, and the sweat was running off him.

Shole said, " It's about ninety degrees in here now. I want

to keep it steady at that. Keep going at about a hundred to the minute and in about three hours you'll be quite a nice fatigue subject."

" I shall be dead," said Marriott. " Can you find me anything to go round my head ? The sweat always runs into my eyes and hurts like hell."

" Right at the end we'll do an exhaled air analysis just to see how you're doing, and then we'll put the flies on."

Marriott nodded, climbed on to the stationary bicycle, and gave the pedals a few tentative pushes. They turned smoothly but rather heavily, quite unlike a real bicycle. The room felt like a Turkish bath. Lucy came back with a duster. She said, " This is the best I can do. It's quite clean." She started to tie it round his forehead.

Marriott said, " Where shall I go ? I always like to have somewhere to go on this thing. Let's see—I've got three hours."

" You could just about ride to Staines."

" Too dull. All along the Great West Road. I think I shall go to Welwyn." He looked up at her and smiled rather painfully. She was standing very close to him but her eyes were intent on the bandage. He could feel her hands as she knotted it at the back of his head. As Marriott sat on the bicycle his face was on a level with her breasts. He swallowed and turned his head, and looked sightlessly at the revolution counter.

Lucy said, " Keep *still*, sap." She finished the knot and stepped back. " Slightly Wimbledon."

Shole said, " All right, Bob. When you like. Keep it going as steady as you can at about a hundred."

The revolution counter flickered to and fro between ninety-five and a hundred and five. He had no sense of his legs going round and round. They seemed to go straight up and down like piston rods. The rag round his forehead wasn't working very well and his eyes were stinging with the sweat, so he kept them closed. Sometimes, still pedalling, he took his hands off the rests and sat upright and wiped his palms on his shorts. But his shorts were soaked now and only made his palms wetter. He heard the whirr as Shole switched on the fan, and remembered the vulgar illusion that a fan cooled the air. He rode for some time to the rhythm of " vulgar-illusion," " vulgar-illusion," " vulgar-illusion."

He was making no progress towards Welwyn now. He had gone down Gray's Inn Road and through the junction at King's Cross and along the Caledonian and Holloway Roads. But every time he started to climb Highgate Hill his mind switched away and he had to be careful where it went. His glasses spoiled the Greek effect. Take them off. If Shole and Parkin hadn't been there your skirt spoils the Greek effect if it comes to that. Take it off. But her eyes would have been calm and unexcited and uninterested. They never were interested when he was interested. They spoke sometimes, but they never answered.

The sweat was stinging his eyes very badly. He opened them and looked blearily at the glass panel. Parkin was looking in. Marriott signalled to him and pointed to his eyes and dabbed at them in pantomime. Parkin grinned broadly and nodded, but obviously didn't understand. After a while he waved and went away. Marriott tried to get his head round so as to wipe his eyes on the short arm of his singlet. But the singlet was wet through and it only made them worse. He shut them again and got up the first slope of Highgate Hill as far as the Underground station. But then unaccountably he started to slip back, and travelled rapidly backwards along the Holloway Road, though still pedalling hard.

He glanced down at his wrist watch and found that he had only been going just over half an hour. Yet already the effort of not thinking about it was beginning to be too much. The only thing was to take it out and consider it calmly, as he had always known it would be. A cage of infected flies would be fastened on to his forearm. He said it aloud in a low voice, so as to hear himself say the words. " A cage of infected flies." The revolution counter flickered up to 120, and he had to slow down and to say it again and again with his eyes on the counter, to make sure that he could say it and still keep pedalling absolutely smoothly and regularly. The flies would thrust their maxillæ into the arm. You might feel that, but usually you didn't. Then they would suck with the labia and that was all. He looked down at his arm. The skin was pale and had a down of gold hairs. But on the inside it was smooth and the blue veins showed through it as though the flesh was transparent. He saw the wire cage on it, and the flies inside fixed on his arm by their heads in the obscene way, and suddenly half-retched. He put up a hand to his forehead and found that it was clammily cold instead of hot. But the sickness had gone again for the moment, and he started doggedly again in a low voice, keeping his eyes on the rev. counter. " A cage of infected flies. . . ." It was the only way. To keep on rubbing your own nose in it. Like taking smears of your own blood. It didn't hurt. But there was the moment of jabbing the lancet in. He couldn't make up his mind to do it, and Mr. Rawson was looking at him with that thin, pale, sneering face. " You'll never make a scientist, Marriott, if you make such a fuss about pricking your finger." He had gone away and jabbed with the lancet below his finger nail a dozen times— jabbed till his finger was sore even though he only wanted one smear. That was like the flies jabbing in their maxillæ and then settling down to suck. . . . It came again in his throat and again he swallowed it back. He had been going three-quarters of an hour, and in two and a quarter hours' time he would finish and they would put the cage on. The sickness was getting worse but he knew he wouldn't really be sick because he never was. It was just the price you paid. He knew that he could pay it and a tremendous happiness came up through the waves of nausea. The young experimental biologist, covered in cold sweat, paying the price for those people in the street—for the others—the laymen. His eyes went down to the rev. counter. It was flickering on 120 again, and he slowed down carefully until it hovered round the hundred, and started again. " A cage of infected flies. . . ."

Sewell was standing looking out of his office window. He didn't appear to be doing anything, but when Shole came to tell him that the experiment was under way he just nodded, and it wasn't until Shole said, " Coming to have a look at him ? " that he turned rather unwillingly and went along to the observation room. He stood looking sullenly through the glass panel while Shole talked, but he didn't say anything or make any suggestions. When Shole had finished he nodded towards Marriott on the bicycle and said, " Why does he keep his eyes shut ? " He said it irritably as though Marriott had no right to keep his eyes shut.

Parkin said, " He must do that to see where he isn't going."

It was one of the oldest jokes in the lab. Sewell turned his head and looked at Parkin. He didn't laugh or look irritated. He just looked and then turned back to Shole and said, " You see what I mean about the conchies. They all had just that look."

Shole said, " I expect the sweat's getting in his eyes."

*   *   *   *   *

Sir Guthrie Brewer looked like the junior partner in a successful firm of solicitors. His greying hair and his perfectly-cut dark suit gave confidence and a sense of maturity ; his brown, rather handsome, youthful face a promise of energy. He smiled broadly and easily without bothering to use anything but his mouth. Nobody could deny that he was an able man ; and in fact, nobody even tried to deny it. They just admitted it and added other clauses. At the beginning of the war he had left the Chair of Physics in a provincial university to advise somebody on something ; at the end of it he had been knighted and had remained in government service to advise everybody on everything. His scientific reputation stood high with Members of the Cabinet and the popular press.

Sewell was not a Member of the Cabinet nor a reader of the popular press. Brewer came in and shook hands with him and smiled at him with steady eyes, like a well-trained life-insurance salesman, and said, " Hallo, Sewell. It's good to see you again. This is Frank Childs."

Sewell nodded to the very small man with the very sharp nose and said, " Let's see—you know Dr. Shole ? "

Brewer said, " I don't think we have met," and shook Shole's hand and sold him some life insurance. He turned to Sewell and said, " It's very good of you to let us come."

Sewell said, " That's all right. The most improbable people drop in all the time."

Brewer laughed as though someone had made a joke and said confidentially, " Well, now, look here—I'd better tell you right away why I rang you up." He took out his pipe and jabbed it sharply into the schoolboy face. " I was talking to Frederickson the other day, and he happened to mention that you were doing some pretty startling work here."

Sewell said, " Frederickson—— ? " and raised his eyebrows.

" Oh, of course he didn't know much about it. It's no more in his line than it is in mine. But he told me vaguely the sort of thing you were doing—which, to my shame, I didn't know before."

" Why should you ? " said Sewell blandly. " I've no idea what *you're* doing."

" That's slightly different. You're one of the chaps who do the work. There's no need for you to worry about any one else. But I'm just a parasite. I just flutter round and advise my masters, God bless them, on every damn thing that's going on."

" So I understood," said Sewell. He lit his pipe. " How d'you manage," he said with polite interest, " when it's something you don't know anything about ? "

Brewer smiled. " Luckily I'm working with people who *do* know something about most things." He jerked his head towards the little man. " That's why I asked if I could bring Dr. Childs along. Anyhow, this is the point. You realise that we've got a lot of work of one kind and another going on that . . ." He lowered his voice a trifle. " Well, that we don't shout from the house tops ? "

" I hoped so."

" Well, from what Frederickson told me and from other bits and pieces that I've heard, I think there's a slight danger of our crossing wires."

There was a moment's pause.

Sewell said, " You mean that you're doing similar work to what we're doing here ? "

" Not altogether. And certainly not from the same point of view. Let's say something that may be—complementary. So it seemed to me that the only thing was to come to you and put our cards on the table and suggest that we might get together."

Shole said, " What are you doing exactly ? "

Brewer glanced at Childs. " That's the snag. I can't tell you until I'm sure that—that I must." He turned to Sewell. " This all sounds frightfully phoney, Sewell. I'm sorry. But frankly, the stuff we're working on is very hot from a security point of view, and I couldn't tell even you without permission from my masters."

Sewell said, " So what you're suggesting is that we should show you our work, but that you shouldn't tell us anything about yours ? That isn't putting cards on the table. That's just making us dummy."

Brewer laughed very heartily and said, " Oh, nice. Very nice."

Sewell smiled for the first time.

Shole said quickly, " But that is what you're suggesting, sir ? "

Brewer's smile vanished. " No," he said. " It isn't. What I'm suggesting is that you should show the *Government* your stuff, which is a very different thing." He paused for a moment. " Look, Sewell, in the days when I was a scientist and not a general factotum, I was a physicist. This stuff's right out of my line. Childs here is a biologist, but he's a Government servant. You can hardly suspect that either of us wants to—to steal your stuff for our own advantage. All I'm asking is that you should have a talk with Childs here, and tell him broadly what you're after and where you've got to. If it doesn't affect our work, then we go away and that's the end of it. If it *does* . . ." He hesitated. " Then we shall probably have to come and ask your help and—and so on. That's all."

Sewell stared at him reflectively for a moment. " Well," he said, " we've nothing to hide. In fact, if you like to wait a month or so you can have the lot. We've got a paper going off for publication now and it's all in that."

Brewer said sharply, " It's not gone yet ? "

" No. But it's ready to go."

Brewer and Childs exchanged glances. Brewer said slowly, " That's fine. Well, now—are you prepared to let Childs skim through that paper before—before it goes off ? "

Sewell said, " We could send him a pull of it if he likes."

" No. That's rather the point. I'd particularly like him to see it to-day."

Sewell shrugged. " All right," he said rather irritably. " I don't see that it matters." He suddenly stood up and said to Shole, " Take Sir Guthrie and Dr. Childs and show them the damn paper and anything else they want to see."

He turned sharply away. There was a moment's rather embarrassed silence. Then Brewer smiled and said, " Thank you very much, Sewell. I'm sorry to be a nuisance." As they started for the door he added, " And then I can come back and have a word with you afterwards, eh ? "

" If you like," said Sewell ungraciously. " But Shole can tell you all about it. He knows it better than I do nowadays."

In the corridor Shole said, " I take it you know the general set up ? This is the Frank Evans Foundation Wing of the Haughton. The whole of the biological side comes under the Professor of course, teaching as well as research. But I'm just the Frank Evans Reader, and we only handle the Professor's personal research stuff. It's quite a small group. Only about a dozen of us. This is the colorimetry room on the right."

As he opened the door there was a loud tinny crash and a slam. Parkin turned round and smiled shyly. A long piece of coloured flex was draped round his neck like a tailor's tape measure.

* * * * *

Sewell stood staring out of the window. His pipe had gone out but he still had it clenched in his teeth. It was quivering slightly.

Brewer said, " Nobody could regret this more than I do, Sewell."

" Just tell me *what* you regret," said Sewell. " I haven't quite got it yet."

" Well—I'm afraid this will interfere with your plans for publication."

" How will it ? "

" I've told you."

" No, you haven't. All you've told me is that your man thinks our work has got a bearing on yours and that yours is very hush hush."

Brewer nodded in silence.

" Well, so what ? " said Sewell impatiently. " Are you suggesting that in some way you can stop me from publishing ? "

Brewer said, " I don't want to talk about ' stopping ' you. But from what Childs says I certainly think we should *ask* you not to publish."

" And supposing I just tell you to go to hell ? "

" Look," said Brewer, " you're talking as though this were just me. Or me and Childs. Forget us. What I'm telling you is that you've got something here which has a bearing on the safety of the country. . . ."

" Bunkum ! " said Sewell rudely.

" I assure you it isn't bunkum. I wish it were."

" The trouble with you boys who get mixed up in defence work is that you can't think about anything but wars." Sewell wheeled sharply. " What we've done here is to make some fairly original studies of the mechanism of epidemic. Even now we don't know much about it. We just know a little more than the next man. If our work has any meaning at all, it's that the hygiene boys may eventually be able to take it and apply it so as to save hundreds of thousands of lives. Now you come along and say, ' Oh, but disease could be used as a weapon. If you publish, some potential enemy would learn more about disease, and he might turn it upside down and use your knowledge against us.' " He gave a loud snort. " Damn it, man, it's lunacy ! "

Brewer shrugged. " It's a lunatic world."

" Maybe. But can't you see where this is taking us ? If what you say is true, all medical research is a defence weapon and must be kept a dead secret in case it strengthens someone else."

Brewer hesitated. " You're exaggerating. Of course it doesn't apply to most medical research. But what you've got here is . . . Of course you've been thinking of it purely from the point of view of preventing epidemics. But surely you can see that you've only got to turn it upside down to get some damned useful information on how to cause them ? "

" And you really suggest," said Sewell slowly, " that in the middle of the twentieth century there are scientists who'll read that paper and rub their hands and say, ' Boy—this shows us how to start a typhoid epidemic ? ' "

" I don't just suggest it. I know there are."

" Well, with due respect I should need more than your say-so before I believed that."

" Surely you realise that there are quite a few people about who don't love us much ? "

" What about it ? There are a hell of a lot of people about that *I* don't love much. But I don't go round trying to give them bubonic or typhus."

" That's not quite a parallel, is it ? " said Brewer patiently.

Sewell said, " All this ridiculous suspicion. . . . I suppose it's your job to be suspicious. But it's not mine. I think it's deadly."

" It's not entirely suspicion. There are a certain number of facts too, you know."

" Oh, yes—I know the sort of thing. God bless me, there's nothing new in the idea of disease as a weapon. You'll find it mentioned in Holinshed's *Chronicles*, and in yesterday's papers. Maybe one day some lunatic will even try it. I don't know. But you can't hold up progress because the new thing may be used in the wrong way. *Anything* can be abused, however good it is in itself."

There was a long pause. Then Brewer said, " Well, look here—it boils down to this. I think your work could be a danger if it's published. You think that's crazy. Who's to decide between us ? "

" Nobody," said Sewell briefly.

" How d'you mean ? "

" Because it happens to be my work and I'm not parti-cularly interested in your opinions. Or your man's. What I publish is my responsibility."

Brewer sighed. " There's no point in making it more difficult than it need be," he said. " I don't like this any more than you do."

" Then why do it ? I didn't ask you here."

" Because it's my job."

" Then get another. Try scientific research. Interesting work."

Brewer said, " All right. If you will have it like that." He stood up and said formally, " I must report officially on this visit, Sewell, and in the meantime I must ask you for an assurance that you won't try to publish that paper or communicate its contents to anybody."

Sewell smiled his brightest smile. " And if I don't take your orders ? "

" They won't be my orders. I don't give orders. I only advise. But if you want to fight the Government . . ." He broke off and said wearily, " Oh, come, Sewell. I don't have to reel off a lot of stuff about the Official Secrets Act, do I ? "

They looked at one another for a moment in silence. Then Sewell said quietly, " I don't know anything about the Official Secrets Act, but I don't imagine they let you walk round and apply it to anything you like, whether you understand it or not. As far as I'm concerned you've no standing in this matter at all, and the only assurance I shall give you is that I shall go right ahead as though you'd never been here."

" You mean you'll send that paper off ? "

" Of course."

" I'd rather you didn't . . ."

" I dare say."

". . . because I'd prefer it not to go in the post. But, anyhow, you must realise that none of the normal journals will publish it."

" What makes you think that ? "

Brewer sighed. " Because of course we shall get in touch

with them and tell them not to publish anything from here without consulting us. You don't seem to realise that this is an important matter." He glanced at Sewell's face and said hastily, " I think you'd better come and see my master, you know, Sewell. I can see you're—you're getting it all wrong."

IV

RALPH PEACH carefully measured a teaspoonful of powder into the glass, added water, and stirred steadily for about half a minute. Placing his left hand on his diaphragm he raised his eyes to the ceiling and slowly drank.

Mab said, " Strictly speaking, there should be a soft organ voluntary while you do that."

Peach washed out the glass, replaced it, put the bottle back in the cabinet, closed the door and then said, " Why ? " in his deep, marzipan-rich voice. He threaded the black tie round the hard collar and began to tie it with slow, precise movements, tilting his chin so as to keep his pointed Imperial out of the way.

Mab looked at him in her dressing-table mirror and said, " You know Lucas will come in an ancient sports jacket that's through at the elbows ? "

" I do."

" Then is it proper for the host to wear a dinner jacket ? "

Peach stopped tying his tie and considered for some minutes in silence. Then he said, " Yes," and went on tying his tie.

" Why ? "

" Your f-father is not a seeker of uniformity but of c-contrast."

Mab said, " How much do you hate having Lucas here ? "

" I find him very stimulating." Peach stared at his reflection for a moment and then passed a hand over his completely bald domelike head. " My head," he said heavily, " dissatisfies me."

" What's the matter with it ? "

" The surface is neither matt or g-glossy. It should either be powdered to the one, or polished to the other."

" You could rub it up with a shammy leather, darling."

Peach said, " The more common and convenient way is to have it done by a b-bootblack. *He* sits in the chair and one kneels."

Mab swung round on her stool and said, " Why don't you ever say things like that to Lucas ? He'd like it."

Peach looked at her with his brown, mournful, cow-like eyes in silence for a moment. " Not in character," he said briefly.

" But that's the whole point. You say he thinks you're dull and a bore. But you deliberately go out to make him think so."

" I t-try to please," said Peach mildly.

" But it isn't fair to him. It means that he gets it all wrong and can't see why I married you and so on."

Peach slipped gently into his dinner jacket. " What your f-father can't see," he said very slowly indeed, " is—why—you—didn't—m-marry—*him*. It—r-remains—a—fascinating—puzzle—which—he—doesn't—want—solved."

" Oh, of course he shows off to me. But that's nothing. He shows off to everybody. That's no reason for leading him up the garden about you."

" I have always disliked c-competitive games and particularly social squash racquets. I propose to provide your father with a bottle of drinkable claret, a reasonable cigar, a doubtful Armagnac. If, in the course of the evening, F-Flanagan feels the need of the platitudes of Allen, I shall supply them. I hope he will go away happily w-worried about your married life. I can do no more."

Mab said, " You despise Lucas, don't you ? "

" I understand that he is the greatest biologist in the country."

" Yet you're quite wrong. Lucas is only to be despised over things that don't matter."

" As a Civil S-Servant, those are the only things I under-stand."

Mab said thoughtfully, " When Lucas is dead, you'll be the most arrogant man in England. I'm not even sure that you'll have to wait till then. Do you want to kiss me before I put on my lipstick ? "

Peach considered for a moment and then shook his head. " No," he said briefly. " But I should like an option on that for a f-few hours. Is there a clothes brush anywhere ? "

Sewell drank his excellent sherry with appreciation. He was fond of wine, and Mab had always hoped it would be a bond between him and Ralph. But it wasn't. Without actually saying so, Sewell had always managed to imply that Peach's taste in wine was nothing to do with Peach—an accident of birth, background or environment, not exactly to his discredit, but certainly not to his credit.

Mab said, " Have you smoked your pipe yet, Lucas ? "

" Pipe ? " said Sewell vaguely. " Oh, *pipe*. Yes, marvellous. Best pipe I ever had, darling."

" Liar. I'll bet you've never even unwrapped it."

" Then why ask me ? Why make yourself an *agent provocateur* of a lie ? " He turned to Peach. " Does she do that with you, Ralph ? The business of asking a question so as to be able to contradict you ? Maddening habit. More men cut their wives' throats for that than for any other single cause."

Peach thought for a while and said, " I don't smoke a pipe p-personally."

" Ah, I *see*," said Sewell, with his brightest smile. " Of course if you don't *smoke* a pipe . . ." The smile faded from his face and he leant towards Peach confidentially. " Tell me," he said in a slightly hushed voice, " how is your indigestion ? "

Peach looked at him with the mild, sorrowful brown eyes. " Variable," he rumbled. " It comes and it goes. It has been suggested that the t-trouble is psychosomatic."

68

" It is," said Sewell tensely. " Take my word for it. When I read medicine if one had a belly-ache one had a belly-ache. But modern science has changed all that. Nowadays, if you have a belly-ache you can bet your boots it's really a headache."

" The body-mind equation . . ." said Peach helpfully.

" Exactly," said Sewell with joy. " The body-mind equation. What d'you take for it ? A slide rule ? "

" Just m-magnesia."

" Why ' just magnesia ' in that tone ? What's wrong with magnesia ? You're not *ashamed* of magnesia, are you ? I like to see a man who'll stand up for his own remedy against the world and . . ."

Mab said, " How's work, Lucas ? How about those five million lives you were going to save when I saw you last ? "

Sewell drained his glass and put it down. " Oh, that ? Yes—I wanted to tell you about that." He turned to Peach. " You've got a man in your outfit named Brewer," he said accusingly.

" Brewer ? "

" Yes. He advises people."

" What about ? "

" Everything. He was a physicist who found there was no money in it."

" Oh—*G-Guthrie* Brewer ? "

" Yes." Sewell leant forward. " Well, I want you to do something for me over him. Have him put in a bag with some bricks and drop him in the Thames. Can you arrange that ? "

Peach considered. " No," he said at last. " You see, he's not in the T-Treasury."

" Oh. Pity." Sewell turned to Mab. " This Brewer turned up yesterday and asked to look at my stuff. Like a fool I let him. Now he's turned round and started some ridiculous nonsense about security."

" What sort of nonsense ? "

" Oh, some song and dance about the stuff being valuable to a potential enemy."

" What did you do ? "

" Told him to go to hell. So now he's gone off to talk to whoever it is he works for. The Lord President of the Council I think it is. Anyhow, it's some red-tape outfit or other."

Mab glanced at Peach. He was looking at Sewell with wide, grief-stricken eyes. He nodded fractionally without looking at her.

Mab said, " But *why*, Lucas ? How does security come into it ? "

Sewell flung out a hand. " My dear, it's no good asking me. The whole thing's complete nonsense. There's a dozen years' work in that paper, and the basis for one of the biggest advances ever made in preventive medicine. But because Brewer and his politicians think it might have a remote application to the war they're so busy manufacturing . . ."

Mab suddenly said curtly, " Stop playing the fool, Lucas, and tell us about it. This is interesting."

Sewell looked at her angrily for a moment. Then he smiled. " Very well," he said, wriggling round in his chair till he was facing her, with his back half-turned to Peach. He closed his eyes. " What d'you want to know ? "

" What's the paper about ? "

" Bit difficult to say in a word. I suppose you'd call it the mechanism of epidemics."

" Why they happen ? "

" More how than why. Have you ever wondered why, once an epidemic starts, it doesn't just go on and on until it wipes out the human race ? "

" No. Why should it ? "

" You're very like your mother in some ways. Anyhow, various other people *have* wondered about it. About a hundred years ago a chap named Farr worked out a formula to describe how a typical epidemic runs its course. It seems as though after a certain point infectivity begins to fall. In other words, the bugs find it more difficult to get going. Decadence sets in. Like the human race only quicker. I'm sure this is boring Ralph."

" Well, what have you done about it ? Made them get decadent quicker ? "

" You really are absurdly like your mother. No. Just made life more difficult for them. You see, in certain conditions and in certain animals you get super-bugs. Still like the human race. Dictator bugs of great infectivity and great virulence that kill things off like flies. But also very occasionally you get a super-animal that even the super-bug can't kill. It produces something that enables it to fight the super-bug. Now, obviously, if an animal can fight the super-bug, the ordinary everyday bug is child's play to it." Sewell paused for a moment and frowned slightly. " All we've done," he said with sudden impatience, " is to increase virulence as far as we can, find the animals that are resistant to the super-virulents, and breed from them, thereby getting exceptionally powerful antibodies."

" Nobody's done that before ? I mean—it sounds fairly obvious."

" It is obvious. People have messed about with it a lot. But it's a bit tricky technically."

" *Could* it have anything to do with security ? "

Sewell hesitated and frowned. His eyes were still closed. " I suppose it *could*. If anybody was crazy enough to look at it from that point of view."

" Had you always realised that ? "

" Good God, no ! Never entered my head."

" So they're right in a way ? Brewer and people ? "

Sewell opened his eyes. " Of course they're not, fool."

" Why not, if the stuff could be used—— ? "

" Because if we're so scared of our own skins that we can't give information of this kind to the world, the sooner we're

71

wiped out and replaced by a more gutful lot the better."
He sat up with finality, and turned to Peach. " D'you know
the set-up ? Who will Brewer go back to ? "

" It's r-rather out of my line," said Peach doubtfully.
" But as I understand it the Lord P-President has a Cabinet
Committee on s-scientific development and Brewer is his
adviser. P-presumably he'll take it to them."

" What sort of a committee ? "

" Oh, just a committee, you know. The Lord President
and the L-Lord Privy Seal, and the Chancellor of the Duchy
of Lancaster and p-probably the Paymaster General. Anybody who's got the t-time for that sort of thing."

" Anybody who's got the time . . ." Sewell repeated
bitterly. He sat staring in front of him for a moment in
silence. He suddenly looked very old.

Mab said quietly, " Supposing they back Brewer up and
want to stop you from publishing ? "

Sewell stared at her for a moment unseeingly. Then he
smiled brightly. " Then I shall go and see them and tell
them they're crazy."

" And if—— ? "

" And if that doesn't do any good I shall go and throw a
brick through the window of No. 10 Downing Street or
parade up and down Whitehall carrying a sandwich board
putting my point of view." He beamed round at them.
" This is excellent sherry, Ralph. Could I have another
half-glass ? "

As the taxi drove away Mab closed the front door and
said, " Look—I don't like this."

Peach stroked his head but said nothing.

" He's worried sick."

" F-Flanagan was certainly a trifle effortful this evening."

" All this vagueness and not knowing people's names or
what the set up is. It's complete bunkum, of course. He
knows the whole thing backwards—all about the Lord

A Sort of Traitors

President's Committee and so on—and he thinks they're going to clamp down on his precious paper."

"From what he says, they p-probably are."

"Well, if they do, they don't know what they're starting."

Mab took and lighted a cigarette. "I know he's silly and irritating in some ways, but he's getting old and I wouldn't like him to get into a—a mess. It'd break him up."

Peach said, "I don't think he really *would* throw a b-brick at No. 10, you know."

"That's where you could so easily be wrong. In anything else you could be sure that Lucas would be—sensible. He might make a fuss and be very dramatic, but in the end he'd just laugh and shrug his shoulders. But on a scientific thing I wouldn't answer for him." She drew at the cigarette. It had not lighted properly and she threw it irritably into the fire. "Who is the Lord President, anyway? Bennett?"

"B-Bennett's Lord Privy Seal. The Lord President is Gatling."

"What sort of person? Would Lucas get on with him?"

"Gatling," said Peach sonorously, "started life as an oil and colourman's traveller and has been t-travelling ever since. I don't know whether Lucas would get on with him. I don't know who Lucas is. But if they ever stopped gilly-gillying one another and talked, they might get on very well."

* * * * *

A desk had been moved into the observation room so that Marriott could work, but the only things on it were *A Handbook of Epidemology* (closed) and an old copy of *Esquire* (open).

Marriott took his glasses off, stretched himself luxuriously, and began to polish the lenses slowly with his handkerchief. He felt slightly tired, and the calves of his legs were still stiff from riding the bicycle. But he felt very well and relaxed and comfortable. It reminded him of the feeling after a game of squash. You played until you were utterly exhausted and sick, and then you had a bath and changed, and for a few hours there was this wonderful feeling of well-being and peace. Particularly if you had won. And he had won. He had looked at them fastened on his arm, and had gone on looking steadily for as long as he wanted to, and nobody would have known. And now it was over, and apart from the little red patches there was nothing left of it, and there was all life to live again.

He took a small square of mirror out of his pocket and squinted carefully at the corner of his eyes. It was difficult because the eyes kept moving.

Lucy came in and said, " Hallo. Lost your lipstick ? "

Marriott swung round and said, " You know the answer to this is a one hundred per cent lemon."

" Nothing at all ? "

" Not a trace. Temperature normal. My pulse as yours doth temperately keep time. And not a sign of the eye inflammation. I should have thought we could wash it out, wouldn't you ? "

" Doc. wants you to carry on till to-morrow morning."

" What for ? It's quite obvious."

" Might be a delayed action."

Marriott shrugged his shoulders. " It's a most extra-ordinary thing," he said happily, " but I can never do any work when I've got time. Whenever we do one of these isolation things I always think it'll be a grand chance to do some work in peace. And I never do it."

Lucy glanced at *Esquire*. It was open at a picture of a blonde with legs about five feet long, in a brassiere and knickers. She said, " You've been catching up with your anatomy, anyhow."

Marriott hesitated and then said very casually, " I think she's rather nice." He picked up *Esquire* and displayed the blonde. " Don't you think she's nice ? "

" She's a rather odd shape—not a very *practical* shape, I mean. And somebody's blown her up with a bicycle pump

74

in places. But she'd be all right if you only wanted her on the wall. Now I must do your readings."

" I've done them. Temperature normal. Pulse seventy-two."

Lucy said, " I'd better do them again." She sat and stared at him with the greeny-brown eyes while he had the thermometer in his mouth. It made Marriott uncomfortable, and he began to make faces and to pretend to swallow the thermometer. Lucy said quietly, " Don't fool about," and went on looking at him, her eyes searching his face without ever pausing on his eyes—as though she was looking at an object, not a person. She took the thermometer out and said, " It isn't normal. It's a quarter of a pip under. Pulse."

Her fingers were very light and slim on his wrist. Marriott said hoarsely, " Your hands are warm now. Usually you say they're cold."

She had her head down looking at her watch, and she did not look up until she had finished taking his pulse. Then she said, " I make it eighty-two, not seventy-two."

" What an extraordinary thing," said Marriott sarcastically.

" You say there's no eye inflammation ? "

" No. But you'd better look."

She hesitated and said, " All right. Turn round to the light."

Her eyes were very close to his but not meeting them. She put out a finger and gently drew the lid aside. As she did so Marriott leant forward and kissed her somewhere between her top lip and her cheek.

She drew back a little way and shut her eyes for a moment, like somebody who had suddenly been licked by an affectionate puppy. But when they opened they were still looking intently at the corner of his right eye. She said calmly, " Not a thing, as far as I can see." Marriott put his arms out quickly but she turned very slightly to avoid him and said with a little smile, " Well, if there is a sub-infection it's very sub indeed." It was an entirely friendly smile.

Marriott said, " What *is* affected is my libido. When I get out of this place I shall . . ."

Lucy said, " It comes of spending your time looking at pictures of blondes. I should think Doc. will let you out to-morrow."

* * * * *

Shole stood with his short legs planted rather wide apart and read the letter. It seemed to take him a long time. When he had finished he put it back on Sewell's desk and nodded without comment.

" Well ? " said Sewell.

Shole rubbed his chin. " Pity," he said briefly.

Sewell picked up the letter, tore it into small pieces and flung it into the wastepaper basket. He said, " I was a bloody fool ever to let that bastard come near the place." His voice was shaky.

" I don't think it's anything much to do with Brewer," said Shole reasonably. " He only took what Childs told him."

" It's Brewer who's made the fuss."

" Well . . . that's his job, isn't it ? I mean—if the security people think—— ? "

Sewell jumped up so suddenly that his chair went over backwards with a crash. He said, " The bloody impudent . . ."

Shole picked the chair up and stood it on its legs. He said, " I don't think it gets us anywhere to lose our tempers."

Sewell stood for a moment in silence. He was a very big man and he seemed to be quivering all over. Suddenly he dropped his hands limply to his sides and said, " All right. Then we won't lose our tempers. But what *shall* we do ? "

Shole reflected. " Might be worth while to go and see the Minister. I doubt if you'll get any change, but——"

" Yes," said Sewell quietly. " I shall go and see him. And I shall see him without Brewer."

" I doubt if you're right there. I'd rather see him *with* Brewer. But it's up to you. Apart from that, it's a matter of—of detail. There are some bits of the thing that they can't be interested in. They might agree to those being published separately."

Sewell was silent.

"And then again—this business about our getting together with Childs and his people—I don't know what you think of that ? "

" What do you ? "

Shole frowned. " Well . . . personally I don't think it's quite in my line. During a war it's different. Everybody must do what he can. But in peace-time—even this sort of peace-time—it seems rather a waste to mess about trying to work out how somebody might give people typhoid or anthrax or what have you. Plenty of people get them already."

Sewell passed his hand over his eyes and said, " I'd give anything for your capacity for understatement." He raised his head. " But the main point is—are we going to lie down and let these lunatics stop our paper—the paper that's got twelve years of first-class experimental work in it—that—— ? "

" What else can we do ? " said Shole, with a trace of impatience. " They're the bosses when it comes to the point. If they want to stop you they can, and we may as well face it."

" And you're prepared to accept that ? "

" I don't see what you're getting at."

" You're prepared to accept that Brewer is the boss ? Our boss ? "

" It isn't anything to do with Brewer."

" Then some precious committee that knows damn all about it ? "

There was a moment's silence.

" This is all rather out of my depth," said Shole rather helplessly. " I'm a scientist, not a politician. I may think this is wrong. But there are a lot of other things that I think are wrong and I don't do anything about them. They're not my business, and I don't understand them. If the people who know about security and the political situation and so forth think this paper shouldn't be published, then I've got to take their word for it, just as they'd have to take mine about the proper pH for a culture. After all—we've got to trust somebody."

*　　*　　*　　*　　*

The Lord President of the Council wore a soft-collared shirt with a bright green tie in a rather large knot. His hair, which was beginning to grey now, was very thick and rather shaggy, and his old double-breasted suit was buttoned up so that it was strained across his thick body in creases. Privately, he had a passion for neatness. But he had been before the public now for twenty-five years in those clothes, and like the old-fashioned package of a popular brand of cigarettes, the soft collar and the big tie and the old suit had a goodwill value that forbade change. Once he had dressed like that because he couldn't afford anything else. Now, as a prominent Minister of the Crown, he still couldn't. In fact, the total effect was oddly impressive. Myers, his private secretary, and Sir Guthrie Brewer were both intelligent looking, handsome, well-dressed men. Gatling had a thick-featured peasant face with small, bright eyes and very thick, dark eyebrows, and he carried too much weight for a man still under fifty. But looking at the three of them, nobody could have doubted who was the master.

The Minister said, " The main thing is—we don't want any trouble." At the age of twenty-two he had adopted a slight Scots accent as being the most acceptable to any company, democratic or aristocratic. " If it gets round that we've had any sort of row with Sewell, we might just as well publish the thing and done with it."

Myers said, " What sort of trouble do you mean ? "

" Well, if he comes here and we tell him he can't publish his stuff and he goes away sore, the next thing'll be a question in the House asking whether His Majesty's Government is interfering with the spread of scientific knowledge. And that'll be followed by a supplementary about Professor Sewell of the Haughton Laboratory, and there we shall be." He looked up from under the thick eyebrows and smiled. " I shall have to butter him up." He looked at Brewer. " Does he like butter ? "

" He thrives on it, Minister."

" Most of us do. Well, then—what sort of butter ? "

" Could you get him a K ? " said Myers tentatively. " He's a senior man."

" I dare say it could be arranged. What d'you think, Brewer ? Would he come quietly for a knighthood ? "

Brewer hesitated. " I don't doubt that he'd be very pleased. He's an ambitious man. But . . ."

" But what ? "

" I think there might be a good deal of—of feeling in scientific circles." Brewer met the Minister's bright little eyes and added hastily, " In any case it would draw attention to Sewell and the work at the Haughton which is surely exactly what you want to avoid."

The Minister stared at him for a moment in silence. " Well, I know I haven't got the right idea about titles," he said contemptuously. " But if I'd done a piece of work like that and you offered me a K.B.E. if I didn't publish it, I should laugh in your face. If I didn't slap it. But of course the scientific mind may be different." He waited for Brewer's flush to reach its maximum temperature and then added gently, " Nothing personal intended, of course, Sir Guthrie."

Brewer, who disliked the Lord President of the Council more than any other man in England, smiled briefly and painfully. " I'm not at all sure," he said, " that Sewell will be an easy man to butter—*effectively* that is. He has the reputation of being as obstinate as a mule. But is the buttering process really necessary, Minister? After all— you're not asking for a favour. You're giving an instruction in the national interest. Sewell may be a well-known man but he must realise that in the last analysis he can't fight the Government."

Myers said, " There's something in that."

The Minister shook his head. " What you mean is that he can't beat it. But he can fight it, and it's the fighting I want to avoid."

Myers said, " But surely, Minister, if you make it clear to him that this is a serious matter . . ."

" The trouble is," said Gatling suddenly, " that you two have a proper respect for governmental wisdom. This chap may not have." He grinned broadly. " I haven't myself."

Brewer smiled at Myers and began, " I think the Minister underestimates . . ." He realised that Myers was still looking at Gatling, and cursed himself inwardly for the breach of etiquette. Gatling, who never missed an opportunity of that sort, had turned away pointedly and was looking out of the window.

Brewer went very red and said, " I'm quite sure that if you simply tell him the decision, Minister, he'll . . ."

Gatling turned back and said inquiringly, " You're talking to me now? You've finished with Myers?"

" Yes, Minister."

" And you're for toughness, eh?"

" Firmness. I think it will pay with Sewell."

The Minister looked at him for a moment and then nodded briefly. " All right. Thank you, Sir Guthrie."

When Brewer had gone the Minister said, " See how these Christians love one another," and then relapsed into silence, staring down at his blotter. Then he looked up and said, " I suppose there *is* something in this, Percy? It's not just Brewer and Co. ganging up on someone they don't like?"

Myers said, " Oh, no. They're quite right. I hate to say it, but they are. We couldn't risk letting him publish. I've seen Childs' report."

The Minister sighed. " I don't like it," he said savagely. " I don't like it at all. It's not the right job for me." He walked over to the window and stood gazing moodily out. " You fight all your life for something and then before you know where you are you're on the other side of the fence fighting against it, with a lot of boot-lickers like Brewer to help you."

He turned back and stared at Myers with a face like a sulky bulldog's. " It was a wonderful life," he said regretfully, " in the days when you weren't responsible for anything except cracking the Government. You could be reasonable and broad-minded and advanced and bold, and what have you. You could stand up in the House and make the Government look like worms. Clumsy worms. There was no danger that anybody'd take you seriously. You knew they couldn't *do* the things—or even tell you why they couldn't. But that was their headache. Now all I can do is stand around and agree with the Civil Service. It's a waste of my talents." He shook his head. " You don't think there's any chance of our being kicked out at the next election?"

Myers said, " Not the next one. Maybe the one after that."

Gatling shook his head. " By that time I shall be finished. God help me, I shall be seeing the *Treasury's* point of view about things by then."

* * * * *

Sewell accepted the big armchair, but he sat upright in it with his back very straight. The sun on his silver hair made a sort of halo.

Gatling said, " Do smoke if you'd care to. I'm going to."
He had a reputation as the rudest and most short-tempered
of men on the public platform. It was of great value to
him in personal contacts. His quiet friendliness was always
such a pleasant surprise.

Sewell inclined his head politely, but his hands stayed in
his lap. The Minister fumbled in his pocket and took out
his pipe.

" You know, Professor Sewell, I've always wanted to meet
you—and for a reason you'll never guess." He started to load
his pipe. " I hadn't much chance of ordinary education—
not as much as I wanted, anyhow. So I had to educate
myself as best I could." He smiled. " The good thing about
that is that you can work on what you like. One of the
things I wanted to know about was Biology. And one of
the first books I bought was called *Elements for Biological
Students*. Remember it ? "

Sewell said, " That little book ? . . . That was written
thirty years ago."

" *Sewell's Elements for Biological Students*," said Gatling,
smiling. " I remember it well."

Sewell smiled slightly. " You remember the photographs.
They were rather fine."

The Minister frowned. " I don't think there were any
photographs in my edition," he said doubtfully.

" No, no. There weren't. I was thinking of another book,"
said Sewell expressionlessly.

The Minister glanced at him sharply and then smiled.
" I'm sorry to find you a cynic, Professor," he said gently.
" I really did work from that book, you know."

" I'm very gratified to know that," said Sewell coldly.

Gatling put a match to his pipe and said between puffs,
" Well, now . . . though I read your book . . . I don't know
much about these things nowadays. . . . But the people who
do tell me that you're just finishing a . . . wonderful piece of
work."

" I should prefer to say that I was just beginning it," said Sewell. He was saying all his words very carefully, sounding all the consonants fully.

" In fact," said Gatling, flicking his match away, " the trouble from our point of view is that it's a damned sight too good. You've scared my people out of their wits."

" In what way, Minister ? I see no reason why any man should be alarmed at the prospect of not having typhoid fever or bubonic plague." Sewell rolled the words out in his best prize-reader manner.

Gatling's lips tightened slightly. " Well, I think they've told you that, haven't they ? I thought I saw a letter to you setting out our point of view ? "

" Yes," said Sewell briefly. " I was sent a letter."

" Then we needn't spend time going all over it again. The point is that here's something that everybody agrees is a fine piece of work, but which is felt to be too mixed up with defence matters to broadcast in the present state of the world. So we're asking you not to publish for the time being. We don't like the position any more than you do, but there it is. Now then—if you want to ask me about that decision, fire ahead."

Sewell hesitated. " You wish me to be frank, sir ? "

" Of course. Say what you like, ask what you like. I want you to go away from here happy. Or at least, not happy, because I'm not happy about it myself. But convinced."

There was a long pause. Then Sewell lifted his head and said, " By whom was this decision made ? "

" By the Cabinet. Advised by its committee on scientific developments."

" Which in turn was advised by you ? "

" Up to a point—yes."

Sewell nodded. " But you, sir, despite your early reading, wouldn't claim to be a scientist. You were therefore advised by—— ? "

" Sir Guthrie Brewer is my scientific adviser."

" Quite. But Sir Guthrie Brewer is, or was, a physicist. This matter is quite outside his field."

" The Government employs quite a few biologists, you know."

" Exactly. And Sir Guthrie Brewer was advised by them ? "

" Yes."

Sewell smiled faintly. " Then the fact is that, though this is a Cabinet decision, the Cabinet is only the mouthpiece for some comparatively junior man in a Government department ? "

Gatling frowned at the bowl of his pipe. " That's a very nice piece of debating, Professor. But you can see the hole in it as well as I can. The Cabinet wasn't considering the scientific side of your work. The Cabinet aren't experts on science or any other technical subject—and I can tell you that if you ever do get a technical expert in the Cabinet he's a damned nuisance. On the technical facts we have to rely on our advisers. But on the *policy* arising out of those facts we have to make up our own minds. The advice we got—quite unanimously—was that your work, directly or indirectly, could be used by a potential enemy against this country. Now—do you dispute that ? "

Sewell hesitated. " I don't dispute that it is possible. But I dispute whether it is at all likely."

" But that's nothing to do with you, is it ? That's not a scientific matter but a matter of judgment. And matters of judgment are *our* business."

" But can you divorce knowledge and judgment quite as easily as that ? " said Sewell. " Are men who admittedly have no technical knowledge the best judges of the reaction of other technicians in other countries ? "

" I don't know," said Gatling bluntly. " But that happens to be the way government's carried on."

Sewell nodded. " Now, supposing," he said reflectively,

" that, thinking that decision to be wrong, I refuse to accept it ? I mean, supposing I just disobeyed your orders and publish my work ? "

" Need we go into that ? " said Gatling, peering up under his heavy eyebrows with a smile.

" I should prefer to go into it," said Sewell coldly.

" All right. Then the answer is that you would bring the full force of the law against you. The Government, however inadequately, represents society, and if you defy the Government you defy society."

" But I might easily feel that since an ignorant Government was acting against the interests of an even more ignorant society, it was my duty to defy both."

" Then we should just have to put you in jail as a public menace," said Gatling curtly. " And that goes however good your intentions might be. All the worst public menaces have good intentions."

" Oh, yes. I quite realise that. If I defy you, you have the power of revenge. But how does it help you ? You can't arrest me and keep me locked up for the rest of my life because I *might* prefer my judgment to yours. And if I once do so, and communicate my work abroad, the harm, from your point of view, is done."

Gatling's small eyes were very bright. He smiled broadly and said, " Look, Professor—this is a very interesting theoretical discussion, but where can it get us ? You're not the sort of man who commits treason just to have his own way."

Sewell had gone very pale. He said, " Treason. . . ."

" Yes," said Gatling, misunderstanding. " It's a nasty word. But that's what it would amount to, you know."

Sewell threw up his great head. " You don't seem to realise, sir," he said very quietly, " that you are placing me in a position in which treason is unavoidable."

Gatling frowned. " I don't . . . ? "

" I am not a patriot," said Sewell in a low voice, staring

straight ahead of him. " I have never felt that because I happened to be born in this country, it was the only country that mattered. I have tried to give it a fair return for what it has given me. But after that my loyalty is to the world. I seem to remember a time, sir, when you and some of your present colleagues in the Government felt the same in your sphere. You seem to have changed your minds. I haven't."

Gatling said quickly, " Don't answer this if you don't want to. But are you a member of—of any political party ? "

" No," said Sewell savagely, " I'm not a Communist nor a Socialist nor a Fascist nor any of your precious ' ists,' except a scientist. But more particularly I'm not a nationalist. You tell me that I mustn't publish my work because there's an outside chance that some vague enemy might use the stuff to kill Englishmen. But I *know* that that stuff, properly developed, can save half a million lives a year all over the world. You say it will be treason to publish it. I say it will be treason to those half a million people if I don't."

There was a moment's pause. Then Gatling said quietly, " Professor Sewell—do you realise the present state of the world ? "

" No, sir," said Sewell bitterly, " I don't. Except that I assume it's in its usual mess. But who made it in that mess ? People who took my line or people who took yours ? We're told every day that what's wrong with the world is fear and suspicion and lack of goodwill. You all go round deploring it. And then you do things like this just to make sure that everybody's got something to be frightened and suspicious about." He paused for a moment and closed his eyes. Then very quietly and politely he said, " What I am asking, sir, is why I or any other scientist should allow our work to be hindered and suppressed and wasted by what we know to be criminal folly. You asked me to speak frankly."

He opened his eyes. Gatling was staring at him with the bright little eyes, but he was not smiling now. He said slowly, " That's right. I'm glad you *have* spoken frankly. Mind if I do the same ? "

Sewell bowed his head with conscious dignity.

" Right," said Gatling briskly. The Scots accent had disappeared and was replaced by the merest trace of Cockney. " Professor, if I came to your laboratory and admitted I knew nothing about biology and then lectured you about it, you'd be angry. And quite right. But you come here and tell me you're not interested in politics— sounding proud of it, mind you—and then tell me my job." He raised his hand as Sewell was about to speak. " Wait a minute—let me finish. The trouble with all you experts is that you want it both ways. You spend a lifetime learning to do your particular sort of trick or cross-word puzzle and at the end you're very good at it—much better than any of the rest of us. But you don't feel that that makes you any less qualified to do other things. In fact, you think it makes you *better* qualified. After forty years in a laboratory, you feel quite capable of coming out and telling the politician his business—though he may have spent those forty years learning it."

Sewell said, " If the scientist has spent forty years learning to think properly and logically . . ."

" I know. I know. I read an article by Professor Booth the other day. He was saying it too—only scientists know how to think and it's high time they took over the running of the world. . . ."

" I really can't take responsibility for Booth," said Sewell with a slight smile.

" Maybe not. But his argument is the same as yours. You may not agree on any other single damn thing—scientists hardly ever do as far as I can see—except that scientists know all the answers better than any one else."

" On the contrary—I have no great faith in scientists as such."

" Haven't you ? Well, I have. I think they know a lot

87

about science. And if they'd stick to that it would be fine. But when they start talking about the ' scientific mind ' and ' logical thinking ' as though they were the only people with minds above the two-plus-two-equals-four level then I get angry. And it makes me rude."

Gatling leaned forward with his hard, bulldog grin. " Everything you've told me," he said, " I'd thought about and talked about and argued at street corners by the time I was twenty. For the last thirty years, while you've been studying biology, I've been learning what's wrong with that point of view—by studying people. Let me tell you what I've learnt. . . ." He leant back in his chair and stared at his blotting paper with the bushy eyebrows puckered.

" You think," he said slowly, " that people are funda-mentally decent and just and peaceful and that they want decency and justice and peace. You're right. They do. But what you forget is that they want them on their own terms. And their own terms don't add up. They want decency and justice without interference with their liberty to do as they like. They want peace without risks—and so on. You think the politician makes opinion—that he twists the people round his little finger by exploiting their simple ignorance. Well, there are a lot of politicians about who think that too. You'll find them losing their deposits at elections, or hanging from lamp-posts all over Europe. The men who survive—the ' leaders,' as they like to call themselves—are the chaps who've spent a lifetime learning to compromise between a set of demands that are all very reasonable in themselves but that don't add up. How to do less work and have more money. How to spend more, reduce taxation, and balance the budget. How to be strong if there's a war but not to prepare for it, mention it, or even think about it beforehand. You talk to me about logical thinking, Professor—give me a logical problem—give me something in which two and two are allowed to equal four and haven't somehow got to equal five—and I'll agree with you. But until then—it isn't so easy."

Sewell hesitated. " I don't quite see the application. . . ."

"You say," said Gatling moodily, "that you'd be prepared to take the chance that this stuff of yours might be used against us, in order to give it to the world. Fine. So would I. So let's do it and feel really big and bold and generous. Then there's a war and it comes back at us and kills us. That's all right. We took a gamble and it didn't come off. But it also kills Mrs. Jones of Tooting, and her cousin Harold. They didn't feel big and bold and generous. They just got killed."

" But surely if government is going to be any good it must take responsibility for doing the right thing," said Sewell. " You've got to explain to Mrs. Jones and Harold what you're doing and why you're doing it."

Gatling sighed. " D'you know what they'd say ? " he said wearily. " They'd say—' Go ahead. That's fine. We're all in favour of generosity and boldness.' And then, just as you were going out of the door, they'd say, ' But of course, mind you, if you take the slightest risk with our safety, you're a scoundrel.' " He spread out his hands. " Look, Professor. You're an idealist and an internationalist and all the nice, admirable things that make you feel good inside. And to-morrow you can go back to your laboratory feeling that you've stuck to your principles and that if only the bloody politicians would follow them everything would be fine. I used to feel just like that. But like a fool I never arranged to have a laboratory to go to. I stuck around in politics. And after a while they got tired of my telling them what to do and said, ' All right. You know so much, you have a go.' And here I am."

He shook his head. " Now I don't mind your thinking that I'm wrong about this. I may well be. But what I mind is your thinking that you and people like you can be right just by some sort of instinct. Every man's got a right to his own view of how to run the world—and even to try it, if anybody'll let him. But what he hasn't got a right to do is to think himself so superior that he can do it with one hand —without knowledge—without experience—without any damn thing except plenty of confidence."

" I have no such illusions," said Sewell coldly.

" Or," said Gatling gently, " that he can suddenly wash out the Government, the law of the land, and anything else he likes, just because they don't fit in with his theory, and act as a pure individualist answerable to nobody but himself."

Sewell hesitated. " Frankly, I can't say I'm prepared to abandon my own judgment in favour . . ."

" I'm not talking about your judgment," said Gatling sharply. " Everybody's entitled to his own judgment. I'm talking about your actions." He peered up at Sewell from under the heavy brows. " We're talking frankly, so I'll tell you something. Before I saw you I was advised by two lots of people. One lot suggested that you should be offered the K.B.E. and the other that you should be threatened with the Official Secrets Act. Both quite reasonable suggestions in their way—for some people." He paused. " But for you I'd rather just say this—what you'd like to do is what *I'd* like to do—as an individual. But as a Minister of the Crown, knowing what I do about the international situation, I can't do it without betraying a trust. I ask you to accept that as my honest verdict—as the verdict of a man doing his best with a difficult job." He paused and then added, " It's one of those cases where people like ourselves have to accept that the world's very imperfect and get on and improve it, instead of acting as though it was perfect already."

" The world will never be perfect enough, sir, to make it unnecessary to take risks."

The spotlight of the sun was full on the silver halo. Gatling hesitated for a moment and then shook his head.

" That might be a good thing to say in debate, Professor. It doesn't mean anything, and it sounds as though it means a lot. But this isn't a debate."

Sewell flushed. " I would remind you, sir, that to you this matter is a small administrative point. To me it is the fate of twelve years' work and twenty years of thought. It is unlikely to be I who am doing the debating." He threw out a hand. " I simply disagree with you about the nature of your responsibilities. Surely I am entitled to do that without being charged with insincerity ? "

" Of course you are," said Gatling curtly. " It's a free country. Anybody's allowed to disagree with anybody. But if you want to *do* anything about it I'm afraid you'll have to go and ask the electorate to put itself in your hands instead of in the Government's. And until you do that your opinion's just—an opinion." He passed a hand over his eyes. " Come on, Professor," he said wearily. " The system's all wrong. The world's all wrong. The politicians are all wrong. But they're all *there* and we've got to do the best we can with them *now*. Forty years in a laboratory learning to face the facts. Help me face this one."

Sewell made no reply. His face, turned towards the window, was slightly sullen. The sunlight emphasised his wrinkles, making him look very worn and cold. After a short silence he made a helpless gesture. " You criticise me," he said, " for trusting my own judgment when I don't know the facts. But you expect me to trust yours still not knowing them."

" What facts do you want to know ? "

" What's the reason for your alarm ? Is it based on anything specific or just on vague suspicion ? Whom do you fear, and why ? Are you just worrying on principle or have you got something to worry about ? "

Gatling hesitated. " All right," he said. " That's fair enough. If we want you to co-operate we've got to convince you. I know you'll understand that this is in the strictest confidence, but here are the facts as we see them."

*   *   *   *   *

Myers came silently in and stood waiting. For some minutes the Lord President did not look up. Then he said, " Not so good, Percy."

Myers said, " He was difficult ? "

" Bloody difficult."

" In what way, Minister ? "

" He's a spoilt old man who's used to having his own way. He's given plenty of orders, but I doubt he's been given one in twenty years. I tried being nice and I tried being tough, but neither really helped. He just doesn't see why he should take anybody's word for anything."

" You told him what would happen if he doesn't ? "

" Oh, yes. I mixed up knighthoods and jails very nicely. But I didn't really sell him."

" You don't think he'll do—anything silly ? "

Gatling thought for a moment. " No, I don't think so. But he isn't convinced, and as long as he isn't convinced he's a risk." He shifted restlessly in his chair. " He's one of those damned people with a mind like a bright boy of eighteen. And it's very difficult to show a famous old man that he's all up in the air and immature."

There was a short silence. Myers said, " You think we should put the dogs on him ? "

" We must put them on the place, anyhow." Gatling frowned. " I don't want him to come to any harm," he said thoughtfully. " He's bogus all through, but he doesn't know it."

" Bogus ? "

" As bogus as hell. He can't even sit down sincerely. And all this stuff about humanity. He wouldn't know humanity if he met it in the street. . . ." He reflected. " Maybe it was me. Maybe he'd be all right if he was talking to someone else in his own line. I expect that's it. He just thought that I was a politician and played up to me. Otherwise I don't see how he could ever do any good in his job, play-acting like that." He got up and flicked a paper clip irritably off his desk. " Why did it have to be him ? Why couldn't it have been some nice respectful little bloke instead of that old prima donna ? We'll have to get somebody to talk to him . . . somebody he'll listen to."

" Brewer ? "

" No. He may be a nuisance, but he hasn't deserved to be talked to by Brewer. Besides, he'd act Brewer off the stage. No. Somebody he can talk to without thinking about the audience all the time." He knocked his pipe out into the ash-tray. " Have a think about it, Percy, will you ? We don't want any trouble."

V

A FINE rain was falling as they came out of the Tube station. Lucy said, " Half a mo'. Coat."

" Not worth it for those few yards," said Ivor. He hated having his coat put on in public.

" But you can't sit about all day in wet things." She took the old raincoat, draped it over his shoulders, and did up one button. " There. That'll just keep it off till we get there. What you really want is a cloak."

Ivor walked quickly with a curious stiff turning of his body.

Lucy said, " How much are you going to hate this evening ? "

" The party ? Why should I hate it ? The last one was damn funny. The people are so wonderful."

" The people who—come in ? "

" Oh, yes. Not the boys. I suppose they're funny too, but you get tired of the joke when you see them every day. There are two of them—Lee and little Billy Cadman—who just add up to one complete man between them. Lee's got no legs but good arms, and he can see. Billy's blind and he's only got one working hand, but his legs are fine. As a team they're wonderful."

Lucy said, " What sort of people do come in ? "

" Nice people," said Ivor. " They're all nice. If they weren't so nice they wouldn't be so funny." He smiled to himself. " Their big line is tact. It's a sort of game—how to deal with a man with a few bits missing without even *noticing* that there are bits missing. The first one I went to I spent about an hour longing for a drink because everybody was too tactful to pick my glass up and give me one, and nobody'd thought of straws."

Lucy said, " I ought to come. I can't think why you won't let me."

" Not on your life. This is my private comedy. Besides, it gives you an evening off, and God knows you need it." He turned the sunken face towards her, which made his walk odder than ever. " What're you going to do with yourself ? "

" I don't know," said Lucy casually. " I might go to the flicks."

" That's right," said Ivor gently. " Something like that. Spot of relaxation." He was smiling at her with peculiar sweetness. Lucy kept her eyes straight ahead and said, " You're sure about their bringing you home ? "

" Oh, yes. They always do from these shows. You can forget about me till bed-time—and till to-morrow morning if you want to."

Lucy said, " There's some money in your top right-hand waistcoat pocket. Cigarettes and matches right jacket pocket. Want a cigarette now ? "

Ivor shook his head in silence. His eyes were fixed on the big building that they were approaching. He was very pale.

Lucy said in a matter-of-fact way, " We'll just pop down the alley."

They turned aside down a small opening beside the high building. A notice on the wall said, " Commit no Nuisance." Lucy whipped out her handkerchief, wiped Ivor's face and straightened his tie. She said, " Good-bye, darling," and kissed him. Ivor said nothing but he smiled painfully.

They came out into the street again and went to the big building. Lucy rang the bell. A little man with a bent back, wearing a porter's uniform, opened the door. Lucy said, " Here we are. Good-bye, darling. Have a nice evening."

" And you," said Ivor. He did not look at her as he went inside.

* * * * *

Shole came into Sewell's room, and said, " They're all
95

there now, having tea, if you'd care to come. I think it's better to do it like this than to make a special song and dance of it."

Sewell said, " Right," and got up. He stood for a moment staring thoughtfully in front of him.

Shole eyed him rather doubtfully. " If you'd rather," he said, " I can quite well do it. Might even be better."

Sewell shook his head. " Why should you do all the dirty work ? Besides, some of them are going to be disappointed. I'd rather tell them myself."

As they went towards the door Shole said, " I think the less said the soonest mended."

" Definitely," said Sewell off-handedly. " That's what I intended."

Besides Lucy, Marriott and Parkin, there were only Lane and Silkin, the biochemists, and Drake and Levers from the pathology side. Marriott had drawn a chalk circle on the bench and he and Drake were playing " covering the spot " with Petrie dish lids. They stopped as Sewell and Shole came in.

Sewell looked round and said, " I thought you were going to have everybody in ? "

Shole said, " We may have to later, I suppose. But I think the main people concerned are all here."

" How about Arthur ? "

" I thought I'd talk to him."

Sewell shrugged. " As you think," he said indifferently. " I only want to do the right thing."

Usually when Sewell wanted to speak to his staff he took a mug of tea and drank it rather noisily as he talked, sitting on a bench. To-day he walked a few paces away and stood facing them and said, " Ladies and gentlemen . . ." His face was cold and expressionless. Shole noticed for the first time that he was wearing a suit that was almost new.

There was a moment's pause as they sidled into a little group facing him. Marriott passed a hand over his hair and pushed his spectacles more firmly on to his nose.

Sewell said, " I have some news for you, and I'm afraid you may find it disappointing." He spoke curtly and formally, as though he was addressing an unfriendly public meeting. " You all know that Dr. Shole has prepared a paper on the mechanism of epidemic disease, which embodies the results of work in which you have all been engaged, and which has been going on in various forms in the Haughton Laboratory for over twenty years." He paused for a moment. Marriott breathed in Lucy's ear. " He's going to funk it again."

" Three days ago," went on Sewell expressionlessly, " when that paper was ready for publication, the authorities —the Government, that is—asked to see it. They then informed me that since our work impinges on matters of national defence and security they would prefer it not to be made public. I saw the Minister yesterday and he repeated that view." Sewell closed his eyes for a moment. " There is, of course, no alternative but to accept the official verdict," he said, if anything even more dryly and coldly than before. " I am sorry if it is a disappointment to you. It is one to me also."

There was a moment's silence. Sewell half-turned towards Shole and raised his eyebrows. Shole nodded.

" That's all," said Sewell briefly. " There are some other results of this development which Dr. Shole will tell you."

As he turned to go Marriott blurted out, " How does national defence come into it, sir ? Is it the Ministry of Health who—— ? "

Sewell turned back and snapped, " I am telling you our orders. It isn't my job to explain why they were issued. Official Wisdom has spoken. It isn't for the likes of us to question it."

Drake, who had a voice like a man with a violent cold, croaked out, " But what'll happen to the work, sir ? "

" I've no idea."

" I mean—shall we go on ? "

" Oh, they're very anxious that we shall go on. Whether any of us will want to is another matter."

Marriott's face was bright pink. " But didn't they give any *reason*, sir ? I mean—it's all bunkum surely about defence and—and so forth ? "

Shole said quickly, " Look—don't let's start a discussion about it now. The Professor's got an appointment. I'll try and explain afterwards."

Sewell hesitated for a moment and then nodded curtly and went out.

There was a moment's silence. Then Parkin looked round with his bright, rather startled smile and said, " Well, well, well, well, well ! "

" So there it is," Shole concluded. " As far as I can see, nothing can be done, so we've just got to swallow it and get on with our jobs."

Marriott said again, " They must be crazy ! "

" For God's sake stop saying that," said Shole without heat. " It may look crazy to us, but we don't know all the facts. They do."

" It's all very well to say we must get on with our jobs, Doc.," said Drake gloomily. " But what *is* our job ? What's the good of doing the work if it can't be used ? "

" Oh, they'll use it all right," said Shole cheerfully.

" What for ? " said Marriott. He looked round at the others. " I don't know about anybody else, but if they think like this about it I should want to be *very* sure what I was doing before I did anything for them."

" That'll all come out in the wash. I don't suppose they'll ask anybody to—to do anything he doesn't want to. In the meantime they want to put the work on the secret list, which is a nuisance because it means all sorts of frills and fal-lals."

" Oh, God ! " said Levers, who had worked in the Ministry of Supply during the war. " Back to the good old Top Secret racket ! "

" I'm afraid so."

" Is it going to apply to the whole lab. ? "

" I don't know yet. Anyhow, it'll certainly apply to everybody here."

" And to Phillips," said Lucy, speaking for the first time. " Phillips is a secret agent. I've always known it."

Parkin turned the lapel of his white coat back and said, " Sheriff ! Stick 'em up ! "

Shole said, " I shouldn't think there'll be much to it. I don't know how they work in peace-time. I suppose we shall have to classify papers and keep a proper eye on them."

" And carry passes and have a bobby at the door with a revolver and pass things by hand, and use scrambler 'phones and take turns at night duty, and never never take sweets from strangers," said Levers.

" Brilliant young scientist," said Marriott, " seeks post amongst comparatively sane and civilised society. Hottentots preferred."

" I expect they'll send somebody along to talk to us and tell us what to do," said Shole. " They usually do that."

" Why wait for him ? " said Levers. " I can do you the whole song and dance. I must have heard it fifty times."

Shole waved him gently aside. " In the meantime," he said in his slow, rather soft voice, " I think the only thing to do is to try to be fairly grown-up about the thing and to take it seriously."

" That's easy enough, Doc.," said Marriott bitterly. " I take it very seriously indeed. In fact, it terrifies me."

" It may sound silly to us and it may be disappointing," said Shole, ignoring him. " But things like this are for the

Government to decide. That's their job. And it's up to us to show a sense of discipline and—and responsibility."

" Responsibility—— ! " said Marriott.

" Not you, Bob," said Shole without even looking at him. " Because you know it all, of course. But the rest of us who aren't so gifted. We can think what we like, of course. But don't let's shout our opinions around too much. Let's keep our mouths shut until we see how it's all going to work out. Then, if we think the job's become pointless—well, it's a free country. We can always go and find ourselves something else. And for God's sake——" He turned to Marriott. " Don't go and badger the Prof. about it. He can't help you, and he doesn't like it any more than you do. And if you think it's a waste of all your work, just remember that he's been on this as many years as some of us have months. He stands to lose much more than any one else, and there's no need to rub it in."

Lucy and Marriott had been taking blood smears all the afternoon. Lucy always found something fascinating in the relationship between Marriott's hands and the rest of Marriott. For one thing, the hands were surprisingly big and firm compared with the rather pretty transparency of the rest. They seemed older—more assured—more competent. He seemed to sit there, staring at them through his glasses, watching them work, like an earnest student watching a demonstration. Marriott never spoke while his hands were working. He just sat staring at them with a slight frown, and if somebody dropped a rack of test tubes behind him, neither the face nor the hands seemed to notice. About once an hour the hands would stop, and then Marriott would come out of his trance, sigh, blink, stretch himself, and talk very fast and rather irritatingly for five minutes. Then the hands would begin again and he would settle down to watch them with that fierce concentration.

As Lucy took back the twenty-fifth and twenty-sixth

guinea pigs and grabbed the twenty-seventh and twenty-eighth, her question was still unanswered. From 2 p.m. till 2.55 Marriott had worked, and it had all seemed clear enough. From 2.55 till 3 he had repeated, with variations, that everybody must be mad, unless the whole thing was just a conspiracy organised by Brewer. That had seemed to settle it the other way. From 3 till 3.45 he had worked again and Lucy had weakened. But at tea-time he had told her what he would have done in Professor Sewell's place, and the prospect of spending an evening with him had seemed appalling. Rather unhappily, but quite firmly, Lucy made up her mind. She would say nothing. She would just go home and sit by the fire and read until Ivor came in. It was rather a grim prospect, but not as grim as an evening listening to Marriott—particularly now he had something to grumble about. It had always been the wise decision. Now it seemed the pleasanter one.

When she went back with the guinea pigs Marriott had stopped working. He had taken his glasses off and was polishing them. Lucy waited hopelessly for him to say that everybody was mad, but for some reason he didn't. Instead, he smiled at her rather wearily and put out a long finger and stroked the head of the twenty-seventh guinea pig. Without conscious volition Lucy said very casually, " By the way, I promised you I'd say when I had a free evening."

Marriott's lips parted. She suddenly panicked and said coldly, " In fact, I shall be free this evening till about ten, but I don't suppose that's any good to you." It hadn't occurred to her before that it would sound quite like that. She found herself blushing with the simplest sort of shame and self-disgust.

Marriott said eagerly. " Then we can . . . ? "

Lucy handed him his guinea pig and said calmly, " Twenty-seven. Presumably I shall have to eat and—and put in a couple of hours somewhere. If you're at a loose end —on a strictly fifty-fifty basis—and you . . ."

Marriott had gone a bright pink. Lucy reflected thankfully that, however clumsy you were, it was always easy to be in charge with Marriott. It was only his hands that were older.

Marriott took the guinea pig and tossed it gently from his right hand into his left. " Yo ho ! " he said, softly and happily. " Yo bloody ho ! "

" Why do the tables in Soho restaurants always *rock* ? " said Lucy thoughtfully.

Marriott said, " Half a mo'." He seized a spoon and dived down with his head under the tablecloth. The table tilted violently. " Careful ! " said Lucy, grabbing at her soup plate.

Marriott reappeared, very red in the face. He said, " I think that's fixed it," and pushed the table gingerly. It rocked gently on the other axis.

" Don't bother," said Lucy. " It's supposed to be like that. Instead of spooning up the soup, one keeps the spoon still and rocks the table." They both kept the spoon still and rocked the table for some while very happily.

" Isn't it interesting," said Marriott suddenly, " how the knowledge of personal inadequacy will come out ? In a man like Doc. Shole for example."

" Is Doc. Shole inadequate ? "

" But surely ? I'm not saying he isn't a very nice chap, and quite sound within his limitations. But he hasn't *got* anything. No flair. No spark. And, of course, underneath he knows it."

" I should have said he was one of the few people who've got more in the shop than they put in the window."

" My dear girl," said Marriott kindly, " that's exactly what you're *supposed* to think. The still water that runs deep is Shole's line. (There's a pun there, by the way.) But in fact he doesn't run deep. He's just still. And as soon as you get a thing like this, you see it."

Lucy said, " I don't see how the Patent Rocking Table helps in eating curry."

" The Doc. Sholes of this life have a passion for authority —for being told what to do. They don't care much who gives the orders or whether the orders make sense. But without orders they're wretched. They know they can't trust their own judgment, so they cling to the boss. You see, it lets them out. Whatever happens, it's not their fault. It's somebody else's responsibility. Doc. Shole would have made a grand Charge-of-the-Light-Brigade soldier. There was one moment this morning when I thought he was going to start ' Ours not to reason why. . . .' "

" That table over there," said Lucy, " has chutney. We have no chutney. Is this fair ? Is this reasonable ? "

" No," said Marriott, " it's a damned scandal. *Aux barricades*." He clicked his fingers and said loudly, " Waiter —chutney. Before this curry gets cold."

" Talking of somebody else's responsibility," said Lucy, " I've been trying all my life to work up enough courage to say ' somebody's else.' "

" Yes," said Marriott. " But that's quite true, you know, about Shole. He's the born subordinate. Most scientists are. In fact, it's one of the curses of science." He glanced at her quickly. " One doesn't doubt that Leonardo da Vinci was quite content to think of himself as a minor employee of Cesare Borgia."

" *Was* he an employee of Cesare Borgia ? Popping the ground glass in the stew and so on ? "

" He was his military engineer. But the point is that he was a *scientist*. So of course he had to have a boss."

" Well, presumably he had to have someone to sign his pay cheques," said Lucy curtly. She glanced at her watch. " You know, I don't think I shall have time to go to a flick. It's after eight now."

Marriott looked at her anxiously. " This damn place is so slow," he said, craning his neck round for the waiter.

She had frightened him now, and he gulped down the scalding hot, bitter coffee at express speed, before she could do more than sip hers. But he wouldn't let her leave it and while he waited he said, " Mind you, it's not really modesty, this longing for a boss. People like to think it is, but in fact it's just a refusal to face responsibility. If I'd been in Prof. Sewell's place . . ."

Lucy put down her coffee cup and said firmly, " Listen— I don't care. See ? This is my evening out and I won't be lectured about responsibility. Say the word ' responsibility ' or ' scientist ' once more and I go home."

For a moment Marriott stared at her blankly. Then he slowly flushed bright red. He said, " Oh. . . . I'm sorry. I didn't realise I was being a bore. . . ."

He looked so dashed and confused that she felt as though she had slapped his face. She said gently, " Sorry. I didn't mean to be beastly. I only meant . . ."

" That's all right," said Marriott. " My fault. Talking shop all the time." He looked down at his plate for a moment in silence and then raised his eyes rather shame-facedly. " Only, you see, I can't get out of my head those poor bloody Indians and people—where you get bubonic and things like that in a big way. It was such a—a damned good feeling that we could *do* something—or might be able to. And this seems such nonsense—being stopped on a thing like that. . . ."

Lucy said, " Of course you're quite right. You're a better person than I am and a better scientist, so you mind more. That's all."

He was pleased. He pushed his glasses on more firmly and said reasonably, " Oh, no. I wouldn't say that. The female point of view is different. . . ." He stopped abruptly and added, " Still—that's enough about it. How about this flick ? "

" Bit late, aren't we ? "

" Not if we go now."

Lucy put a ten-shilling note on the table and got up. " Well, let's go away, anyhow. Will you pay ? I'll be with you in a minute."

They were very silent as they walked down Shaftesbury Avenue. Marriott's hand was still on Lucy's arm, and he slipped it a little further round and tightened his grip. He could not tell whether she had noticed or not. As they reached the Piccadilly subway entrance she hesitated for a moment, but when Marriott gently pressed her on she came at once.

As they settled into their seats the screen showed a picture of a broad bean. A voice was saying, ". . . and this pressure is sufficient to split the tough outer skin of the seed." The radicle of the bean emerged and began to grow rather jerkily downwards.

" Oh, God ! " said Marriott. " The wonders of science."

They were sitting in the back row. Immediately above their heads was a dim red light. Suddenly Lucy turned her head and looked at him. He could see the outline of her face in the red light, but not its expression. He stared back at the shadowy face, feeling his heart thumping quickly. She seemed to look at him for a long time, then she turned her head slowly away and looked at the screen. Marriott hesitated for a moment and then slipped his arm round her. He was hoping that she would turn her head again so that he could look full into the shadowy face for the next step. He was not afraid of her now. But she did not turn.

" What we need is air," said the voice humorously as the plumule jerked its way upwards. Marriott left his arm round her for a while and then firmly and decisively brought his hand up until the palm was on her breast. She neither stiffened nor slackened. He could still see her face in profile as she looked at the screen and the growing bean plant. There seemed to be something odd and statue-like about her face. As he leaned towards her, peering at it in the shadows, he realised why. She had her eyes closed. For a moment he had an absurd and mortifying idea that she had gone to sleep. Still looking at her closely, he whispered, " You *said* we'd hold hands." Her eyes stayed shut and for a moment she did not move. Then he felt a slight touch on his knee and looked down and found her hand lying on it, palm upwards. He put his own spare hand on it. It was very cold.

They had only been in the place half an hour, but as the liner went down the slipway and the film faded into the signature of the News Reel company Lucy turned, and said, " D'you mind if we go now ? "

It was surprising to hear her voice again. Marriott looked at his watch and said, " It's only nine."

" I know. But if we go we can have a cup of coffee before I have to beat it."

Marriott hesitated and then said, " All right," rather reluctantly. He tightened his arm for a moment so that her breast was right in his hand. She was looking at him now and he wanted to be sure that there was no misunderstanding —that she hadn't just let his arm stay there by accident. Lucy merely said, " Fine. Then let's cut our way out." She disengaged her hand, stood up, and began to fall over feet on the way to the door. As they came out into the air she said, " Two cups of coffee and one opportunity for a personal statement. There's a Slaters next door almost."

When they had ordered their coffee Lucy sat back and looked at him with a smile. Marriott was glad that she smiled, but at the same time a little disconcerted. It was an entirely friendly smile, but neither as shy nor as con-spiratorial as it might have been. All the time they had been in the cinema he had wanted her to look at him, and she had gone on looking at the screen ; and now, when the lights were bright she was looking at him and he rather wished she wouldn't.

Lucy said politely, " Thank you very much for a very nice evening."

To his horror and fury, Marriott found himself blushing. " Oh, that's all right," he said awkwardly.

Lucy said, " You can have my sugar. I don't take it." She tipped it into his saucer and added, " I don't know that a personal explanation's necessary, but I don't want to take any chances. . . ."

Marriott said, " Chance of what ? "

" Well—you do realise that I'm just a bitch, don't you ? "

" Why are you ? "

" To come out with you and hold hands and so on."

Marriott swallowed. " You mean—because of Ivor ? "

" No," she said slowly. " Ivor's a—a special aspect of it. He's my affair. No. To—to take something from you when I haven't got anything to give back."

Marriott suddenly felt very angry. He said, " That's absolute bunkum. You enjoyed it."

" Of course I did," she said in surprise. " That's just what I'm trying to say. I just took whatever was going and enjoyed it like a—a . . ."

" I don't see what you're getting at. If you don't mind about—about Ivor, what else is there to worry about ? " Marriott took off his glasses. " I mean," he said, with a frown, " surely we're neither of us at the stage where we think there's something *wrong* about ordinary sexual feeling ? I *like* touching you and—and so on. You like it. Why shouldn't you ? If we *didn't* like it there might be something to worry about."

" And that's all right with you ? I mean—you've enjoyed yourself ? Got what you wanted ? "

" Not all that I wanted by any means," said Marriott gallantly. " But I've certainly enjoyed myself." He was feeling much more confident now. " I hope you don't suspect me of being a—a romantic type with delusions about my personal charms. I got over that when I was eighteen."

" Well," said Lucy calmly, " I just wanted to be sure." She smiled at him again—the same friendly, slightly crooked smile.

Marriott put down his coffee cup. " You're not easy to deal with," he said gravely. " Partly because one can never really believe how fantastically young you are. It only comes out occasionally and it's always quite startling. You know, when you started talking about ' a personal explanation ' it took me quite a time to believe that you were speaking seriously. I mean to say—if you're going to start having a conscience, at least let's arrange for there to be something to have a conscience *about*. After all, this is the twentieth century, Gawd help us."

He had picked up the three spare lumps of sugar and piled them into a small column. Rapidly and dexterously he shifted the top two and whipped the remaining one on to the top, staring at them through his glasses with blank intensity. Lucy looked at the long, quick, powerful fingers for a moment in silence.

" I must go now," she said suddenly. " It takes at least half an hour at this time of night."

VI

As Big Ben began to strike six o'clock Harris left his room and walked with measured tread along the corridor to the door marked " Ralph W. Peach." The walk took him exactly as long as it took Big Ben to strike the hour. Harris tapped and entered. Silently Peach closed the file that he was reading, placed it in his " Pending " tray, rose, and unlocked a steel cabinet. From it he took a chess-board on which was set out a nice, sticky middle game with Black playing a solid but rather constipated French Defence. Peach carried the board carefully to his desk and set it down. They drew up their chairs in silence. Harris pushed his spectacles up on to his forehead and Peach passed a hand over the smooth dome of his head. " White to move," he said in his deepest contra-fagotto voice. Harris gave a little grunt and wriggled down more firmly into his chair.

At six twenty-five the telephone rang. Harris, whose hand was hovering over his Queen, withdrew it and said, " Damn ! " He looked at the telephone in an offended way and said, " Must be a wrong number. It's nearly half-past six."

Peach considered for a moment. " If I answer it," he said thoughtfully, " it might create a dangerous p-precedent. On the other hand, our concentration is now broken, and if it happened to be the P-Permanent Secretary I should gain m-much credit." He went to the telephone and gave a staccato grunt of " Peach." After some while he said, " Oh," He then listened for some time and said, " Yes," and put down the receiver rather hesitatingly. He turned to Harris and said, " I'm afraid we shall have to adjourn. That was P-Percy Myers."

" Who's he ? "

" He assists Gatling. He appears to want assistance in assisting Gatling."

" What, *now* ? " said Harris incredulously.

" Yes."

Harris said, " The only things that could really have helped Gatling should have been done forty years ago. The palliatives that remain will keep till to-morrow morning."

" P-Percy doesn't seem to think so. He sounded Most Urgent Most Secret." He sighed. " I think I shall have to go. Pity, because I had a slight moral ascendancy which will now be dissip-pated."

" Oh, all right," said Harris grumpily.

Myers said, " Then I remembered that you were married to his daughter. The Lord P. cottoned on to that and here we are. He was going to talk to you himself, but as the whole thing's a bit backstairs we thought it was better if he kept out of it."

Peach said nothing. He was looking at Myers like a mildly startled cow.

" When was this ? "

" That the Minister saw him ? Day before yesterday. How well do you know Sewell ? "

" We m-meet occasionally. Very occasionally."

" Have you any influence with him ? "

Peach considered. " Only in a p-purely negative sense."

" You don't get on ? "

" I don't think he cares for me."

Myers frowned. " That's a pity. I hoped . . ."

" His attitude to me is rather b-biological."

" What sort of biological ? "

" S-systematic. He regards me as a specimen of a rather dull g-genus."

Myers said, " Well, this is really rather important from

his point of view. The Lord P. has done all he can to make him see reason. But he feels that the old man's still rather up in the air about the whole business. What we want is somebody to talk to him like a Dutch uncle and to make him see that if he tries to throw his weight about he'll only get hurt."

Peach pulled gently at his beard. " I don't think I'm the right m-man," he said rather pathetically. " I can't conceive of a more d-difficult Dutch nephew than my father-in-law."

" Well, of course it's up to you," said Myers, looking rather hurt. " My master wants to avoid trouble, but of course we can't *make* you do anything about it." He paused. " How about your wife ? Can she handle him ? "

Peach stopped pulling his beard and sat staring at him for a moment.

" I should like notice of that," he said slowly. " She certainly has a strong effect on him. But I'm not sure if it's the right *sort* of effect."

" He hasn't got a wife himself ? "

" Not an op-operative one."

Myers shrugged. " Well—it's up to you. But I don't mind telling you this—in strict confidence. We're putting the dogs on. We must. And if it turns out that he's not playing properly we shall run him under the Official Secrets Act p.d.q."

Peach suddenly said irritably, " That isn't the way to do it."

" What isn't ? "

" Telling me things in strict confidence and then expecting me to spill them. If you want him to believe the dogs are on, why not tell him so ? " His eyes were no longer cow-like.

Myers hesitated and then smiled rather wryly. " I'm sorry, Ralph."

Peach slowly shook his head. " In any case my f-father-in-law wouldn't react in the right way," he said regretfully.

III

" The mention of the dogs would m-merely lead him to wear a false beard and carry a water-p-pistol."

Myers said, " Look, old boy—it is now seven-thirty, and I've got a dinner date. I was told to put this to you and I have. Personally, I couldn't care less whether old Sewell comes unstuck or not. If you do—then you'd better do something about it. If you don't—then forget it. That's all."

Peach nodded mournfully and rose.

" In the meantime," said Myers, " what shall I tell my master ? I suppose I shall have to tell him something."

" Tell him," said Peach, weighing every word, " that I shall do my best." He stopped and thought about it. " Whilst reminding him delicately that it isn't s-strictly a Treasury matter. Would it be in order for me to see the dog-men ? "

" See anybody you like and God bless you. I'll ring up and fix it now."

* * * * *

Ivor Gates stood in the entrance to the Tube station carefully scanning the slow trickle of people coming in. It was easier at this time of day than during the rush hour. He knew exactly the sort of person he wanted. Women talked and were a nuisance. It must be a man, and not too friendly and expansive a man, or one with too much time to spare. Somebody who looked as though he had business of his own and could be depended upon to mind it.

Two plump, chubby men carrying brief cases looked at him curiously, but he stared back blankly and let them go. He had no desire to be called " old man." Just behind them was a very tall, thin, hatless person in an old raincoat. He had a long yellow face and looked tired. As he paused for a moment and fumbled for his money Ivor moved forward and said, " I wonder if you'd be good enough to buy a ticket for me ? I want to go to Russell Square."

The man with the yellow face looked at him for a moment, saw, and said, " Sure." He fumbled in his pocket again.

Ivor said quickly, " The money is in my top right-hand waistcoat pocket."

The man hesitated for a fraction of a second and then, with a quick nod, slipped his fingers into the pocket and took out a threepenny piece. Ivor heaved an inward sigh of relief. This was going to be all right.

When the tall man had bought the ticket he turned to Ivor and said, " Same pocket ? "

" No. Breast, please. Sticking out. That's fine. Thank you."

" You're welcome," said the tall man briefly.

They got into the same compartment, but sat some distance apart. The man was reading the midday paper. He did not look at Ivor during the journey, but at Russell Square he looked up as Ivor heaved himself out of his seat and made for the door. Their eyes met. The man raised his eyebrows and Ivor nodded. The man winked unsmilingly and went back to his paper.

Marriott was examining his blood smears. His spectacles were pushed up on his forehead, and he did five with his right eye and then five with his left. For years he had tried to learn to keep both eyes open when using a microscope, in the proper way, but he could never do it. If he kept both eyes open he saw nothing but a vague mixture of the bench and his specimen. It was a failure in elementary technique of which he was deeply ashamed.

Arthur came in and said rather doubtfully, " There's a gentleman . . ." and held the door open very wide.

Ivor turned and said, " Thank you," to Arthur with a very charming smile before he looked at Marriott.

Marriott dropped his spectacles back on to his nose with a quick contraction of his forehead and slipped off his stool. As the door closed behind Arthur, Ivor said, " My name's Gates. . . ." He hesitated. " I am in the right place, am I ? "

Marriott's face was very red. He said, " Are you looking for Miss Byrne ? This is where she usually works but . . ."

" You're Mr. Marriott ? "

" That's right. I work with Miss Byrne. . . ." Marriott forced his eyes to stop looking at Ivor's sleeve and to look at his face instead. ". . . but she isn't here at the moment. She's . . ."

" I know," said Ivor. His face was pale, but he was smiling a curiously sweet and intimate smile. " That's why I've come." He suddenly stopped smiling and muttered, " Mind if I sit on this ? " and collapsed rather awkwardly on to one of the stools.

Marriott said, " I'll get you a chair . . ." and looked round helplessly.

" No, please. This is fine. Higher the better for me." Ivor was smiling again now. He said, " I'm sorry to barge in on you like this. I would have rung up for an appointment but ringing up's rather a business. . . ."

" That's all right," said Marriott. His heart was thumping hard. He fumbled in his pocket, produced a battered packet of cigarettes and hesitated.

Ivor said, " Thank you. You have to light it for me, I'm afraid."

There was something peculiarly unpleasant in putting the cigarette between his lips. As he opened them, Marriott was reminded of a fish taking a fly. When he held the match to the cigarette Ivor looked up at him under his lashes like a coy woman and said, " Can you spare ten minutes to talk to me ? "

" Sure," said Marriott. With a sudden rush of courage he added, " What about ? " But as soon as he had said it he blushed again.

Ivor rolled the cigarette skilfully to one side of his mouth so that it stuck out rakishly, and said, " I think Lucy's told you about me ? "

" Yes."

" Then I needn't go into all that. You know she lives with me and looks after me, and so on." Ivor closed his eyes and frowned. " Now you'll probably agree," he said thoughtfully, "that Lucy's a very attractive young woman? "

" Yes, I do," said Marriott. His voice came out oddly loud and rather husky.

Ivor nodded. " You'll probably also agree that looking after the remaining bits of me is no job for an attractive girl of twenty-four ? " Ivor smiled. " In fact, you've probably told her so ? "

Marriott forced himself to stare hard back at the sunken face. " Yes, I have," he said. " It isn't."

" I quite agree with you," said Ivor gravely. " I've told her the same. It probably won't be for long, but even so it's a waste of her time. And women can't afford to waste time. Lucy ought to be going round falling in love and falling out again—going out with people and meeting a lot of men. Finding herself a husband and having children, and so on. That's what she ought to be doing. Incidentally, she'll make somebody a marvellous wife." Ivor smiled. " She has *all* the qualities."

Marriott had a queer feeling in his stomach that reminded him of sea-sickness. He said, " Yes."

" I thought we should agree about that," said Ivor with his secret, intimate smile. He paused and then said suddenly, " Did you have a good time the other night ? "

Marriott hesitated and said, " When d'you mean ? "

" When you took her out ? " Ivor paused with his eyebrows raised. " Oh, I see—sorry. You're not sure whether she told me that she went out with you. Well, she didn't, and I didn't ask her. It was quite unnecessary. Please don't think I'm trying to trap you—I'm all in favour of her going out with you or anybody else she likes."

Marriott suddenly felt quite satisfactorily angry. He said, " There's no question of trapping me. I did take Lucy out.

I'm glad you're in favour of it, but I shouldn't care if you weren't."

" Excellent. And *did* you have a good time ? "

" I did. I don't know if Lucy did. We didn't do anything very exciting."

" Well, now, that's rather the point," said Ivor. " I think she enjoyed herself very much. And though it may not have been very exciting for you, I think it was for her."

Marriott looked up and then hesitated.

Ivor said, " You must remember that in many ways she's very inexperienced."

There was a pause.

" Well, what about it ? " said Marriott sullenly. " I don't see what you're getting at. You say you want her to—to go about and enjoy herself. I don't see what—what you're trying to say."

Ivor said, " Do you mind throwing this cigarette away for me ? It's a wicked waste but I can't smoke more than half, or the smoke gets in my eyes. . . . Thank you." He watched as Marriott crushed the end under his foot and pitched it into a bin. " What I'm trying to say is that in this whole matter, there's not the least need for you to worry about me." He smiled. " You say you *weren't* worrying about me, but I doubt if that's altogether true. People are incurably sentimental about the maimed, even when they realise that it's illogical. My view—and I should like to feel it was yours— is that sexual competition should be open and completely rational. I realise that I, who am sick and damaged, can't hope to compete with you, who are fit and whole—and I don't even want to do so. I prefer to face the facts. As a scientist and a biologist you'll agree that I'm right."

Marriott poked his glasses a little more firmly on to his nose and cleared his throat. " From the purely objective stand-point," he said rather apologetically, " of course I agree. But not many people can—can *be* objective about these things."

Ivor smiled. " Then perhaps that's a way in which I'm lucky. I don't suffer from too many illusions." The smile faded from his face and he added, " But the trouble is, as you say, that other people—and especially women—are not objective."

" You mean Lucy ? "

" Lucy," said Ivor thoughtfully, " has been trained as a scientist. For all I know she may be quite good at her job. People seem to think so. But the training hasn't gone very deep."

" No," said Marriott. For the first time he found himself answering Ivor's caressing smile.

" Underneath she remains as unobjective and sentimental as most women. She's incapable of a calm, scientific assessment of any emotional matter. That is your problem. And mine."

Marriott nodded. He was beginning to feel a good deal more at home. The words had the right sort of sound even if the meaning wasn't altogether clear.

" That's why I've come to see you," said Ivor. " Because I wondered whether, as a scientist, you realised quite how this whole business must look to—let's say—the unscientifically minded." He looked at Marriott thoughtfully. " You, as I say, are young, fit and whole. I am—as you see me. You can carry on your life quite reasonably by yourself, or if you want a woman, you can go and pick any one that suits you. I'm not quite in that position." Ivor's voice was still very quiet, but he was breathing rather quickly. " There are certain things I can do for myself, but not many. For the rest I have to be treated like a child in arms. I have to have my food cut up for me and put into my mouth. I have to have my face washed and my hair done. I have to be dressed and undressed. Sometimes I can't turn over in bed and have to be helped. . . ." He paused and added breathlessly, " There's a lot more of it but I won't go into it all. Use your imagination and you'll see. . . ."

Marriott said huskily, " I realise it must be . . ."

" She does all that," said Ivor, more breathlessly than ever. " Every day. Every night. Whenever she isn't actually at work here. And what she gets back isn't sweet patient gratitude. I give her hell. Complete hell. I can't hurt her physically. Often I should if I could. But I make up for it in other ways. By God, I do ! "

His voice suddenly cracked, but he gave a sort of choking cough and went on more loudly now. " So you see what you're asking her to leave when you want her to come to the pictures. And you see what a sentimental person who wasn't a proper scientist might think of it—might even think of you. That's why I asked you whether you had a good time the other night. She was off the lead, you see. She knew I shouldn't be home till late. I was at a party for bits of men —the bits that're left after a war has had a go at them. So she could come out with you and—and kiss and— and . . ."

" I didn't kiss her," said Marriott foolishly.

" Why not, you fool ? " Ivor's whole body seemed to be shuddering. " She'd have liked it. She wants to be kissed and handled, and taken to bed and the whole bloody lot. . . ." His voice rose triumphantly and hysterically. " But if she does she'll remember. And she won't like it. Because she isn't a proper scientist like you. She's sentimental. Damned sentimental. Shall I tell you why she stays and looks after me ? Because she likes it. It makes her feel good. That's what I can do. You can't do that. You can only make her feel a bitch. Remember that. It's funny. You can't compete because you can't make her feel good. . . ."

He started to laugh and sob at the same time. Marriott saw him sway and said, " Here—steady," and jumped forward just in time to catch him as he fell outwards from the high stool. The stool went over with a crash. Marriott managed to hoist Ivor so that he was propped against the bench. His body was surprisingly and rather horrifyingly light, as though it was empty. Marriott shifted his grip and said, " Easy now—easy," rather helplessly. Ivor had gone limp and boneless, and he could not let go of him to pick up the stool. He was trying to hook it on to its legs with his foot when Lucy came in.

She said, " What——? " and then ran forward and grabbed Ivor and said, " All right. I've got him. Stool there. All right, darling, steady a minute. . . . That's fine."

Ivor's eyes were closed. There were tears on his cheeks and his nose had run, but he sat on the stool, leaning against the bench, quite quietly.

Lucy said over her shoulder to Marriott, " D'you mind getting out ? I can handle this better by myself."

Marriott went into the animal room and leant against the wall by Phillips's cage. Phillips came and hung on to the bars and peered at him hopefully, but as Marriott stood still he soon lost interest and went to the back of the cage and sat down with his eyes closed. Marriott felt cold and realised that his shirt was wet through with sweat. He went along the corridor to the lavatory and took his shirt off, and dried himself with a towel and washed his face. But when he put the shirt on again it was still wet and clammy. He stayed in the lavatory for some time, and then went back to the animal room. Phillips came up again and this time Marriott chucked him under the chin.

Lucy came out and said, " Sorry about that."

" Is he all right now ? "

" Oh, yes. I shall have to take him back, but he's all right. He very much wants to see you before he goes. Can you bear it ? "

" Of course," said Marriott unhappily.

" He wants to apologise. I told him I'd apologise for him but that wouldn't do."

Marriott said, " There's nothing to apologise for."

" I expect there's a good deal," said Lucy calmly. " But we'll talk about that later. Make it as short as you can. I want to get him home." She sounded very matter-of-fact and rather cold.

Ivor was standing by the bench looking quite calm again. He smiled at Marriott ruefully.

Lucy said, " Here's Bob. Now say your piece and let's go home."

Marriott realised suddenly and distractingly that it was the first time she had ever used his Christian name.

Ivor said, " I just wanted to apologise for that deplorable exhibition. . . ." He said it easily and without embarrassment.

Marriott said, " Not at all," and smiled awkwardly.

" A beautiful example of being carried away by words," said Ivor. " I completely lost the thread of what I was trying to say, and then suddenly it all seemed very sad and I was weeping with what I can only assume was self-pity." He smiled the secret smile and said, " Showing the value of scientific objectivity."

Lucy said, " Never mind about scientific objectivity. Let's go home."

" But I wouldn't like him to think I was always like that," said Ivor protestingly. He turned to Marriott. " Look—we must have a talk sometimes. Come and—and see us. Bring him back some evening. Lucy, and—and . . ."

" All right," she said coolly. " We'll see. Now, come along."

Ivor turned to Marriott and bowed slightly with his brightest smile. " Good-bye," he said. " And once again, apologies."

Marriott went to the window and saw them emerge into the street. Lucy signalled a taxi. Ivor seemed to be protesting but she opened the door and pushed him gently in, putting an arm round him to steady him into his seat.

* * * * *

The address just off the Strand was a seedy office building. A bomb had landed next door during the war and had torn a hole in it. The repair showed as a red brick patch on a grey surface. In the hall was a large board with a long list of tenants. Peach noticed, with appreciation, Harmony General Holdings Ltd., and Gerald Peaman, Sykes and Sly, solicitors. Besides the dangerous-looking rope-lift was a door with a notice saying, " Bunnett Bros. Enquiries." Peach went in.

The room was entirely unfurnished except for a desk at which an elderly commissionaire was working on a football coupon. Peach said, " I want Mr. Prince. I'm not sure whether he's Gerald Peaman, Sykes and Sly or Harmony General Holdings."

The commissionaire said nothing but turned his head to one side as though he hadn't caught the words.

Peach said, " My name is Peach. I think Mr. Prince knows I'm coming."

The commissionaire got up and said, " Peach," rather contemptuously, nodded, and went out, shutting the door behind him. When he had been gone about five minutes Peach sat down at his desk and began to study the football coupon. The commissionaire appeared to be hesitating over Blackpool at home versus Arsenal. Peach took out his pen and firmly gave Blackpool to win, and then went over and looked out of the window.

Mr. Prince worked in a small office with a blank wall six feet from his window. His desk was lit from above by a daylight tube which made his big red face look so blue that at first Peach thought he was suffocating.

Peach said, " What I want to know is whether there's anything to w-worry about, apart from what he may have said to the Lord President."

" Worry about ? " said Mr. Prince. " Never worry about things. It gives you ulcers." He rubbed his eyes wearily. " I don't know what happened till the day after he saw the Lord P. We weren't in it till then. But he must have written to Sir Nicholas Pelly, because two days later Pelly comes back with this." He tossed over a typewritten sheet.

Peach read, " Dear Sewell. Thanks for your letter. I am most distressed to hear of your experience, but I'm afraid it is not an uncommon one at present. Quite rightly you give no details but, even in principle, I don't think the Society could possibly interfere. Security is absolutely a matter for the Cabinet, who alone know all the facts. Yours sincerely, Nicholas Pelly."

Peach put the letter down and said, " That's all right."

Mr. Prince put his head on one side and looked dubious. " Well . . ." he said. " Let's say *just* all right."

" He's only consulting the head of his professional body on a matter of p-principle."

" I dare say. But what he'd been told to do was to keep his trap shut. Well, anyhow, then he saw his lawyers and they told him not to be a fool."

" You had a m-man under the desk ? "

" He wrote to a Professor Bird in the States, but that letter was destroyed. It may not even have been about this. He's talked about it a couple of times at his club. Nothing much —just dirty cracks about bureaucratic interference with science. And he's been to see . . ." Mr. Prince turned over a paper. " A Dr. Rupert Haggard of Wimpole Street. Does he mean anything to you ? "

" He's just his doctor."

Mr. Prince grunted. " Apart from that he's talked to his staff and made it pretty clear that he disagrees with the decision. That's the most serious thing of the lot. He oughtn't to have done that. D'you know any of his staff ? "

" No. Except a man named Dr. Shole whom I met once. That's all."

Mr. Prince grunted again. " Well, anyhow, there it is. He's being naughty and he's not playing along properly."

" But he hasn't gone about in Dundreary whiskers meeting women in s-swathed gowns ? "

" Not as far as I know. Why ? Does he usually ? "

" No," said Peach firmly.

" I hate these ' no trouble ' jobs," said Mr. Prince moodily.
" What can you do ? They expect you to stop a man from
doing something, but they won't let you touch him before
he does it. Then they say you're slow."

" But what could you do, anyhow ? He hasn't done
anything illegal."

" Dangerous thoughts," said Mr. Prince. " The old Jap
had something there." He shook his head regretfully.
" What a job you could do with a law like that behind you."

" Look," said Peach, " s-seriously—you aren't worried
about him ? "

Mr. Prince looked at him with lack-lustre eyes. " I never
worry," he said wearily. " Gives you ulcers. I shouldn't
think he'll do anything. Does he get drunk ? "

" Not very."

" Well, if he doesn't get drunk and he hasn't any politics
to speak of he'll probably be all right. He may talk a bit,
but we can look after that. I doubt he'll do anything else.
He's too old. Mind you, though—that's not a prophecy."

" What d'you think I ought to do ? "

" Tell him not to be an old fool or you'll smack his
backside," said Mr. Prince promptly.

VII

THE club valet had brought Sewell his tea at 7.30 and it still stood on his bedside table getting cold. For some years after he had become a resident he had tried to explain that he did not like early morning tea, and each time after he had explained this they stopped bringing it for a few days. But after that the tea would appear again, and for a long while now he had given in and let them bring it, though he never drank it.

He lay there now on his back, staring out across the jumble of roofs. He had not looked at his watch but he knew that the valet would come in at any moment and hesitate and say, " You're still in bed," in that faintly accusing way. But even that did not make his arms push back the bedclothes and his legs kick themselves round, and his body raise itself. He lay there with his arms crossed on his chest and stared out at the grey roofs and the low brown clouds. " Seaman Evans is becoming rather dull and incapable," Scott had written on the Beardmore Glacier. Dull and incapable, on the long struggle back from disappointment. But at least they were struggling for their lives, and if they got through there was something for them. He lay on his back in bed and stared out of the window, not tired, not sleepy, but with nothing to move his arms. He had promised himself that to-day he would see the Vice-Chancellor and ask for an official protest—that he would see Windlesham and get him to ask a question in the House. But he knew now that he wouldn't. He had banged his head against a brick wall for days, and now, like Seaman Evans, he had concussion, and was becoming dull and incapable.

He heard the valet pass the door with somebody else's

tray, and that moved him so that the bedclothes went back and he was sitting on the side of the bed, but for a while he could get no farther. His eyes wandered round the room. It was a nice room, furnished comfortably but impersonally. He had occupied it for twenty years now, and it was Professor Sewell's room. Any of the club servants would tell you so. But all the same it remained one of the club bedrooms. Take the clothes out of the wardrobe and the chest of drawers, stack up the books, and there would be no trace of him left. One day somebody would pack the things and carry out a few suitcases, and they would come in and sweep and put clean sheets on the bed, and it would become Mr. Somebody else's room quietly, instantly, and without the slightest flicker of emotion. . . .

He looked at his watch and it was after eight. That meant that he wouldn't be at the laboratory until half-past nine. He would be half an hour late—he, who was never late. But for a man to be late he must be late *for* something.

It was only nine-fifteen after all when he reached the laboratory. He went in by the side door and the commissionaire stepped forward and touched his hat and said, " Good morning, Professor." Sewell put his hand into his breast pocket and showed a glimpse of his open wallet. The commissionaire nodded and smiled, and Sewell walked upstairs to his office. His desk was clear and there was nothing in his In tray except the current issue of the *Journal* of the Royal Statistical Society. He picked it up and pitched it into his Out tray without opening it, and sat staring at his blotter. Someone had given him a new piece of blotting paper and it was completely clean and grey and blank. He took out his fountain pen and shook it gently over the blotting paper, and watched the drop of ink stain the surface and spread out in a round blue mark like the mark on one of Marriott's Petrie dishes. Becoming dull and incapable. . . .

*   *   *   *   *

For over a week after Ivor's visit Marriott never lunched at the sandwich bar. There was always something he wanted to do which took him farther afield. He still talked to Lucy for the five or ten minutes an hour that his hands stopped working, but it was always about the craziness of everybody or about Shole's lack of responsibility. He didn't even look at her much. It was quite a surprise when he offered to come and help feed Phillips. True, he only leant against the wall and watched Lucy do it. But he did watch her.

After a while he said, " I was always brought up to believe that vague invitations were bad form."

Phillips was holding Lucy's hand and swearing eternal devotion. He always did that before he would eat his food.

Lucy said, " Were you ? " She took her hand gently away from Phillips and said, " Yes, yes, I dare say. Well, now go on and eat it, darling."

Marriott said, " Yes. I understood that I was to be invited to—to come and see you."

" Me ? " said Lucy, genuinely puzzled.

" You and—and Ivor. At home."

She was surprised.

Marriott said, " Don't you remember—just before he went he said . . . ? "

" Oh—I see." Lucy turned back to Phillips for a moment and then said, " Why ? Do you very much want to see Ivor again ? I should have thought you'd have had enough last time."

" I found him very interesting."

Lucy turned and looked at him. He had taken his glasses off, and he was blinking and looking serious.

" Why ? "

" There was something rather magnificent about the way he spoke of—of you and of his position."

Lucy turned away and said curtly, " It didn't look very magnificent when I arrived."

" But that was the whole point. He came here and made

a grand effort to do something that—that was beyond his strength. He tried to be more objective than any man could in his position. Maybe he couldn't manage it in the end. But it was a fine effort."

Lucy looked at him in a startled way and said, " But, my dear man, surely you realised . . . ? " and then stopped.

" Realised what ? "

She thought about it and then said carefully, " You mustn't take Ivor too—too seriously, you know."

" I don't see what you mean."

" Well, when we talked about him before, you told me that he was a piece of human debris or something like that. Anyhow, not at all important. Now . . ."

Marriott flushed. " I hadn't met him then," he said simply. " I suppose I was thinking about the—the whole thing in abstract terms."

" And now you're not ? "

" Now I realise that—that there are some advantages that you can't take. I mean . . ."

" What you *need* to realise," said Lucy coldly, " is that it's Ivor's arms that are missing. His brains weren't blown out."

" They certainly weren't. He's got the—the *wreckage* of a fine mind. For a layman he thinks extraordinarily objectively." Marriott smiled rather ruefully. " After all, it's rather unusual to find a man who can say, ' I realise that I can't compete with you, and I think that's quite right and desirable. Go ahead and don't worry about me. I don't matter, anyhow.' "

Lucy said acidly, " You must remember that I missed that phase. By the time I came in it wasn't at all like that."

Marriott was silent for a moment. Then he said thoughtfully. " Hospital nurse. I suppose everybody gets it."

" Get's what ? "

" I know what you do for Ivor. Nobody could do more for another human being. Yet you talk about him in that— that rather hard, cold way that nurses talk about their patients, as though you didn't care a damn about him. I suppose it's a kind of defence against the—the intolerable. If you didn't put on that act you couldn't stand it."

Lucy said, " Phillips, don't smack your mouth. It's vulgar." She turned away from the cage and started back towards the laboratory.

Marriott uncoiled himself, put on his glasses and followed. He said, " Well, how about my invitation ? "

Lucy stopped and looked at him thoughtfully for a moment. " Want to go to the pictures again ? " she said.

Marriott blushed and said, " That's below the belt. It's a bloody thing to say."

" Why ? You wouldn't have thought so a little while ago."

" This isn't very easy for me, you know," said Marriott. " There's no need to make it any harder."

" Harder ? " she said. " What is there hard about going to the pictures ? It's easy. It doesn't mean anything. I thought we'd agreed that."

" You know quite well what I mean."

" I certainly don't," said Lucy. Her lips suddenly began to tremble.

" Well, anyhow, I gather you don't want me to come to see you," said Marriott huffily. " So . . ."

Lucy picked up the bucket, turned away quickly and said, " Oh, come, and be damned."

" Thank you," said Marriott with dignity. " Very cordially put."

As he passed the general office there was a loud rattling and Sewell shouted, " Bob—have you got a key to this damned thing ? "

Marriott went back. Sewell was yanking violently at the handle of the Top Secret cabinet. His face was flushed and angry.

Marriott said, " Key ? No—I don't have one. But I think I know where Mary keeps the office one."

He went to Mary's desk. The key was at the back of one of the top drawers. Sewell took it and said, " That shows how much good all this nonsense is." He opened the door of the safe and grabbed a couple of files rather vaguely.

Shole came in. Sewell turned to him and said, " I was saying—it just shows how much good all this security fiddle-faddle is. Whenever I want anything it's locked away in this damn thing. Yet everybody knows where the key is —everybody except me, that is."

Shole said, " Have you lost your key ? "

" No. It's probably in another suit or something. Anyhow, it's the same about passes. I haven't had mine with me for days. But Evans never stops me. What's the *good* of it ? "

" Well, of course, Evans knows you. . . ." Shole considered. " I could arrange for him to see it and—and keep you out if you haven't got it, if you think that would be . . . ? "

Sewell said thickly, " The day any one keeps me out of my own laboratory because of this nonsense, I shall resign my chair."

As he turned away Shole said, " By the way, has Bob told you ? He's cleaned up that business about the inflamed eyes. There's nothing in it."

Sewell said, " Did any one ever think there was ? "

Marriott went bright pink. Shole said, " There might have been. Anyhow, he's managed to clear it up rather neatly. Very pretty bit of work."

" Good," said Sewell vaguely. He turned and looked at Marriott for a moment unsmilingly. " Though *why* . . ." he said with sudden anger, " *why* he should waste his time doing good work, or why any of us should, I don't quite see."

He turned and went out. There was a moment's silence. Then Marriott said, " Well, my God . . . ! " His lips were trembling.

" Don't take any notice," said Shole quickly. " He's got a liver to-day." He shut the doors of the cabinet. " Look,

Bob—will you make it your job to see that whatever he's taken is put back in here properly when he's finished with it ? "

" Sure," said Marriott bitterly. " Which false beard shall I wear ? "

Shole grinned and said, " Whichever you think suits you. Shove this key back, will you ? I want to go and have a word with Prof."

Sewell said, " So there you are. I've drawn a complete blank everywhere, and as far as I can see I shall go on drawing blanks." He stared moodily in front of him. " If we had three ha'pence worth of guts we should all resign. Simply shut the place down."

Shole said, " Well, there's nothing to stop us doing that. If you think it's the right thing, I'll make one, of course. It seems rather a pity but . . ."

Sewell smiled bitterly. " Do you know what they'd say if we did ? " He opened his eyes very wide in mock surprise. " Why, whatever did you do that for ? "

" That's right," said Shole. " That's what they'd say."

" Yet surely they must see that, quite apart from the ethics of the thing, you can't get decent work unless people have freedom ? Look what happened to German science under the Nazis. . . ."

" The trouble about freedom," said Shole, " is that there's so little of it that a bit more or a bit less doesn't seem worth making a fuss about."

" Hampden wouldn't have agreed with you," said Sewell with a smile. " ' Twenty shillings would not have ruined Mr. Hampden's fortune, but one-twentieth of twenty shillings would have made him a slave.' " He sat back and smiled, pleased with the aptness of it.

Shole noted the smile, waited a moment, and then said, " What I *do* feel is that if we are going to carry on we mustn't—mustn't discourage the junior people."

" Meaning that I'm doing so ? "

" Not you particularly. It's a thing we've all got to watch. But it's a bit unfair if . . ."

Sewell looked at the earnest brown eyes and then glanced quickly away. There were times when Shole reached the limits of his endurance.

He took a deep breath and said quietly, " Yes. That's quite right. It's a thing we must watch. . . ." He got up hopefully.

Shole rose too, but he planted himself in his solid way and said, " There's just one other thing. This boy from Bristol that we were thinking of taking. Channing. Young, of course, but I think he might be good later on. Leary thinks a lot of him."

Sewell closed his eyes. " Channing ? " he said carefully. " Oh, yes. Channing. I remember."

* * * * *

There were only twelve of the Confidential Security Reports, but Mr. Prince grunted like a man confronted by a mass of toil.

Iverson said, " Have you got Charles Edward Parkin ? "

" No," said Mr. Prince. " Have you got Mrs. Bung the Brewer's wife ? " He shuffled vaguely through the sheets in front of him. " Half a mo' though—yes, I have. Charles Edward Parkin. Nothing known."

" Same here," said Iverson. They both discarded a sheet.

" Robert Clayton Marriott. Nothing known. Henry Samuel Levers. Nothing known."

" Ditto. Ditto."

Mr. Prince picked up another sheet and grunted. " Now this is more like it," he said happily. " Percival Grant Silkin. Was a founder member of the New Party. Later member of the British Union of Fascists. Later member of the Communist Party. Later adopted as prospective Liberal Candidate. Spoke for Scottish Nationalist candidate at last election. . . ." He looked up with some awe. " He's had it all except whooping-cough. Anything about him on your side ? "

" Not a word. Better have a look at him, hadn't we ? "

" I suppose so. But you won't get anything. You'll find he's given it all up and taken to collecting stamps. I know that sort. I was like it myself. I gave ten bob to the Lloyd George Fighting Fund once. Arthur Pike. That's the lab. man. Nothing known. . . ."

Mr. Prince picked up another sheet and paused. Then he gave a little grunt and, raising his head, looked at Iverson in a startled way.

Iverson said, " What's up ? "

Mr. Prince poked a thick finger at the sheet and tossed it over. He said, " Now that's *interesting*, if you follow me."

There was a long pause. Then Iverson said doubtfully, " Yes. Probably nothing in it, but . . ."

" Probably ? " said Mr. Prince. " There isn't one chance in ten thousand that there's anything in it. Let's get on and waste a bit of time on it. I never mind a bob on an outsider like that."

*   *   *   *   *

It was necessary to set an example, and Sewell had meant to stay at least until six o'clock. But it was also necessary not to go mad, and at half-past five he gave it up and went. He did not go round to say good night, but as he went down the corridor he saw Levers and Parkin through an open door. They were sitting side by side on a bench talking. There was nothing odd in that really, but he thought they looked like workmen waiting for the knocking-off hooter.

It was only quarter to six when his cab reached Piccadilly Circus, and he had a sudden vision of the club at that time in the evening, and stopped the cab and got out and walked to fill in a bit of time.

It was raining slightly, and he put his hands in his overcoat pockets and turned inwards for warmth, and to the facts for comfort. There had been a technical hitch about publishing the report. That was all it came to. It was as though he had discovered something that needed further checking, which would hold the thing up. The effect would have been just the same. He remembered with a slight shock of surprise that only a week ago he had been hesitating about letting it go—that he had told Shole how he hated publishing things. And now, because the matter had been taken out of his hands, it was as though life had suddenly stopped.

It was illogical. A delay had arisen, but he was used to delay. And if he was sixty-four, there was nothing new in that. He was a fit man, and there would probably be at least six years to go. Two thousand days. Forty-eight thousand hours. The time since 1943. . . . But quite possibly ten years. Or since before the war. Or since before the war. . . .

He paused to look in a shop window and realised that having his hands in his pockets pulled his shoulders forward in a slight stoop. He had no need to stoop, and he took his hands out and braced himself and walked on with shoulders back and head high like a guardsman, through the drizzling rain.

It was just six o'clock when he reached the club. There were only half a dozen people in the bar and they were talking in compact groups of three. Pilley glanced up and nodded, and said, " Hallo, Lucas." But one of the men with him was a guest ; and anyhow, Pilley was a bore.

Sewell went to the bar and George gave him his whisky and soda. Sewell said, " Very quiet to-night, George." George glanced at the clock and nodded. " Has Mr. Claspell been in ? " Sewell asked, without wanting to know.

George said, " Not since lunch. It's a bit early for him."

After a few minutes Sewell took his drink and strolled into the billards room. Nobody was playing and the cloths were still on the tables. Within the next half-hour the place would fill up, but that was within the next half-hour. Sewell stood and looked at the billiards room for a while and then switched on the lights over one of the tables and carefully removed and folded the cloth. He took his cue out of its case, and placing the red ball midway between the centre and top spots, played the long loser into the top pocket. The white ball clicked neatly in, but the red finished just too far above the middle pocket. He set the balls up and played the shot again. This time it was a shade too firm. The third time it was dead right, and after that he played the shot half a dozen times, getting it approximately right each time. But he was not absolutely satisfied with his cue delivery, and he took to playing the ball straight up over the line of spots, trying to hit it exactly in the middle so that it came back from the top cushion over the spots again. He did this many times, and then stopped and stood quite still gazing at the white ball on the green table.

Pilley came in with his guest and said, " Hallo—here's Lucas mis-spending his youth." He introduced his guest and said, " Lucas is practising for the boys' championship. In a few more years he'll be good if he sticks to it. Shall we have a three-hander, Lucas, or are you waiting for somebody ? "

Sewell said, " No, no. You two go on. I'm waiting." He put his cue in its case and went back to the bar. There was still nobody there that he really wanted to talk to, but as he was buying a drink Newnes came in. Newnes was a fool, but he was possible. Sewell said, " Hallo, Peter. You dining here ? "

" I am, Lucas."

" Then how about splitting a bottle of champagne ? "

Newnes raised his eyebrows and said, " An excellent idea, Lucas. One of the best ideas I've heard for a long time. Celebration or just good old simple extravagance ? What Winston used to call an ' easement ? ' "

Sewell's heart sank but he smiled doggedly and said, " That's right. An easement."

Newnes's face was the face of a stupid man trying to be

134

intelligent. After a few moments Sewell said, " I've just got to make a telephone call. See you in a moment."

He went out to the telephone booth. He had no idea of the number and had to look it up, but Mab answered at once. Sewell said, " Are you free for lunch to-morrow ? "

" I could be, darling."

" Well then, come and have lunch with me. At the Picardy. Quarter to one in the foyer."

" All right."

There was a moment's pause and he was just going to hang up when she said, " Is anything wrong, Lucas ? "

He had half-expected that and it irritated him. He said roughly, " Wrong ? No. Why should there be ? See you there," and hung up.

VIII

As the bus turned into Whitehall Lucy said, " I'm sorry if you'd rather have come back to the flat for a meal, but honestly there isn't anything to see, and Ivor doesn't really like having people in."

" You're sure he won't mind this," said Marriott rather anxiously. " I mean—I don't want to . . ."

" Oh, Lord, no—he'll like it. Half his trouble is that he doesn't see enough people—normal ones, that is. He'll probably talk your head off."

Marriott hesitated and said, " Is there any subject I— ought to keep off ? "

" How d'you mean ? "

" Well, he struck me as being a very interesting person but very highly strung. As though you could easily say the wrong thing."

" Oh, yes. You can. But then, *anything* can be the wrong thing if . . ." Lucy paused for a moment and then said, " Look—I want to tell you something." She turned and looked at him, her eyes searching his face in that queer way that Marriott always found disconcerting. " I don't know why you want to meet Ivor again. But if you're going to, you'd better know certain things about him.

She considered. " The point about Ivor is that he's—is that everything he does is done *deliberately*. Everything's a— a performance. Sometimes it's a performance for some- body else's benefit. More often it's for his own. It's usually a very good performance and he puts his whole soul into it. But it's a performance all the same."

Marriott said, " Isn't that rather sweeping ? "

" I dare say. But it's true." She saw his face and turned

her head away and said, " Damn ! Now you think that's a
criticism, and it isn't."

" Surely you're implying that he's insincere ? "

" It isn't anything to do with sincerity. Being insincere
is saying what you don't mean or don't feel. Ivor doesn't
do that. But he—arranges his feelings first." She looked at
him almost appealingly. " Don't you see what I mean ? "

Marriott said, " Don't you think he may ' perform ' more
when you're there than when you're not ? "

" Why d'you think that ? "

Marriott smiled. " Well—take the day he came into the
lab. There was no performance about when he was alone
with me. That I can assure you."

" Of course there was," said Lucy irritably. " That's
what I've been trying to get into your thick head. The . . ."

" As you weren't there," said Marriott coldly. " I don't
see how you think you know. I may or may not have a thick
head, but I know when a man's sincere and when he isn't."

Lucy hesitated for a moment and then said, " All right.
Have it your own way," rather wearily.

There was nobody else in the side bar of the little pub.
Ivor was sitting at a table talking to the barman. He seemed
completely at home. Marriott had wondered how he
managed about drinking, forgetting straws. Ivor greeted
them very cheerfully and said, " Come on—I'm half a pint
ahead."

Marriott chose beer. Ivor ordered it and a gin-and-lime
for Lucy without asking her. Lucy said, " Have you paid ? "

" Yes. Phil's had ten bob off me." Ivor turned to
Marriott. " When we come in here Phil takes ten bob out
of my pocket and when we've drunk about eight bob's
worth he says we've used it up, and throws us out. Don't
you, Phil ?"

The barman smiled and said, " If you never get less for
your money than you get here, Mr. Gates, you'll do."

"As a matter of fact," said Ivor in a low voice, "we rather have to keep an eye on Phil, or the ten bob lasts altogether too long. Pubs and tarts are the two institutions that always seem to feel I'm a deserving case—oh, and railway porters. They won't take tips."

"Tarts?" said Marriott in surprise.

"Yes. I'm very seldom out by myself at night. But if I am I nearly always get some very generous offers." He bent his head and sucked at his beer through the straws. "Everything has its compensations, you see," he said, with a grin.

Marriott flushed slightly and put out of his mind the sudden unspeakable vision.

Ivor seemed to be in very good spirits. He told a number of wryly funny stories about the Centre. Lucy was silent and didn't seem to be listening very carefully. Marriott suspected that she had heard the stories before. After a while she went away and collected the bar-room cat and sat stroking it, looking down at it abstractedly. Marriott felt uneasy and faintly disappointed. This casual chatter and story-telling was all very well, but somehow after his last encounter with Ivor it wasn't what he had expected. Drawing-room comedy was a poor substitute for tragedy. He had drunk two pints of beer and beer always made him feel rather muzzy and uncomfortable.

Ivor told a story about an Irishman at the Centre. Marriott said, "I didn't realise that you were an Irishman till Lucy told me."

"What?" said Ivor, exaggerating his accent slightly. "Do you not recognise a man from Cork?"

"A *Southern* Irishman?"

"Sir—— !" said Ivor with mock indignation.

"Then how did you get mixed up in the war?" Marriott flushed slightly. "I mean—you just volunteered?"

"That's right. I was one of the Irishmen who said, 'We may be neutral but who are we neutral *against*?' So I joined the army." Ivor smiled brightly. "And just to show how grateful they were the R.A.F. blew my arms off."

"The R.A.F. did?" said Marriott, puzzled.

Lucy tipped the cat on to the floor and said, "Not exactly on purpose, you understand. A slight mistake over the target area. Who's going to buy me another drink? Darling—will your ten bob stand another round?"

Marriott said, "What a ghastly piece of luck."

"Moral, don't interfere in things that don't concern you," said Ivor lightly. "Or else get killed properly and then you're a hero. But it does leave you with a very proper sense of the futility of war. Far more so than if the other side had mucked you up." He sucked at his straws and produced a loud bubbling noise. "The well's run dry," he said. "More beer down here. Personally, I can hardly read the papers now without going crazy with fury at the way we're drifting into another mess."

Marriott pushed his glasses on a little more firmly. "You think we are?" he said.

"Why?" said Ivor. "Don't you?"

"I don't know," said Marriott rather helplessly. "It seems as though everybody's crazy. Absolutely crazy.

Ivor was looking at him closely with those bright, sunken eyes. He smiled and said, "You know, it's one of the odd things about being in a position like mine that you lose this sense of—of being on this or the other side of the fence. I'm not a Communist or an anti-Communist or a Conservative or any of those things—simply because it doesn't mean anything to me. Whatever sort of set-up we have, it doesn't alter my position. I can't earn a living. I'm entirely dependent on other people. Unless we got an arrangement by which people like myself were put in a lethal chamber, nothing that can happen makes much difference. It gives one a curious feeling of being outside the battle."

"*Hors de combat* in the literal sense," said Marriott. Encouraged, he took another drink of beer.

" So I'm left," said Ivor, " with no alternative but to be just a pacifist. I have no views about who's right and who's wrong. All I know is that it's insane for people to fight about these things." He hesitated for a moment and then smiled rather too brightly and added, " You see, my own experience was that if you wish to fight the evils of Nazism you just get your arms blown off by the forces of democracy. I am the *reductio ad absurdum* of war." He was breathing more quickly now. Lucy stirred uneasily and glanced at her watch.

" Look," she said, " it is now seven-fifteen. We ought . . ."

Ivor said, " Shut up. If you're hungry, go and get one of Phil's sausage rolls. And anyhow, get us all another drink. It's your round."

As she went away a man came in and Ivor looked up and said, " Why, hallo, Bill. Come and join us. Marriott— this is Bill Brown. Bill—Bob Marriott. Lucy—another sausage roll and another drink, and come and be introduced."

It turned out that Lucy and Bill Brown had met once before somewhere. Marriott sat rather impatiently while they worked it out and while Brown asked Ivor how he was. Brown somehow reconstructed the party, and he didn't want it reconstructed. It had just been getting interesting. Almost before he decently could, he said, " You know, what you were saying's very striking."

" I can't remember what I *was* saying."

" About being the *reductio ad absurdum* of war."

Brown gave a loud crow of laughter. " He said that to you ? " he asked eagerly.

" Yes."

" Yes—and I'll bet he said it as though he'd just thought of it." He turned to Ivor. " Pinching all my best remarks like that. *I* coined that phrase about him a year ago."

Ivor smiled quietly but said nothing.

" I don't care who coined it," said Marriott. " But it's true." He didn't care much for Bill Brown, who had thick lips and protuberant dark eyes and wore a navy-blue shirt with a bright green tie.

" Of course it's true," said Brown seriously. " I'd like to take Ivor and show him to quite a number of people. . . ." He turned to Ivor. " How would you like to be exhibit A ? Say to a few really belligerent American editors ? "

" Or to Mr. Molotov," said Marriott.

" Sure," said Brown, staring at him with the prominent eyes. " To any of them."

Marriott said, " What I want is an—an objective approach to these things, without a lot of ' isms ' and dogmas."

" There speaks your scientist," said Ivor.

" Oh," said Brown. " You're a scientist ? "

" I try to be. So does Lucy. But it isn't very easy in this world."

" I should have thought that was the one thing it *was* fairly easy to be," said Brown, putting down his mug. " Aren't we always being told that this is a scientific age ? "

" Oh, God ! " said Marriott wearily. " We are indeed. As though every age in history hasn't been."

Lucy said briskly, " Tell them the bit about Cesare Borgia and Leonardo da Vinci and then we simply *must* go."

Marriott flushed. " It's all very well to laugh about it," he said angrily. " But *you* ought to know what science is up against nowadays if anybody does." He turned to Ivor. " Have you heard about what's happened to us ? "

" What, about your stuff suddenly becoming very important and hush hush, and so on ? "

" Yes."

" So hush hush that we mustn't talk about it in pubs," said Lucy, getting up. " Come on, I. Gates. We must go."

" I haven't the slightest intention of talking about it," said Marriott coldly. " Except to say that it shows how far science can ever get with all this international paranoia about."

A Sort of Traitors

Brown was looking at Marriott with marked respect. "Paranoia," he said. "Persecution mania in fact? International paranoia. That's a very striking phrase."

"It's struck a lot of people in its time," said Lucy. "Drink up that beer, Bob."

Ivor said, "Don't bully, Lucy. He doesn't have to come if he doesn't want to." He smiled at Marriott. "Stay and finish your drink with Bill. It's only Lucy clock watching. She always does it."

Marriott hesitated. But Ivor had heaved himself on to his feet and was clearly going with Lucy, and there was a chance of getting back to the original party. He took a last gulp of beer and said, "No, I'm coming," and got up too.

It wasn't very late, but Lucy seemed to want to get Ivor away. As they parted at the bus stop Ivor said, "I'm sorry Bill came barging in. He rather spoiled our talk. But he's one of my few remaining drinking companion, and . . ."

Marriott said, "Oh, that's all right."

"We must get together again—when we can have an evening without Lucy clamouring all the time."

"Clamouring!" said Lucy. "I hardly said a word. Here's your bus, squire. See you to-morrow."

Marriott looked back as the bus started and watched them walking away—Ivor with his queer, effortful walk and Lucy with her quick, neat one. His head was aching and he felt angry about something without being quite sure what. But it was all connected with Brown. Until he had come it had been getting better all the time.

* * * * *

Mab stirred her coffee and went on waiting. Sewell had asked her to meet him at a quarter to one, and as usual he had been sitting in the foyer when she arrived. All through the preliminary glasses of sherry and all through the meal she had waited, saying just enough about nothing in particular to break the long silences ; and now they had got to the coffee and Sewell still sat staring at his cup as though he hardly knew she was there.

Mab said, " Do you realise that this lunch creates a record ? "

He looked up and raised his eyebrows.

" I've now seen you three times in quick succession. Once on your birthday, once when you came to dinner, and now. We haven't been in one another's pockets like this for years."

Sewell said, " No." He considered his coffee cup again and then said, " How's that fellow ? "

" Ralph ? Very well."

" I've been meaning to ask you this for a long time," said Sewell, as though speaking were a great effort. " How d'you get on ? "

" You mean with Ralph ? Darling, you ask me that every time you see me. We get on very well." She waited a moment and said, " Now you ask me if we're going to stay married and I say ' Yes,' and you look incredulous. You're forgetting your lines, Lucas."

Sewell closed his eyes. " I've been thinking a good deal about this lately," he said, with a frown. " And I suppose in some ways it was really my fault."

" What was ? "

" Your marrying Peach. I oughtn't just to have cleared out and left you with your mother. I ought to have taken you with me."

" What on earth's put this into your head ? " said Mab, slightly startled.

Sewell shrugged. " It's obvious enough. The only thing you could do was to get married and get away. Otherwise you'd have gone crazy. But of course it didn't occur to me at the time."

Mab looked at him thoughtfully. " Look, Lucas," she said. " If you want to wish you'd been a better boy, don't let me

143

stop you. I can think of several things you might have regrets
about if you want some. But get your facts right. It was
practically three years after you left Mummie that I got
married. It was nothing whatever to do with you. And
anyhow, I *like* it."

" I'm sure you do," said Sewell indifferently. " Of course,
in the circumstances it was entirely the right decision."

Mab said angrily, " There are times when I could hit
you over the head with a bottle. What's the matter ? "

Sewell hesitated. " I was merely wondering if you were
happy. In so far as anybody can be, of course."

" You're always wondering if I'm happy nowadays. I
don't like it, Lucas."

" Not what you've been used to," said Sewell bitterly.

" No. It isn't. And it's very disturbing. I spend half a
lifetime organising on the basis that you don't give a damn
what happens to me, and just when I've got it all set up
you suddenly want to wade in again."

" I'm sorry, my dear," said Sewell, with a wry smile. " I
wouldn't interfere for the world."

" I'm glad to hear it," said Mab bluntly. " Once or twice
lately it's sounded as though you'd interfere if you got half
a chance."

" How d'you mean ? " said Sewell, genuinely startled.

" You don't seem to realise that all this business you
do about Ralph is unforgivable and damned impudence.
Ralph's my husband and I see him every day. *He's* the person
who matters to me. I see you about once a year when you
don't happen to have enough work to do, and think it would
be fun to be a bit fatherly. And then you do this act about
my happiness as though you and I were hand in glove and
Ralph was an outsider."

" Whereas of course it's I who am the outsider."

" Well, if you are, darling, whose choice was it ? " She
saw his face and said gently, " I'm sorry, Lucas. I don't
want to be beastly. But you do—you do walk in and out so.

I don't really mind nowadays. But I got trodden on a bit by it years ago, and now it scares me if I think you're . . ."

Sewell said heavily, " You're quite right, of course. I've no right to talk to you about these things at all. ' Impudent.' That's the right word. I apologise."

She grinned at him and said, " Darling."

Sewell did not smile back. He dropped his eyes to his coffee cup and said, " One gets old, you know, and then, of course . . . one's values change. . . ." He trailed off into silence.

Mab said quietly, " Lucas—you're all *right*, are you ? "

He looked up and said, " Of course."

" This business about the work worrying you ? "

" In a way. More irritating than worrying."

" Tell me more about what's happened. You saw the Minister ? "

" Yes." He stared moodily at his coffee cup. " It looks as though there's bound to be a—a certain amount of delay. I suppose they're right according to their lights. But, my God, what lights ! "

A shadow of relief passed across Mab's face. " Damned annoying for you, though."

" Yes," said Sewell listlessly. " It makes everything rather pointless. . . ." He frowned and passed a hand across his eyes. " It's a warning, really, against putting all your eggs in one basket," he said. " Concentration on one idea . . . it can let you down."

Mab said gently, " Look—I'm sorry I said that a minute ago. You do know that . . ."

" That's all right," said Sewell indifferently. " Entirely justified. It's I who should apologise." He paused and then said suddenly, " By the way—how are you off for money ? "

" I've got heaps. Why ? D'you want me to pay ? "

" No. I don't mean now. I mean in general ? "

Mab considered. " We exist. In fact, we exist quite a lot, compared with most people. Why ? "

" Would it be a good thing if you had some more ? " Sewell hesitated and added quickly, " I'm asking purely for information. Don't answer if you don't want to."

" You mean—from you ? "

" Yes. Unless, of course, you thought that was—trying to walk in again. It wouldn't be. It's simply that I've got a —a surplus that's no good to me. You'll get it eventually, anyhow. Might have been more sensible to have it now."

Mab said, " Darling, that's awfully nice of you, but you know the answer, don't you ? "

" That you'd rather not ? "

" Yes. But if you've got a surplus, how about Mummie ? Mummie's one of those people who never have enough money and never will. But—she isn't very flush, you know. And she'd *enjoy* it so."

Sewell's face had gone very tired. He said, " Yes. There's something in that. I must think about it." He stared moodily in front of him for a while and then said, " Would it be a good idea if I went down and saw her ? "

Mab hesitated. " It couldn't do any harm. How much good it would do depends on what you say when you get there. Last time she saw you she spent the next week right up in the air and the next two in bed. I don't really know whether that's bad or good." She looked at Sewell's averted face and said, " D'you *want* to see her ? "

Sewell looked at her for a moment and then dropped his eyes to his coffee cup. " Yes," he said heavily. " Yes. It's a long time since . . . I think I'd better go down. Ring her up and say I'm coming. Thursday. Or Friday."

IX

THE train still went from Platform 8, as it had always done. Twenty years and a war hadn't altered that, though it now left at three-fifteen instead of at three-five. It was odd to be in Charing Cross station again. Every day, five or six days a week, year in year out, he had been in and out of Charing Cross ; and then one morning he had come to it, and taken a cab to his club, and never used it again. Sewell glanced round the station to see if it meant anything to him now. As London termini went, he liked it. He always had. It was small and comparatively light. But that was all. He knew that catching trains there had sometimes been good, and more often bad. But now it was just a station, and there was no good or bad left in it.

He was getting used to it now—this negativeness. At first it had been disappointing and oddly frightening. But if he could sit opposite Mab for a couple of hours and feel nothing but a mild irritation with both himself and her, it wasn't likely that Charing Cross Station would be very stimulating. This was the way the world ended. Not with a bang, nor even a whimper, but with a sort of creeping paralysis of indifference.

He was too early, as usual, and when he saw that it was only five to three he asked himself whether it was worth a wait of twenty minutes. It had been a silly idea to visit Rose, and now, if there were twenty minutes to wait, it seemed an absurd one. He offered himself the possibility of going back to the club instead. He could be there by the time the train started, safe with the reality of a shiny magazine, instead of setting out on this journey which had no shred of reality about it. But the offer was refused promptly and without explanation, and he accepted the decision as he accepted everything now, and went and sat in the train.

He hadn't told Mab which train he would travel on, so there was no danger that Rose would meet him. He was glad of that. She had a passion for meeting people and for seeing them off. He could remember with surprising vividness the feeling of bracing himself, as the train drew into the station, to meet Rose's greeting. He had tried a dozen times to stop her from coming. But it was no good. "You shouldn't bother, Rose." "But, darling, I *like* it. It's the big moment of my day." And then again, "I'm always having a nightmare in which I'm meeting you and the train comes in and you aren't on it. I watch and watch and all the people get off, and I still stand there hoping, and then at last the train goes and I realise you haven't come. . . ." And yet, when at last he wasn't on the train, she had been surprised. Rose always knew what would happen, and was always surprised when it did. "You'll leave me one day. I'm not clever enough for you. Don't think I don't realise that." Yet "I could understand it if you were in love with somebody else or if—if there were any *reason*. But just to walk out and leave your wife and child and your home. . . ."

The train started to move at last. Sewell leant back in the corner and closed his eyes. The past was all clear enough—some of it surprisingly clear. But it was a photograph—flat and monochromatic. A series of events, and sometimes one had been right and sometimes one had been wrong. But it didn't matter, and there was nothing in it to think about. All that remained now was to make certain formal, useless gestures. It was quite pointless to go and see Rose. But it cost nothing, and she might like it. One could afford, at last, some small thing that Rose might like. Always, before, what Rose wanted had been something that one couldn't afford.

He must have dozed for some while. When he awoke he was very cold, with a sense of leaden depression. He looked out of the window as the train ran through Hither Green, and was surprised to see that it was not raining. It was some while before he realised that it had been fine all day, and that the puddles and mackintoshes at Charing Cross and the heavy feeling of misery and foreboding belonged to thirty-five years ago. He had quarrelled with Greenhaugh and resigned his lectureship, and that, for the moment, had been the end of the world. The train had run into the station and he had told himself carefully that she wouldn't come to meet him in that pouring rain. He had been carried some way past the barrier, and as his carriage passed it he had seen her standing there in the dripping blue mackintosh cape, looking at the windows with that bright, eager face. He hadn't braced himself to meet Rose's greeting then, but had stumbled out and as she came to meet him he had said, " I've resigned." Rose's face had brightened as though he had brought her a diamond necklace, and she had said, " Resigned ? Oh, darling, what fun ! " and kissed him. And then she had said, " Come on—let's get home out of this. You look as though you'd had enough of it," and suddenly Greenhaugh and his rabbit teeth and the shortage of decent jobs were no longer relevant.

He was coming home now, and the world was coming to an end again, but he wasn't thirty now, and the end that was coming was the real end. He was cold and afraid because he couldn't see the way ahead, and Rose couldn't be at the station to meet him because she didn't know the time of the train. As the train ran into the station he went and stood in the corridor and stared out at the platform, gripping the bar which ran along the windows so tightly that he could feel the muscles trembling in his arms. As his carriage passed the barrier he saw her standing there, looking eagerly at the windows, a handsome elderly woman, unmistakable and entirely strange. It was not raining. Sewell let go of

149

the bar, pulling himself up to his full height, went slowly along the corridor to the door.

She said, " Hallo, Luke, darling," and kissed him. As he kissed her and smelt that faint carnation smell he reflected that nobody else had ever called him Luke, and with luck nobody else ever would.

When they were in the taxi Sewell said, " How did you know what train I was on ? "

" I didn't," said Rose simply. " I just met them all."

" You shouldn't have bothered to do that."

She smiled at him and said, " But I *liked* it. I hardly ever have any one to meet now, and it's nice to have that thrill again—waiting to see if—if somebody gets off."

Her face had worn extraordinarily well. Her cheeks were plump and tight, and she made up so that they still had the soft pink and white that set off the china-blue eyes. It was only under her chin and on her throat that the skin was loose and coarse, and on her forehead that the lines had deepened. Her body was thick and heavy now, but by some miracle her legs and ankles were still a good shape. Looking at her Sewell decided that no one would ever have thought she was sixty. The popular verdict would have been that she was a miraculously preserved seventy.

He said, " You look very well, Rose."

" I *am* a lot better than I was." She looked at him solemnly. " You look a bit tired. Working hard ? "

Sewell hesitated for a fraction of a second, and then he saw the rather blank, china-blue eyes on him and the old hopelessness and laziness and boredom came back. It wasn't there and even to have thought it might have been was sheer fantasy. " Moderately," he said.

When he had bought the house it had been on the edge of the village, with nothing beyond it but the fields sloping down into the valley, with the hills rising abruptly on the other side. Now the valley was a solid housing estate, and up on the hills there were a lot of white houses with green roofs. It was different inside too. The drawing-room was narrower than he remembered, and he had forgotten that it had a round window at the end. Rose saw him look round and smiled, and said, " How it all comes back, eh ? Or doesn't it ? "

" Some of it's very familiar," he said. " But haven't you had that grate altered ? "

" Grate ? " she said vaguely. " No. It's always been like that. Wait a minute though—no, it hasn't. I had the tiles put in. Was that after your time ? "

Sewell said, " I think so." It was all after his time. Far more so than his uncle's house in Cumberland, which he had seen twice, fifty years ago.

Rose looked better without her hat. Her hair was a rather dusty grey now, and, surprisingly, she had neither dyed it nor bleached it. Somehow it made her whole appearance less equivocal.

She said, " There are crumpets and honey, and I managed to get a bit of Earl Grey. Probably by now you hate all of them, but I have no later information."

" I still like them all, but nobody ever gives them to me. You shouldn't have killed the fatted calf, Rose."

" My dear, you can't think how lovely it is to have somebody to kill the fatted calf for." She said it rather tremulously, but then, with careful briskness, " I hear you've been seeing a bit of Mab and Ralph ? "

" Yes. I went to dinner with them and Mab lunched with me. Mab been down ? "

" She comes down occasionally. But I always feel it's an effort for her. After all, she's busy, and there's nothing to bring her here."

" How d'you mean ? " said Sewell unguardedly.

" There's nothing to bring any one here, is there, Luke ? "

Five years ago when he had last seen her in London, it

had been quite different. She had laughed and cried and flattered him and abused him. It had been all the old days and the old arguments. He had come prepared for that again, and now it wasn't happening and wasn't going to happen. He was relieved, but at the same time rather hurt. Except for that fatuous moment in the train he had known that there was nothing to be got from Rose. But he hadn't expected her to know it and accept it. True, she kept implying that she was lonely, and whenever she did so there was the old self-pity. But there was nothing of that waiting pathetically for the reply that never came ; and when sometimes there was a silence, he often had to break it himself with some desperate commonplace. He grew impatient at last and said, " How d'you spend your time nowadays ? Must be a bit solitary." But even then she only smiled faintly and said, " Oh, I don't know. I don't really seem to have so very much. As you get older there doesn't seem to *be* so much time, does there ? "

It wasn't until the tea had been cleared away and she had taken him out and shown him the garden and explained about the man who came in two evenings a week to do it, that she suddenly said, " Mab seemed to think you wanted to see me about something." It was said politely and without excitement. He might have been the vicar calling about a sale of work.

Sewell said roughly, " I didn't tell her so. I just told her I wanted to see you."

Rose smiled. " Oh. That's much nicer. Mab seemed to think . . ."

" I wanted to see you, and I thought you wouldn't mind if I came."

" You know I always want to see you, Luke," she said gently. " If you just came to please me it was very sweet of you and you know I'm grateful. I'm only sorry it isn't more fun for you."

He looked at the soft, plump face and the gentle blue eyes

and for one moment he thought of taking her and kissing her hard on the lips, and saying that he loved her and always had ; and it would have been true enough in its way. But one's truth and Rose's truth had always been two different commodities, and the fatal thing had been ever to mix them. He would go away after it, and she would be left confused and hurt and exalted and agonised, with all that careful pride trodden under foot. There would be no doubt then who was the master, and in an odd, childish way, it still mattered to him that he should be the master. But it didn't matter as much as that, so he did not kiss her, but looked at the grate that she had had tiled after his time, and said casually, " By the way, how are you off for money ? "

There was a slight pause. Then she said vaguely, " Money? Well, I've had rather heavy medical expenses, of course."

" What sort of medical expenses, Rose ? "

" This wretched migraine. I had a bad time with it last winter."

He stared at her for a moment until the blue eyes looked guiltily away and then said, " Mab tells me that you've got a new psychiatrist."

She hesitated and then said in a low voice, " Yes. I have. Dr. Park. He's—he's done me a lot of good, Luke."

" And how much does he cost ? "

" Four guineas a week," she said wretchedly.

He waited again and then suddenly smiled and said, " Four guineas a week ? I should say it was worth it. He *has* done you good."

She should have cried then. She had always cried when he suddenly let her off and was kind. But she didn't cry or even look surprised. She just said, " Worth it ? You can't reckon what he's done for me—like that."

Sewell thought she didn't understand. He said gently, " Look, Rose—four guineas a week is rather a lot for—for

153

you to cope with. I should like you to send Dr. Park's bills to me."

There was a long pause. She was staring at him with her eyes wide open and rather startled. Once she opened her lips and closed them again without speaking. He smiled at her encouragingly, and gradually she began to smile back. "That's—that's very kind of you, Luke," she said politely.

"Kind of me?" he said bitterly. "Four guineas a week that I don't need, so that you can have something that means a lot to you? That isn't kind, Rose. It's magnificent."

She said as though she hadn't heard, "Kind and generous. But there—there isn't any need for it, Luke."

He was startled and said roughly, "What d'you mean? You can't pay this chap four guineas a week out of your income without going without a—a lot of things."

"I can," she said simply. "You'd be surprised. I don't spend much nowadays, really."

Sewell said, "Then you've changed, my dear."

His face frightened her. She said anxiously, "I don't mean I'm not terribly grateful, Luke, because it's awfully sweet of you. But you see, I don't *have* to go to Dr. Park— I mean I shouldn't die or anything if I didn't. It's just that I like it and think it's good for me—and I think I ought to pay for that myself. I'd rather, really."

"In fact, paying Dr. Park money you can't afford is all part of the treatment?" said Sewell contemptuously.

She thought for a moment and then said, "Could you really spare the money, Luke? I mean—without being short yourself?"

"Of course I could," he said. "Did you ever know me give away anything I wanted?"

"Then could . . . wouldn't it be nice if—if you could do something for Mab? I know Ralph earns quite a good salary, but he's got a—a position to keep up and it would be nice for her if she had an allowance of her own. Even if it were just fifty pounds a year or something like that. . . ."

He hardly bothered to say it was not worth while to come to the station. He was past caring now. The loneliness of being with her was even becoming bitterly funny. In the taxi she repeated, gently and sincerely, that it had been nice of him to come, and that she was sorry that she couldn't make it more amusing for him. He said mechanically that it had been nice to see her, and on the platform he kissed her and smelt the faint carnation smell for the last time. The train only stopped for a moment, and he got in and sat gazing straight in front of him until it had pulled out of the station. Then something made him go and look back out of the window. She was still standing on the platform, a heavy elderly woman in an old musquash coat, waving her handkerchief blindly at the back of the guard's van. He did not wave back, but stood there looking until she was out of sight, and then went back to the empty compartment. After he had been sitting for a few minutes he got up and walked slowly down the corridor. In the next compartment was a middle-aged man with horn-rimmed spectacles. Sewell went in and carefully flicked some tobacco ash off the seat before he sat down. " I notice," he said, with his brightest smile, " that, though we now have ' British Railways ' painted on the engines, we still have tobacco ash on the seats."

The middle-aged man looked at him for a moment and then said solemnly, " First things first, sir. The worker's soul must be ministered to before the trouser-seat of the bourgeoisie."

Sewell let out a long, silent breath. It was easy now. " There's the beginning of a French epigram there," he said. " Based on the expression ' sans-culotte.' "

* * * * *

Sewell was poking about round the oven in a vague way

when Lucy got back to the laboratory. He pointed at the dish of melted wax with the stem of his pipe and said, " What's this ? "

Lucy said, " Liver sections from the controls. They're nearly cooked."

" D'you have to do sections yourselves ? Why doesn't Arthur do them ? "

" Arthur'd got a lot of stuff for Dr. Shole, so I said I would."

Sewell said, " D'you like messing about with a microtome ? I always did."

" I like it as long as somebody else sharpens the knife."

There was a long string of filmy sections hung over a wire. Sewell looked at them and said, " You do these ? "

" Yes. They're rather fried. I think the wax was too hot."

" They look all right." He stood and peered at them for some moments. Lucy stood politely waiting.

Sewell looked up and said, " Where's Marriott ? Isn't he in to-day ? "

" He's with Dr. Shole."

Sewell nodded and turned away from the oven. Lucy hesitated and then pushed the dish of melted wax a little farther in and closed the door.

Sewell was standing looking out of the window about four feet away. She paused again. It was difficult to know whether, for working purposes, he was there or not. Lucy carefully picked up the wax ribbon in which the liver sections were embedded and started to break it up into its component squares.

Sewell turned and watched her. After a moment he said, " Going to stain those ? "

" I'm not sure if they're worth it."

He was standing in front of the rack with the alcohols and the xylol on it, and she could hardly ask him to move.

Sewell was still staring. He said, " Did I ever tell you about old J.B. and the pressure experiment ? "

Lucy looked up and smiled politely and said, " No ? "

" Well, it was when J.B. was doing the original stuff on low pressures. He was in the pressure cage, riding a stationary, and the idea was that they gradually lowered the pressure on him to see how it affected his work output. Haines was recording, and as the pressure dropped J.B. was supposed to signal that he was all right. What they didn't realise at that time was that as the pressure falls people get very stupid and dull, and tend just to go on doing what they were doing before. Well, there was J.B. grinding away and every now and again waving a hand at Haines and grinning, and eventually they got it down very low indeed. But still J.B. grinned and waved, so Haines thought he was all right. Then somebody called Haines away for a moment. Well, this was late at night and there was a charwoman going round. She came on the cage with J.B. in it. By that time he'd stopped pedalling and she thought he looked a bit odd. J.B. saw her looking in, and he grinned and waved as he'd been doing to Haines and then fell slap off on the floor, absolutely out. Almost anybody else in the world would have thought this was part of the experiment, or else would have gone and found Haines. But this woman realised that something was wrong and that J.B. was passing out, and she just put her broom through the glass of the cage, and that was the only thing that saved J.B.'s life."

Lucy said, " What extraordinary courage ! "

" That's exactly what I always said. She backed her own judgment, and if she'd been wrong everybody would have been furious." Sewell was sitting on the bench now and the question of whether he was there or not no longer arose. The Prof. wanted to gossip. That was normal. What wasn't normal was that he should do it with her. Usually women were to be touched, but not to be seen or heard.

Sewell filled his pipe and said, " Let's see—how long have you been here now ? "

" Nearly three years."

" Like it ? "

" Yes."

" I've never understood about women scientists," he said thoughtfully. " You must explain it to me sometime, Lucy."

That was new. So was the smile.

She smiled back and said, " What don't you understand? "

" What their attitude can be. Men must speculate. They must be interested in the future because the present is always pointless for them. But women aren't driven by that. They've got a perfectly good job and a completely satisfactory life in the present."

" In the home, you mean ? "

" In producing children. The cow's employed. The bull isn't—except very occasionally. So the bull has to find something to fill up his time or he'd be bored to distraction."

It was a good face—a very alive face for all its age. She said, " I doubt if I could explain much, because I'm probably not a proper scientific woman."

" Oh—splendid. As long as you realise that you're not a scientist in the sense that Shole or even young Marriott is a scientist, it's all right. I don't mean that as a criticism, you understand. . . ."

It went straight on without a moment's pause or hesitation. In fact, he was in the middle of a sentence when he suddenly looked at his watch and broke off and said, " Good heavens—it's half-past six. Come on—you'd better come and have dinner with me now I've kept you as late as this."

Lucy said, " What—to-night ? I—I'm afraid I can't."

Sewell's face fell. " Oh," he said, " going out ? "

"Yes. At least I'm tied up. . . . Thank you very much. . . ."

" Well, some other night. To-morrow night. Could you do that ? I've wanted to have a chat with you for some time."

" It's very nice of you, Professor Sewell. I should like it. But it's a bit difficult for me. . . ."

He passed his hand over his eyes and said wearily, " Well, try and fix it. Try and fix it for to-morrow evening. And let me know in the morning." He looked down at her with a curious brilliant intimacy. " You must make these charitable efforts, you know."

X

LUCY said, " Could you bear it—as long as I got somebody in ? I don't particularly want to go, but it's by
way of being a royal command."

" Of course you must go," said Ivor. " Dinner with the
boss. *Droit du seigneur*, and so on."

" I don't know why he should suddenly have asked me.
He's never had anything to do with me before if he could
avoid it. He doesn't approve of women—not as scientific
workers, anyhow."

" I doubt you're being taken to the Picardy as a scientific
worker, darling. How old is he ? "

" Oh, pretty old. Sixty-fivish, anyhow."

" The prime age for a sugar daddy."

" Of course it may be that he's going to fire me and that
this is a delicate way of doing it."

" Darling," said Ivor firmly, " any girl who's taken out to
dinner by a sixty-five-year-old boss and comes away without
getting promotion or a rise doesn't know her stuff. Even if
he *did* set out to fire her. Shall I give you a few tips ? " He
moistened his lips. Lucy said quickly, " Who would you
like me to get in ? Sam ? "

Ivor reflected for a moment. " No," he said at last, " not
Sam. I don't think I could take a complete evening of Sam."
He smiled suddenly. " I think I'd like Bob."

" Bob ? Bob who ? "

" I can't remember his other name. Your Bob. Your
young man from the Haughton that came to the
pub."

Lucy said sharply, " You mean Bob Marriott ? "

" That's it. Marriott."

She turned away and said, " Don't be a fool, Ivor."

" Why not ? " said Ivor reasonably. " I should like to have him, and I'm sure he'd like to come. You ask him and see."

" I certainly shan't."

" But *why* not, Lucy ? Why on earth should you mind if I happen to like a—a friend of yours and he happens to like me ? "

" Well, for one thing he—he doesn't know how to do things for you. . . ."

" I could tell him. After all, even a scientist can be taught to give a man his food."

". . . and for another . . ." Lucy hesitated.

" Well ? " said Ivor gently.

She turned and faced him, and said, " Look, Ivor—you know quite well that boy's a fool. If you enjoy talking to him it's only because you like embarrassing him and hearing him be silly. It's not good for you or for him, so for God's sake forget it."

Ivor smiled at her and said, " But, my dear, a man can't help being interested in his rivals. Obviously that young man must have *something*—apart from two arms. Otherwise you wouldn't be so interested in him. I want to know what it is. I want . . ."

Lucy glanced at her watch and said, " We shall have to go. Is it to be Sam or Clarry ? "

" I've already told you. I should like you to ask Mr. Marriott."

" Well, I won't, so that's that."

" You bitch," said Ivor dispassionately. " You bullying little bitch. If I had the use of my hands you'd think twice before you spoke to me like that." He beamed at her fondly. " All right, darling. We'd better be starting."

" And—and how about to-night ? You can't stay here alone."

" I shan't," said Ivor calmly. " I shall ring up Marriott

L

and ask him to come along. Oddly enough, you're not the only pair of hands in London."

*　　*　　*　　*　　*

Marriott had got tired of slacking and had found something to do. She wanted to tell him that Ivor was going to ring him up—to advise him to say " No." But she knew that if she did Marriott would look at her in blank surprise and ask for some logical, factual, why and wherefore. And then he would smile his patronising, knowing child's smile, and tell her not to be silly. He would like to spend an evening with Ivor. Ivor had an interesting mind. . . .

When she got back from lunch Marriott was already there and she knew from his manner that Ivor had rung up. She waited to see what he would say, but Marriott said nothing. He just looked at her rather furtively and went on with his work. Probably Ivor had told him that she wasn't to know. That would be very like Ivor. She said, to give him a lead, " Did I tell you that Prof. Sewell had asked me out to dinner to-night ? "

" Really ? " said Marriott politely.

" Yes. I'm abandoning Ivor and going on the tiles."

There was a moment's silence and then Marriott said, " I dare say Ivor'll be glad. He always says you don't go out enough."

Lucy was suddenly furiously angry. She had done her best for both of them and all that happened was that they ganged up together, the knave and the fool, and laughed at her and lied to her. They enjoyed each other's company. Let them enjoy it and go to hell.

" Yes," she said in a voice that was shaky with anger. " Perhaps I've worried too much about Ivor. Perhaps I've worried too much about everybody. Never mind. To-night I'm off duty."

The lavatories were the most modern part of the Haughton

Laboratory. In fact, they were so good and had cost so much money that Sewell had shocked the Council by proposing a chair of Skatological Research, and had threatened to move his whole department into them. " Here, gentlemen, are taps that run—basins that are cleanable—decent lighting—all the things that I've been asking for in my department since about 1920. Let us give up the dull pursuit of science and spend our days in luxurious excretion and lavage."

But they were invaluable if one was going out for the evening direct from the laboratory. Lucy took the dark-green silk frock out of her suitcase, hung it up and examined it carefully. It hadn't creased. She took off the jersey and the old check skirt and started to wash. Sewell had told her not to dress, but one could hardly go out to dinner in a jersey and skirt with a darned sulphuric acid burn in the front. And, anyhow, it was impossible for any one to look over-dressed in the green frock, which was short and at least four years old. She put it on and decided that it looked all right. It never had looked more than all right, even when it was new. But it looked all right, and so did the shoes.

At twenty past seven Lucy stepped back from the mirror and looked at herself sulkily. It was always the same. One's nose was too broad at the base and one's chin was too round. But apart from that there was an absence of slickness that it was impossible to define. Taken bit by bit it wasn't bad. Quite passable legs. Quite a reasonable shape as shapes go. Nice hair, very sleek and thick and heavy. Eyes a bit like the mud at the bottom of a pond but not piggy or boot-buttony. And yet the whole effect was dull and dowdy. She smiled at her reflection, and that was better. She curved her upper lip back so that her teeth showed and that was better still, particularly when she turned her head sideways. . . . After a while she remembered that she was going out with Professor Sewell, not with Mr. Gregory Peck. She gave a faint giggling snort, and composed her face into an expression of alert, amused attention. Gazing at her alert, amused reflection, Lucy decided sadly that twenty-four was a very difficult age. One had neither poise nor youth.

Sewell sat at the glass-topped table staring fixedly at his second whisky and soda. It had been there some time now and the bubbles were only rising in half a dozen slender threads. A man came in and called, " Pietro ! " as soon as he was inside the door. He was tall, with a low forehead, a bristling moustache and an insolent, sneering face. The head waiter came hurrying out of the restaurant room and bowed and said, " Good evening, my lord." My lord gave a lot of rapid instructions in a low voice, and Pietro bowed a lot. Then he went away and my lord threw himself down on a chair and looked round the place contemptuously. Sewell decided that he must be a subtle piece of Left Wing propaganda. He couldn't really be a member of the puzzled and thoroughly frightened aristocracy. " Excuse me," Theodore Hook had said to the pompous-looking stranger, " but are you any one in particular ? " I am Sewell. That doesn't mean anything to you, but if you watch the obituary columns of *The Times* it will eventually.

Lucy came in. She was wearing a dark-green frock and carrying her coat over her arm. She looked very pretty, but rather like somebody's very intelligent typist. Sewell was conscious of my lord's eyes as he got up. He said, " Hullo, Lucy, here you are," and for some reason shook hands with her. She smiled at him rather shyly and said, " Sorry I'm late."

" You aren't. I'm early. Would you like to get rid of your coat ? . . ."

Sewell went back to his table. My lord was staring at him with blatant interest. Sewell looked at him thoughtfully and expressionlessly until he drooped his eyelids and looked away. A middle-aged woman in a big mink coat with very full sleeves came in and cried, " Raymond ! " loudly and rapturously. She hurried over to my lord's table and took his hand in both of hers. He half-rose rather unwillingly, looking at her with his half-closed eyes, and said, " Hallo," and pointed to a chair. Lucy reappeared. She didn't look round the room but kept her eyes on him as she walked towards the table. Sewell got up and said, " Now—a drink. Martini or—— ? "

" Martini, please." She sat down and glanced rapidly at the woman in the mink coat and back to him. Sewell smiled at her and said, " That's a very charming frock." She was uncomfortable, and she was very young. But she had a certain calmness. He had noticed it before.

She said, " Very old and quite unsuitable. But it's the only one I've got."

Sewell said, " On coming to think of it, I seem to have expected you to come in a white coat." He beckoned a waiter. " Dry Martini and a whisky and soda, please."

The waiter said, ", Yes, Professor." Sewell saw the Left Wing propaganda look up. He looked back. I am Lucas Sewell. That doesn't mean anything to you. But if you watch . . .

*   *   *   *   *

Marriott said, " You have the infected flies in a sort of little cage, and you strap it on your . . . you strap it on so that they can get a good bite at you. I'm a good subject. Flies always like the taste of me."

" You know, I just don't think I could do that."

" Why not ? There's nothing to it."

" Perhaps not to you. But the idea of letting something bite you which you *know's* infected . . ." Ivor shook his head with a grimace and sucked at his straws.

Marriott was pleased. " One gets used to it," he said lightly. " After all, it's one's job." He sipped his whisky.

Ivor said, " You like that better than beer, don't you ? "

Marriott hesitated. " Well, yes. On the whole I do. Beer's all right, but . . ."

" But it's got a filthy smell and a filthy taste. Otherwise it's fine, eh ? " Ivor smiled and added quickly, " I feel just the same."

" Do you ? " said Marriott with relief. " I've never liked it much. One *drinks* it, of course, but . . ."

" Beer," said Ivor, " is a drink for the unintelligent. Do you mind catching Phil's eye ? I think there's enough soda." He sucked the dregs out of his glass and sighed. " It's extremely kind of you to have given up an evening like this."

" It's extremely kind of you to have asked me."

" But that's the snag. I can't ask anybody to a meal without its being rather—rather difficult and embarrassing for them. So it has to be somebody whom I know well and like a lot."

Marriott blushed and said, " Well . . ."

" Besides," said Ivor calmly, " I had an idea that you might like it too. One either has something for people or hasn't, you know. Last time I think we both felt that we could have done without the rest of the company."

" Yes. I was sorry when Brown came."

" Oh, not only Brown. It was a nuisance having Lucy there." Ivor was looking up with his odd, intimate, feminine smile. " Women are very nice at certain times and irreplaceable for certain purposes. But, by God, how tired one gets of them ! "

There was no need any longer to play safe and agree. One knew Ivor now. Marriott said, " Living alone in digs one is chiefly conscious of the irreplaceability part of it."

Ivor laughed and stared at him with very bright eyes. " I dare say," he said. " I dare say one's *very* conscious of it. I wonder how Lucy's getting on with her Professor ? "

Marriott said, " I wonder. I can't quite see why he suddenly wanted to take her out. He's never taken *me* out."

" I don't think it's very odd that anybody should want to take Lucy out," said Ivor, with his white-toothed smile. " Can't you see his point of view ? "

Marriott blushed, but it was quite easy to grin back. " Oh, come," he said. " The old boy's well over sixty. As far as I can make out he used to be a hell of a lad. But surely nowadays—— ? "

" Nevertheless," said Ivor solemnly, " we mustn't underestimate him. Many a good girl's found something fascinating about white hair. And then where should we be ? " He grinned again. " Partner, I look to you to keep an eye on our interests."

" Leave it to me," said Marriott, with a conspiratorial gesture. It was quite easy when one knew Ivor and had got used to his way.

The white wine had an indescribable roundness and smoothness. Sewell was saying, " It's a matter on which it's practically impossible to be objective. But trying not to be a sixty-year-old diehard or, worse, a sixty-year-old radical, I feel that there has been progress in practically every direction that doesn't matter. When were you born ? "

" Nineteen twenty-four."

" Good heavens ! You make me feel like a patriarch. Well, now, my mother was born in eighteen fifty. She was an intelligent, well-educated woman—in fact, she took quite a part in the movement for the New Education for women. I remember well her ambitions for women. The vote. Higher education. Entrance to the professions—all the usual feminist programme. Well, we're just about a hundred years from her birth and here are you—the young woman she dreamed about. I wonder what she would have thought of you ? "

" I doubt if I'm a very good sample," said Lucy apologetically. " I'm not very—very modern really. I often think I should have done better in—in the nineties, say."

Sewell said, " You talk about the nineties as history. They were part of my life."

There was a moment's silence. Sewell was staring away

across the room. The lines of his face seemed suddenly to have drooped and sagged. He turned his head suddenly and said, " Why do you think you would have liked the nineties ? "

She had been thinking of the clothes, but that was childish. " It always sounds rather colourful," she said feebly.

" You'd certainly have looked very nice," said Sewell without a moment's hesitation. " Now let's see—what would you have worn ? Your hat would have been . . ."

The waiter was removing the plates. Lucy leaned back in her chair with an inward sigh of contentment. It was so easy. It was all taken and done for you. It wasn't particularly brilliant or exciting, but there was no tension—no fear—no watching points. It was the *calmness* of the old that was so attractive.

" Your views, like your waist, would have been tightly laced into the corsets of the period. But the mental and physical corsets of one's own day are never intolerable. One accepts them as part of life." Sewell cut his cheese. Lucy noticed with foolish surprise that his hands, though beautifully shaped and kept, were an elderly man's hands, and that they shook slightly. He looked up and said, " What interests me is whether the removal of the nineteenth-century corset—the mental one, I mean—has brought greater happiness. It has certainly brought greater *freedom*. But they're not necessarily the same thing."

" I don't know," said Lucy thoughtfully. " I should have said happiness was a—a personal thing—that you either had it or not, and that the—the conventions didn't make much difference."

Sewell shook his head. " You may be right, but I doubt it. Look at yourself. I don't know anything about the life you lead. But you've got a job. You can keep yourself. It's not necessary, if you want to remain a lady, to sit meekly at home waiting for somebody to come and marry you. It's not necessary, when you do marry, to go into marriage completely ignorant of what it means." He looked down at his plate for a moment and then turned the fine grey eyes full on her. " Let me try to show you what I mean. You are a very attractive young woman of twenty-four. You have chosen so far not to marry. In my day, to have suggested to you that you were not a virgin would have been a gross insult. Nowadays it's merely a glimpse of the obvious."

Her eyes were a curious greeny-brown. She had a certain calmness. She smiled slightly and said, " It's rather disconcerting to be told that it's as obvious as all that."

Sewell laughed. " I don't mean obvious when one looks at you—though of course it is, if it comes to that. What I mean is that it's obvious from the situation. Or, at least, highly probable. Whereas virginity until marriage was the norm of female social behaviour, now it's rather the exception. Now that's a tremendous change—a step towards what is loosely called ' freedom.' But is it a step towards happiness ? "

" I don't know," said Lucy simply. " I've no—no standard of comparison. Do *you* think so ? " Whatever happened, it was essential to go on looking straight at him—to go on talking quietly and thoughtfully—to justify the compliment of being talked to as one grown-up person to another.

" I don't know either," said Sewell, " from the female point of view." He gave a sudden startlingly boyish grin. " From the point of view of the lascivious male, of course, it's an admirable reform."

*　*　*　*　*

Bill Brown was still wearing a navy-blue suit and a green tie. Judging from their condition they might easily have been the same ones. His eyes bulged even more than Marriott had remembered. He said, " Let's have another drink. What is it ? Whisky ? "

Ivor glanced at Marriott and said, " Well, I don't know.
You're rather behind the party. We've had several already."

" Never mind. I'll drink doubles and catch up."

Marriott said, " Given A and B have drunk three single
whiskies, and that on each succeeding round A and B
continue to drink single whiskies whilst C drinks double
whiskies, how many rounds will be necessary before C has
drunk as much as A and B ? "

" Three," said Bill Brown with surprising promptness.

" Correct," said Marriott, looking at him with new
respect. He was feeling in excellent form, though he still
disliked the way Brown's eyes bulged, and wished he would
go away.

As Brown went to the bar Ivor leaned over and said
quietly, " Watch Bill on drinks. He's got a head like
concrete."

Marriott nodded sagely. It was pleasant to feel that he
and Ivor were together whereas Brown was something
outside the party. When his drink came he merely sipped
it and put it down. In fact, he had never felt more clear-
headed in his life—far more so than he usually felt after a
pint of beer. But Ivor was quite right.

On the next round Ivor insisted on drinking plain soda
water, and Marriott did the same. Brown grunted something about getting them a nice cup of cocoa, but it didn't
matter what Brown thought. He drank his drinks in a
peculiar way, letting them stand on the table for some time
and then taking them off at a single gulp. But he was
certainly a good deal brighter than Marriott had thought.
He seemed to have a slight bee in his bonnet about Americans.
" What was it old Jowett said ? ' Let us not create for ourselves any new necessities.' That might be a definition of
American civilisation—the creation of new necessities."

" Isn't it a definition of civilisation in general ? " said
Ivor.

" Define a necessity," said Marriott. He pushed his glasses on more firmly and looked at them challengingly. It was obvious that they couldn't. " A necessity is something you *think* is necessary. That's all. Even food is only necessary because we think we must go on living. In fact, it doesn't matter a damn whether we go on living or not—not in any absolute way."

" Talking of food—— ? " said Ivor.

" There's no hurry. Why interrupt perfectly good drinking just to eat ? " Brown nodded at Marriott and said, " That's where the scientist scores. He takes these social questions and puts them right down on bed-rock."

" Yes," said Ivor. " It's a capacity which I always find completely terrifying."

They both sat and looked at Marriott in silence for a moment. He sat and smiled quietly and inscrutably at them in turn—the Spirit of the Summit.

" And yet that young man," said Brown to Ivor, " has no more power than you or I. He thinks in a different way—a much *better* way. Yet as society is organised his opinion counts for no more than ours—or any crossing sweeper's." He gazed at Marriott reflectively with the bulging brown eyes.

" Except that the scientist draws the blueprint of the future of civilisation and the crossing sweeper doesn't," said Marriott, slightly offended.

" But forgive me," said Brown excitedly. " That's just what I wanted to get at. When we were in here the other night you yourself were complaining that you weren't *free* to do your work. That it was censored and controlled. . . ."

" He's free to do the work," said Ivor. " What he isn't free to do is to publish it."

" Well, where's the difference ? He's free to draw his blueprint, but he can't show it to anybody. Who stops him ? Presumably some Government department. Drawing power from the vote of the crossing sweeper. Or so I

171

gathered." He turned to Marriott. " Don't talk about this if you don't want to. God forbid that I should ask about your State Secrets. It's the *principle* that I'm interested in. Have I stated it fairly ? "

Marriott hesitated. " Yes. Up to a point."

" I think you're on rather awkward ground," said Ivor to Brown.

" Exactly. He can't talk about it. Even the principle, let alone the details, isn't discussable. The power of the crossing sweeper . . ."

Marriott said, " I don't see that there's anything secret about the principle. It is simply a fact that scientists are stopped from publishing valuable work for—for political reasons."

" Quite. And of course the scientists accept that. They daren't do anything else. See what's been happening to them in America. . . ."

" They *don't* accept it," said Marriott curtly. " At least I don't. And nor do plenty of others. But what can they do ? "

Brown shrugged his shoulders. " It's always easy to suggest heroism for other people. But I should have expected that somewhere there would be a scientist who'd snap his fingers in the crossing sweeper's face and publish and be damned."

" It's odd that you should say that, Bill," said Ivor with a thoughtful smile. " The same thought had occurred to me—that that would happen. But I suppose it's too much to expect. Even scientists have to live and keep out of jail and so on."

" I suppose so," said Brown wearily.

There was a moment's silence. Brown was staring moodily at his glass. Ivor smiled quietly at Marriott with a reassuring wink.

" It's all very well," said Marriott with sullen anger. " But even if any one were prepared to—to risk all that, he couldn't do any real good. It's not a question of publish and be damned. Nobody *could* publish the stuff—or print it or distribute it."

" Why not ? "

" Because the Government would stop it. They've got complete control. . . ."

" Yo-ho ! " said Brown. " *Have* they ? " He leaned forward. " Laddy—I'm in the publishing business. And I can tell you that there isn't a damn thing you can't . . ." He stopped abruptly and looked at Marriott for a moment with the bulging dark eyes. Then he pushed back his chair and said curtly, " Look, I'm tired of this pub. Let's go round the corner to my place. It's only a few yards."

There was a moment's pause. Ivor's eyes met Marriott's. He said, " I think Bob and I had better go back and rout out some food. . . ."

" That's all right. We can find something at home. Bread and cheese is the Chef's Own Dish to-night, I expect. If there's any cheese."

Marriott began, " It's very . . ." But before he could get it out Ivor said, " Well, that's damn nice of you, Bill." Marriott was surprised and disappointed and he tried to catch Ivor's eye again. But Ivor was looking at Brown and Brown was saying, " Fine. Then let's go. Only a few yards."

*　　*　　*　　*　　*

Sewell talked on. She was easy to talk to, with that lively, intelligent face and the quick smile, and she was not shy of him any more. But he had to be careful now—had to listen to himself more critically. That he should disgust himself was inevitable and accepted. But he must not disgust her. And it wasn't an easy face to read.

" And then there comes a day when the mere facts about your age no longer mean anything. You know that you're no longer young. You know that your hair is grey—that you can't see print so well without your glasses—that you no longer have the strength you once had. You know that you will probably die within a comparatively few years. Sometimes you catch yourself acting like an old man. But most of the time, because it's all come so slowly, you don't feel any different. I used to think when I was a young man that when a man's hair went a venerable white all the rest of him went a venerable white too—that he no longer felt the things that I felt or needed the things that I needed. I thought he wanted to go slowly and peacefully to sleep. . . ."

She was listening attentively enough, but she didn't see. Interest in the idea. Nothing else. Not even pity. Not even that. Sewell suddenly grinned his boyish grin and said, " Do you see the *New Yorker*? There was a cartoon in it the other day showing an old stage-door Johnnie at dinner with the typical *New Yorker* gold-digger girl. The caption was, ' But, Mr. Hammick, seventy-five isn't *old*.' This is really your cue to say ' but sixty-four isn't *old*.' "

Lucy said, " Are you really sixty-four? "

" Yes," said Sewell quickly. " Whereas you thought I was sixty-six."

For the first time she looked confused.

" There you are, you see," said Sewell bitterly. " The facts are that I'm forty years older than you. To me, those facts mean nothing in particular. I therefore fail to realise that they mean a great deal to you."

" I don't quite see what you mean."

" My dear girl, you're a very attractive young woman. If a man—*any* man—of under forty, say, had sat and looked at you and talked to you as I've been doing for the last two hours you would have assumed, shall we say, that he was very interested in you—that he wanted something. Wouldn't you? "

" Well, yes," said Lucy, still puzzled.

" But that—that would have been completely different, wouldn't it? "

She looked at him uncertainly for a moment. " Look, I'm

sorry, Professor Sewell," she said, with a rather tentative little smile ; " but I've rather lost the thread of what you were saying and I particularly want to get it because it was very interesting ? . . ."

Sewell closed his eyes. " No, no," he said. " It was just that I was being obscure. All I was trying to point out was that age has its compensations. I can take you out to dinner and talk about life at large, without any danger that you'll misunderstand my intentions. . . ."

" Oh, I *see*."

". . . as you might with any man under forty." He opened his eyes and smiled at her. " The privilege of age—to be harmless, even to pretty girls."

Lucy said, " Oh, yes. Sorry. I was being dense." She looked at the handsome old face and the silver hair, and it was on the tip of her tongue laughingly to question the harmlessness. But that would be cheek and he mightn't like it.

Sewell said, " Would you care for some fresh coffee ? "

She glanced at her watch and said, " It's getting rather late. Oughtn't we to—— ? "

" No, no," he said heavily. " I've brought you out and talked all the time, whereas the whole idea was that you should talk." He pulled back his shoulders with a curious bracing movement and smiled his most brilliant smile. " Come on now—tell me all about yourself. Name—Lucy Byrne. Age twenty-four. Married or single ? Single. How single ? "

He was easy to talk to. His eyes were always calm and unsurprised and he knew a lot. He asked a certain number of questions about Ivor—mainly technical ones about his arms. But he didn't ask why Ivor didn't go into a home for the disabled. He knew about Marriott too. " I take it that he's in love with you ? "

It was quite easy to say, " He probably thinks so."

" And that you're very little, if at all, in love with him ? "

That wasn't so easy, but if one was to be treated as an adult one must act like one. She said levelly, " I find him attractive physically. I don't know why."

" Why not ? " said Sewell. " He's a good-looking boy." He was staring away into the distance. His face had dropped into the rather sullen elderly lines.

" Oh, yes. But there's something rather—rather humiliating about a purely physical attraction. If you're a female, anyhow." She was staring down at her coffee cup. " There are plenty of people whom I *like* a lot more than—than I like him. In a lot of ways I think he's irritating and—rather childish. But . . ."

Sewell looked at the bent head and the shining black hair and the young breasts. Something was aching at the bottom of his throat so that he instinctively pressed at it with his hand.

He said very gently, " All men are childish to women, you know, just as all women are childish to men."

She looked up with a slight smile and said, " I suppose so. He's always telling me very solemnly and pompously that I'm a—a sort of child in arms. . . ."

Sewell smiled back at her and said, " Of course. From his point of view you are." But he could do no more, and when she looked away he added wearily, " I shouldn't worry about it." Any man under forty. Armless men and harmless men, as long as they were under forty. But nothing to warm King David.

*   *   *   *   *

From the state of Bill Brown's shirt Marriott had expected him to live in digs or a bed-sitting-room. But he took them to a Mews house not far from Ivor's flat, and though there were children running and screaming in the Mews and most of it looked battered and slummy in the lamplight, the house itself was all cream paint and glazed chintz and speculative modern art. There was an excellent cold meal on the table.

Brown said, "Excuse me a moment," and went out. They heard him shouting "Mitzi!"

Ivor said, "Old Bill doesn't do himself badly, does he? He got this house for an absolute song."

Brown came back carrying a bottle. He said, "No Mitzi. Must have gone out." He seemed rather pleased about it. Marriott never gathered who Mitzi was, but the table was laid for two.

Brown displayed the bottle and said, "You will observe that the label says whisky. A small prize is offered for the best guess at what's in it." He had remembered straws for Ivor.

The drink tasted very like any other whisky to Marriott, except that it had a slightly smoky flavour.

Ivor said, "It's a sort of stage Irish, with a bogus accent."

"*I* think it's that stuff they make from rum. Anyhow, you drink it at your own risk. The management takes no responsibility." He swallowed his own in a quick gulp and said, "That's the best way to drink it. Then you don't get the taste of paraffin."

Marriott lay back in the big comfortable armchair, took his glasses off and began to polish them. One of his eyes seemed to be playing tricks, but he couldn't be sure which. He closed them in turn, but either by itself seemed to be all right. It was only when they were both open that there was a slight difficulty over focus.

The evening paper was lying on the table. Brown glanced at it and gave a snort. He said, "You will be astonished to hear that the Council of Foreign Ministers has broken up without reaching agreement on the agenda. My God, they can't even agree about the things they're going to disagree about. Come on, let's eat this food. It doesn't seem to belong to anybody."

As they sat down he said to Marriott, "Have you any politics? *Do* scientists have politics? Or do they think it's all nonsense, like most intelligent people?"

M

Marriott pushed his glasses on firmly and put one hand over the eye that wouldn't focus. " In proportion as they have political views," he said, " they're bad scientists. Strong political views mean that you can't have an open mind."

They were both looking at him with interest. He felt very clear and authoritative, and it was irritating about his eye.

" That's true," said Brown. He leant over and rapidly cut Ivor's ham and galantine into conveniently sized pieces and put a piece to Ivor's mouth. There was nothing embarrassing about it. He just did it. It was an acceptance of a fact. Marriott didn't mind at all.

He said, " There are certain facts and there are certain things that everybody wants to do. Politics is just an opinion about how to do them."

" Oh, wait a bit, Bob," said Ivor. " *Does* everybody want to do the same things ? "

" Yes," said Marriott firmly. " Everybody wants everybody to have enough to eat and nobody wants war. Things like that." He noticed that there was a plate of food in front of him. When they had been in the pub he had been hungry. He wasn't hungry now, but he started to eat.

" But if politics is just a question of method," said Brown, " surely the scientist must be a politician ? He must have some ideas about how his work should be used." He gave Ivor another mouthful. " This stuff of yours—you must know what ought to be done with it ? I mean—that it ought to be kept for England, or shared with America or . . ."

" I don't give a damn about England or America," said Marriott loudly. The suggestion was somehow peculiarly irritating. " How much bubonic or typhus is there in England or America ? It's in Asia that it's wanted. Let England and America have the bloody atomic bomb. It's no good—no constructive good—anyhow. Let Brewer and

178

the physicists play around as much as they like as long as they don't blow the world up. But this could *save* half a million lives a year."

" Oh, come ! " said Brown, with a smile.

" I tell you it could. Why, in India alone there've been years when a million people died of bubonic."

" He's probably right, you know," said Ivor. " We've no conception of the size of these things."

" Of course you haven't," said Marriott rudely. " But I have. It's my job."

Brown stared at him for a moment with the bulging dark eyes very wide open. Then he shrugged his shoulders. " Well," he said quietly, " I'm damned if I'd like to sit quietly eating my dinner with the lives of half a million people in my hands."

" They're not in my hands," said Marriott bitterly. " I wish to God they were. If I were in old Sewell's place. . . ."

" Who's old Sewell ? "

" My Professor."

" Oh, I see. So it's really his work ? "

" No, it's not," said Marriott angrily. His eyes were focussing better now. " If it's anybody's it's Shole's and mine. And another chap who's dead. We've done the donkey work. But Sewell's responsible. If I were in his place I'd tell them to go to hell. But of course he's got no guts. And Shole's worse. He likes being bossed about. He's got no—no sense of responsibility to "—he hesitated—" to everybody."

" To mankind," said Brown gently.

" Well, that's what it comes to," said Marriott defensively. " Doesn't it ? It's no good saying you're a scientist if you haven't got a sense of responsibility." Suddenly and inexplicably he felt his eyes blur with tears. He blinked hard and reached for his glass to cover his surprise and confusion.

Brown said, " Look, don't drink any more of that muck. It might easily poison you. Let's have some coffee."

" Sure," said Marriott, smiling. He had blinked his eyes clear. Apart from their sudden watering, he had never felt less like crying in his life. While Brown was getting the coffee Ivor said, " Personally, I can do with some coffee after all that hooch. You all right ? " He was smiling that queer smile of intimate affection.

Marriott said, " I'm fine." The food had been a good thing.

When Brown came back he handed round the coffee and then sat down and stared at the carpet for a long while in silence. Ivor said, " Penny for your thoughts, Bill." Brown took no notice but continued to stare at the carpet. Then he suddenly raised his head and looked at Marriott and said, " When we were in the pub you said a queer thing. That scientists were completely under the thumb of governments."

" Well, aren't they ? "

" Nobody's ever under anybody's thumb unless he chooses to be."

" Bunkum ! " said Ivor briskly.

" I'm going to ask you some questions," said Brown, ignoring Ivor still. " And I particularly don't want you to answer them if you think you shouldn't. But if you feel you can, then I'm going to tell you something that may interest you." He paused, lit a cigarette and put it between Ivor's lips. His face was serious and abstracted. " This work of yours," he said slowly, " has been stopped—or at least publication of it has been stopped—for security reasons. As a scientist you think that's wrong. But you're not only a scientist—you're an Englishman. As an *Englishman* do you think it wrong ? "

" I don't quite get you," said Marriott, frowning.

" Well, do you think the security of this country would be—would be compromised if it were published ? "

" It's knowledge," said Marriott. " And any knowledge can be misused."

" But as a patriotic Englishman . . . ? "

Marriott smiled. " I'm afraid I'm not a patriotic English-man," he said sarcastically. " At least, not that sort, thank God. I'm a scientist and science doesn't stop at the English Channel. I happen to think that people who live in India or—or China matter too."

" Then you can lay your hand on your heart and say that if you were the—the Cabinet or whoever it is, you'd publish this stuff and take the chance ? "

" Of course I would," said Marriott rather irritably. " I've already said so. If I were in Sewell's place . . ."

Brown nodded. " Right. Now, if you were going to publish it, what would you publish it in ? Some scientific periodical, I suppose ? I mean—you don't want to put it in a—a newspaper? You just want it to get to other scientists ? "

" Yes. And chiefly research people at this stage."

Brown squashed out his cigarette. " Well," he said calmly, " if I were to tell you that it *could* be put in the hands of other scientists in every other country in the world, would you be interested ? "

There was a dead silence. Then Marriott swallowed and said, " Of course I should be interested. But . . ."

" But what ? "

" Well—I mean . . . how ? "

" This isn't my line of country," said Brown. " I'm a publisher, and I don't know anything about science. But I *do* know that this problem of yours has cropped up before and that there's some sort of an organisation which exists to cope with it. That's all."

Ivor said, " What sort of organisation ? "

" I think it's called the International Scientific Exchange. I gather that it's got members amongst scientists all over the world—people who believe that there ought to be no national barriers in science. And it exists for the private exchange of information between scientists. I don't know who runs it or where its headquarters are. Probably in America, I think."

" I've never heard of it," said Marriott.

" Maybe not," said Brown dryly. " Nor have many other people. But you probably know some people who—*have* heard of it. Do you know Grossman ? "

" Grossman of Harvard ? Yes, of course. Does he belong to it ? "

" I didn't say he belonged to it, I was only asking if you knew him." Brown lit a new cigarette. " I was shown some of the papers they produce—one thing, anyhow. It was about plastics. It didn't mean anything to me, but apparently it was rather important and somebody was sitting on it, so it—leaked."

Ivor said, " You know, Bill, this is one of the most cheering things I've heard for a long time. The scientific boys are just refusing to be muzzled, eh ? "

" Apparently."

" But how do they get away with it ? " said Marriott. " I mean, why doesn't somebody get run in or—— ? "

" Who is there to run in ? The stuff isn't signed and there's no printer's name on it. It's just—information. I thought you might possibly know about the whole thing, being in the scientific racket."

Marriott shook his head. There was a metallic taste in his mouth and he drank some coffee. He said, " How's the stuff obtained ? I mean—who does what ? "

" I don't know. As I say, I don't know much about it. But if you're interested I can introduce you to someone who does." He blew down his nose and stared at Marriott almost defiantly.

Ivor said, " But one could hardly expect Bob to . . ."

" I'm not expecting him to do anything. He was complaining that it wasn't possible to get stuff published without official blessing and I'm saying it is. That's all."

There was a long silence. Marriott was staring at the

floor. His eyes were focussing properly now. After a while he looked up and met the bulgy dark eyes.

" That's very interesting," he said mildly. " Awfully interesting. One hands over the information to—to somebody ? . . ."

Brown said shortly, " I've no idea what one does."

Marriott took out a cigarette and lit it slowly and with care. His hands were hardly quivering. " It's a thing that one would have to be a little careful about, isn't it ? "

" Of course. I don't suggest that its legal in the usual sense. . . ."

Marriott smiled slightly. " I wasn't thinking so much about that. I mean you'd want to know who you were dealing with." He stared straight at Brown, but the bulgy eyes never flickered.

Brown said, " Naturally."

" Still," said Marriott coldly, " it's an interesting idea and one I'd like to think about. Thanks for telling me." He glanced at his watch and then at Ivor. " Oughtn't we to go ? "

It was only a few hundred yards to Ivor's flat. Brown walked with them to the door, and it wasn't until they were going upstairs that they were alone. Marriott took the key out of Ivor's pocket and let them in. Ivor said, " Light switch on the right," and walked across to the gas fire. He pushed the tap on with his foot and flicked the self-lighter with a quick movement of his toe. The gas lit with a pop. Glancing round, Marriott saw a handbag on a shelf. It was a brown leather bag, rather worn. He recognised it and remembered for the first time that this was where Lucy lived. He had always wanted to see the flat and he should have been interested in it. But for the moment he was too excited.

Ivor smiled at him rather wryly, and said, " Before we

183

talk—I wonder if you'd do something for me? I can't take my own shoes off and these are too tight. . . ."

Marriott blushed and said, " Sure. . . ."

" It's the sort of thing I hate asking—and have to ask all the time. . . ." Ivor sat down with the odd lurching movement and held out his foot. It was difficult to pull the shoes off, and Marriott was stupidly afraid of hurting him. Ivor's slippers were beside the gas fire and he put out his feet in turn and skilfully hooked his toes into them. He smiled at Marriott and said, " You can't imagine what a relief it is to—to have things like that done by male hands."

" Why? " said Marriott uncomfortably.

" If you'd ever been entirely dependent on a woman you'd know. Light us both cigarettes, will you? I'm extremely sorry I let you in for that."

" What—with Brown? Oh—that's all right. Very interesting."

" *Very* interesting," said Ivor. He smiled in that almost coy, feminine way as Marriott lit his cigarette.

Marriott hesitated and then answered the intimate smile. " What I'd really like to know," he said, " is what his game is."

" Brown's? "

" Yes. I mean—it's a very pretty story, this business about an International Scientific Exchange, but there's one obvious hole in it, which he'd realise if he were a scientist. Even if stuff were published without being signed, everybody in the same line would know which lab. it had come from by the *sort* of stuff it was. Or at least that it had come from one of two, say. This stuff of ours—everybody would know it came from Sewell's department whether it was signed or not."

" But would that help them? "

" They'd know that one of half a dozen people had let it out."

" Quite. But they wouldn't be able to *do* anything because they wouldn't know which."

" Well, frankly, I didn't believe a word of it. Or not much of it, anyhow."

Ivor closed his eyes. He was still smiling to himself. " But were you *intended* to ? " he said gently. " After all, it was a nice story. You mustn't be carpingly critical."

" You think—he didn't *mean* me to believe it ? "

Ivor opened his eyes. " Come, come, Bob. He knows that you're a person of the highest intelligence. Surely he'd assume that you'd read between the lines ? After all, he doesn't know you very well. You could hardly expect him to slap all the cards on the table."

Marriott hesitated. " He's a—an agent for somebody who wants to get hold of the stuff ? "

" Presumably," said Ivor calmly. " Of course, this is all as new to me as it is to you. I only know him as a pub. acquaintance. But that would be my guess."

" And mine. Then who's he working for ? Is he an Englishman ? "

" I don't know. But does it matter, anyway ? "

Marriott reflected for a moment.

" What d'you think I ought to do ? " he said rather helplessly. " Go to the police ? "

" The police ? " said Ivor, raising his eyebrows. He hesitated for a moment and then said carefully, " Well, of course you could do that. . . ."

" I don't suppose anything he said to-night would—would prove anything, he was too careful. But it might put them on the track of something."

" It might. If you thought it was the right thing to do."

" Why ? Don't you ? "

There was a long pause. Ivor was staring unseeingly at a corner of the room. His face was oddly puckered, as though with pain.

" I—have no opinion," he said in a low voice. " How could I have ? I've told you—I don't come into any of these things any longer. I'm not personally concerned. . . ."

He smiled rather painfully. " I'm not even an Englishman."

Marriott said, " I should think you've earned the right to regard yourself as an Englishman if anybody has."

Ivor flashed him a quick look of gratitude. " Thank you, Bob," he said quietly. " *Half* an Englishman, anyhow. But even so I've no right to an opinion."

" I don't care whether you've got a right to one or not," said Marriott impatiently. " I want to know what you think. You don't like the idea of going to the police ? "

Ivor hesitated. Then he turned his sunken face almost defiantly and said, " All right then. No. I don't."

" Why not ? "

" Because, you see, you—you led Brown into this to some extent. You implied that if you had your way you'd publish your stuff at once. You told him that science wasn't something that stopped at the English Channel—and so on." Ivor smiled. " Of course *I* realise that that was just conversation. But he wasn't to know. You might really feel like that."

Marriott frowned. " But I—I *do* feel like that," he said slowly. " So does every intelligent person."

" Quite. But that doesn't stop them from going to the police if there's any question of stuff *crossing* the English Channel." Ivor smiled wryly. " The world's full of people who're internationalists—as long as their own country stays on top."

There was a long silence.

" But surely it's quite a different thing ? " said Marriott doubtfully. " I mean—if there really were an International Scientific what-not, there might be something to be said for it. But if he's just working for another country . . ."

" Well ? " said Ivor gently.

" Well, why *should* anybody give it to him ? I'm not a— a sort of Kipling patriot. I think the world matters more than England. But I don't think any particular *country* does."

" And so you think that unless they can be given to the whole world the good things should be kept exclusively for England ? If the Indians are to go on dying of bubonic, the Chinese should die of it too ? "

" Of course not."

" But isn't that what you're saying ? Surely that's where you land as soon as you stop thinking about people and start thinking about ' countries ' ? If a thing ought to be generally known, isn't it a good thing for *anybody* to know it, whatever his nationality is, and whether he's black, white or grey ? " Ivor shifted himself restlessly in his chair and closed his eyes. " I tell you," he said with weary bitterness, " I see these things differently from you. I've nothing to lose or gain any more. It's easy for me to—to think of people just as people and—to wish them well. . . ." He suddenly threw up his head. His eyes were still closed but there were tears on his cheeks. " If it could only have been me . . ." he said in a half-strangled voice. " If only I could have been in your place. It would have been so much easier for everybody. . . ."

" Why ? " said Marriott. His throat was curiously dry.

" Because I've nothing to lose," said Ivor huskily. " Because I'm beyond the reach of nationalities. Because nobody can touch me and I should only have to think of— of what was the right thing. Whereas you've got—two arms. And if you've got two arms they can tie you up. . . ." He shook his head sharply as if to clear it and opened his eyes. " You'd better go home, Bob, my dear," he said quietly. " It's getting late."

Marriott swallowed something. " Let me get this clear," he said. " You're saying that you'd give this stuff to Brown ? . . ."

" Give it to Brown ? " said Ivor, with a tiny smile. " I'd never give anything to Bill except a drink. He's a no good."

" No. But that you'd be willing to hand it over to—to a foreign power ? If you were in my place ? You'd think that was right ? "

Ivor slowly shook his head. " No," he said. " That's not what I'm saying. I'm saying that if I were in your place— but in my state, mark you—I should be able to work out what I thought was right and then do it. I shouldn't have to bother about what the Government thought or what the Blimps thought or what any other damn person thought. I should just have to take the responsibility of trusting my own judgment, wherever it led me. I don't know what the answer would be—I haven't really thought it through properly. . . ." He paused. " On the other hand," he added, smiling, " if I were a fit young man with a life and a career in front of me, I should certainly feel as you do and stay safely on the side of the big battalions."

" It's not a question of—of being safe," said Marriott. " It's . . ."

" All right. Then let's say I should act like a proper patriot. Going to the police, and soon."

" No, I can quite see what you mean about going to the police. I said that without thinking. It's—it's just the way one's been brought up. . . ."

" Exactly. The whole thing's a matter of how one's been brought up."

" And I can see you're right about its not really mattering who Brown's working for. Everybody ought to have the stuff. But—well, a chap you meet in a pub, who tells you some childish yarn—it's all so—hole-in-the-corner. Dirty. Seedy. D'you see what I mean ? One can't feel that *that* could be the right way of doing anything. You half-expect the next thing'll be that he'll offer you ten pounds as a bribe, or some black market cigarettes."

Ivor laughed. " That's it. That's Brown exactly. ' Hist ! Want any petrol coupons, mister ? ' " He shook his head. " But that's the snag. The whole thing *is* dirty and seedy. But what made it dirty in the first place was the refusal to let you publish—the refusal to let other nations have something that they ought to have. As soon as you get dirt on one side you get dirt on the other. And here, for once, there's no doubt who started it."

" It's that bloody man Brewer and the physicists," said Marriott moodily.

" No, it isn't," said Ivor gently. " It isn't Brewer on one side or Brown on the other or even our beloved Government. It's just you and me, Bob, and all the other people like us—the people who won't think, and if they do, don't trust their own answers." He threw himself restlessly back in his chair. " But can you blame them ? " he said bitterly. " I thought there was a job that wanted doing and I went and tried to do it. And look at me now. . . ."

He closed his eyes and his head fell forward on to his chest. " Keep out," he muttered indistinctly. " Keep out. You'll only get hurt if you don't. Let somebody else take the responsibility—and get the kicks."

Marriott said suddenly, " Of course the person who ought to do something about this is Sewell."

Ivor raised his head. His eyes were very bright and his smile showed the brilliant white teeth. " That's right, Bob," he said. " Sewell. He ought to do it. There's always somebody else who ought to do it, thank God."

As the bus trundled up to the stop Marriott could see a bent head with a shock of fair hair at one of the windows. The head was raised. He saw the thick glasses and realised that it was Root, and instinctively he stepped back so as to be out of the light. Even as he did it he knew it was ridiculous. There was nothing to hide from Root or anybody else. But he didn't get on the bus. He stood and saw Root go back to his book, and watched the bus lumber away, and then started to walk slowly towards Victoria. It kept dividing itself into two different problems, and though the answers to both of them were there, they wouldn't add up to give a single answer. A quadratic equation, with two entirely different values for x. There was Brown, and there *x* equalled nought. He thought of the bulgy brown eyes and the fake sincerity and suddenly felt that it would have given him great satisfaction to kick Brown's behind—with his toe, so that it would hurt, as he hadn't kicked anybody since he was a small boy. But then again there was the thing that was nothing to do with Brown—the thing to which Brown was utterly irrelevant—the thing that Ivor could see, sitting there with his eyes shut and his tortured face and the tears swelling out from under his closed lids ; Ivor, with that infinite detachment and fairness that came from being outside the battle, criticising nobody but " people like you and me, Bob . . ." and yet crying bitterly, " Keep out, or you'll get hurt." And there *x* equalled . . . He didn't know what *x* equalled, but it wasn't zero.

He was quite sober and his head was clear. Yet something of reality was missing, and as he walked along the crowded pavements at Victoria he remembered the thriller in which men went to the moon and lived inside a sort of glass bubble. There was that feeling about it—the feeling of being inside some transparent casing and looking out at a world with which one made no contact. He stood at the corner of Wilton Road and looked across at the lights of the Victoria Palace and at the cinemas and the buses and the people, and tried hard to feel a sensible, workaday part of it all. But it did nothing to recognise or welcome him. The throng of people passed him, but it opened as it reached him and closed again behind, leaving him untouched. He suddenly felt desperately and terrifying alone, and he would have given anything for somebody to bump into him—to feel the friendly weight of another body and to hear a voice saying " Pardon " with tipsy politeness. But the stream opened and closed without touching or heeding him, and left him standing there alone inside the glass bubble.

XI

SIR GUTHRIE BREWER was used by now to co-ordinating people who didn't want to be co-ordinated, and advising people who didn't want advice. Rudeness and surliness only made his handshake firmer and his smile more easy. The air of well-dressed reason and good-tempered commonsense that he carried with him and dumped on the desk under one's nose were almost as material a professional badge as a doctor's black bag. He said, " I've come to thank you," and sat down as though he proposed to take some time about it.

Sewell leaned down and knocked his pipe out into the wastepaper basket. He had only just filled it, but the movement made it unnecessary to look at Brewer for the moment, and he didn't want to look at Brewer.

" Nobody could have been more helpful than your people here have been to Childs and Ross. You know how it is when you've got to poke about round somebody else's work —it's not all sweetness and light as a rule. But your man Shole couldn't have done more for us."

" I'm glad of that," said Sewell politely.

" And I'd just like to say this—if it's any satisfaction to you, the stuff you've given us may make a big difference to—to our whole defence position in that field." He paused as though expecting Sewell to say something.

Sewell nodded and began to search in the drawers of his desk for his tobacco.

" I say that because I don't want you to think that there's any question of the work just being wasted." Brewer smiled at his fingernails. " Incidentally I've taken the opportunity of pointing out to the Minister just how much we all owe you."

" Thank you, Sir Guthrie," said Sewell respectfully.

Brewer smiled. " Well, there's no harm in rubbing into these people what they get from the scientist, you know. You mustn't be cynical."

Sewell leant back in his chair and closed his eyes. " Well, what do you want ? " he said. " I'm only trying to say the right thing. I'm glad Shole has been helpful and I'm glad some use is being made of the stuff. In other words, if we've got to wear a muzzle it's no good barking our heads off. But you don't expect me to say I *like* being muzzled ? "

" Of course I don't. But I hoped you might see by now that—that the whole business is *necessary*, and that we're not such God-awful Philistines as . . ."

" I think it's necessary to prevent disease," said Sewell moodily. " You think it's necessary to prevent disease in England in wartime. That's the only difference between us. Anyhow, need we talk about it any more ? You're getting all you want ? "

Brewer said, " Well, that's rather the point."

" Ah. I thought there must *be* a point."

" We've been given—and I repeat it whether it gives you any pleasure or not—the most generous co-operation. We've got and are getting all we can—as things are arranged now. But if the set-up were changed, we could get more."

" Meaning what ? "

" We don't only need your information—we need your active help." He paused and smiled slightly. " Can I be blunt or will you jump down my throat ? "

" I want to know what you've got in mind."

" All right. At the moment we've got Childs and Ross and their staffs working in this field—purely from the point of view of defence. They've got a lot of stuff on hand which hasn't any connection with this work of yours. But where modified virulence is concerned they tell me you're a mile ahead of us in knowledge, technique and everything else. Now obviously our whole approach is different from yours. We're concerned with war circumstances and you haven't been. If we're going to apply the information we've got from you it'll mean a lot of experimental work. We're not set up to do it and we haven't anybody who *can* do it—at least, not without wasting a lot of time learning what your chaps know already. Are you prepared to help us out?"

"How?"

"Well, in this sort of way. You've never taken very much interest in the artificial super-virulent strains that you've produced—except for the production of anti-bodies. You've assumed that what you've got to deal with are the natural strains. So they would be in peace. But in war anybody who was going to use bacteria as a weapon at all would go all out to produce artificial virulence. So you see, to us the most interesting part of your work is the part that you've followed up least.

Brewer sat back and examined the bowl of his pipe carefully.

Sewell said, "You want us to spend our time here studying something that's never killed a man—and never will unless some murderous lunatic gets hold of it—instead of on work that——?"

"No, I don't," said Brewer calmly. "I think that would be quite wrong. It's not your job and it's probably right outside the Haughton's charter. I'm suggesting that *we* should do it—but that you should help us. You see, apart from anything else, there's bound to be a security snag in a place like this. I'm sure Shole and his people will do all they can, but the security people tell us frankly that if the stuff's really hot it ought to be somewhere else which is more under their hand. You don't want to be in a position where you can't take on a new lab. boy without having him vetted for security. Well, at our places that's all lined up already...."

N

" So what ? "

Brewer smiled more reassuringly than ever. " I want to borrow some of your people," he said. " There are only three of them that we should really need, Shole and young Marriott and a shock-headed boy—what's his name ? . . ."

" Parkin."

" Yes. We shouldn't want them for long. Probably about six months. We should set out quite openly to pick their brains and to get them to train our people. After that they could come back." He examined his pipe again. " I know it's a lot to ask, Sewell. Perhaps I'd better say all over again that I'm not asking for a personal favour. It's simply . . ."

Sewell's face had broken into a queer, confident smile. " That's all right," he said briskly. " A very reasonable suggestion. Ask them. Go and ask old Shole if he'd like six months on a job of that sort. I'll be interested to hear what he says."

Brewer frowned. " You must realise that I can't do that. He's your man. I can't approach him unless I've got your agreement."

" Come, come ! " said Sewell reprovingly. " You underestimate your powers. Surely you can tell him that his wife'll disappear or that his old mother's pension will be stopped if he doesn't do as he's told ? Why should I come into it ? "

" Look," said Brewer, with a patient smile, " don't waste it on me. I'm only a poor stooge with rather a difficult job to do. Will you agree to my talking to Shole and getting his reaction ? "

" I can't stop you."

" And will you agree to let him make up his own mind ? In other words will you *not* try to persuade him to refuse ? "

Sewell said, " I'll go further than that. I'll tell him that if he thinks it's sensible to drop what he's doing now and come to you he certainly ought to do it." He got up. " And if he comes I'll buy you a dinner for two. You and whoever else you like."

* * * * *

The elderly commissionaire was still filling in football coupons in the empty room, but this time he said, " Let me see, it's Mr. Prince you want, isn't it ? " and took Peach straight up. Peach said, " You've got a good memory."

The commissionaire said, " Ask me what won the Derby. Any year you like. Or who won the Cup. Or the Boat Race."

" You mean you can remember ? "

" Ask me. Any year you like." The lift came to a stop, but the commissionaire didn't get out. He just stood there invitingly.

" All right," said Peach politely. " Who w-won the Boat Race in 1923 ? "

What appeared to be a spasm of pain crossed the commissionaire's face. " Damn it ! " he said. " Nineteen-two-three. . . ." He closed his eyes, opened them again, smiled and said, " Oxford. Am I right ? "

" I'm sure you are."

The commissionaire opened the gates and said, " They call me Jumbo. Elephant, see ? Never forget."

" It's a remarkable gift."

" Always had it," said the commissionaire. " Long as I can remember. It's that door straight ahead."

Mr. Prince's memory was not as good as the commissionaire's. He looked at Peach warily and said, " Yes, sir ? " with aggressive respectfulness.

" My name's P-Peach. I got a message . . ."

" Peach ? " said Mr. Prince. " Oh, yes. Man with a father-in-law. Have a chair." He picked up a file from a tray and opened it. " Well, I'm sorry to have to tell you that your father-in-law's being a bit naughty. Nothing much, mind you, but a bit naughty. He wrote a letter to

Sir Nicholas Pelly. Must have done because here's a copy of the reply. . . ."

" Wait a minute," said Peach. " I think this is where I c-came in."

" Came in where ? "

" I mean you told me about that last time. Unless it's another letter ? "

Mr. Prince reflected. " No," he said at last, " it's the same one. Must be something else. . . ." He turned over the leaves of the file. " Oh, yes. Here we are. Do you know any of your father-in-law's staff ? "

" Only a man named Dr. Shole. This is still where I came in."

" Don't know a girl named Byrne ? "

" No."

" Pity. Then you wouldn't know a man who's a friend of hers ? "

Peach hesitated. " Well, I might. But I shouldn't really know if she knew him, should I ? I m-mean . . ."

" That's true," said Mr. Prince. " Well, don't let's worry about it." He turned his purplish face and the watery blue eyes on Peach and looked at him for a moment in silence. " Your father-in-law talked to you about this ? "

" He hasn't talked to me about anything. I haven't seen him since I m-met you last. He had lunch with my wife one day."

" Yes ? "

" He didn't mention this business, but she was rather w-worried about him. She said he seemed rather odd."

" She shouldn't worry. It's a bad thing. What was she worried about ? "

" He seemed very s-silent and depressed, I gather."

Mr. Peach grunted. " How old is he ? "

" Sixty-five, I think. Or sixty-four."

" Fit man for his age as far as you know ? "

" Oh, yes."

" Take any interest in women ? "

" I d-don't know."

" You don't know much, do you ? " said Mr. Prince regretfully. " Well, is he the sort of man who *would* like women ? "

" Oh, yes. I've always understood that he was one of the finest amateurs of his d-day. But that will have been some time ago."

" I don't know," said Mr. Prince dispiritedly. " Some of these old boys get better the longer they stay in cask. I never see how it's done myself. But there it is. You don't know a man named Marriott, do you ? On the staff there ? "

" No," said Peach. " Shole is the one I know."

" That's right. You said so before."

There was a long silence.

Peach said, " I take it nothing new's happened ? I mean my father-in-law hasn't—— ? "

" No," said Mr. Prince. " I wouldn't say anything new's happened. Though God knows how *I'm* expected to know if it has. He didn't say anything to your wife about his health, did he ? "

" Not as f-far as I know. Why ? "

" Why not ? I always talk to people about mine. Anyhow, thanks for coming in."

Peach rose and picked up his hat. " I g-gather," he said mildly, " that it's all right so far ? "

Mr. Prince blinked his watery eyes. " It's so-so," he said. " Just so-so, you know."

" More so-so than it was ? "

" I don't know," said Mr. Prince irritably. " How the hell *could* I know ? You never know anything on these jobs."

" Nothing I can do ? "

" Not at the moment. I'll tell you if there is. This Shole's a good man, eh ? Reliable bloke ? "

" I should say v-very. I don't know him very well."

" Good," said Mr. Prince cordially. " Fine. Well, don't

you worry. I never do. It doesn't do any good. . . ." He paused rather helplessly. " There was something else I wanted to tell you but it's gone for the moment. . . . Oh, yes—mind that damned lift. It sticks and then they have to get you down with a crane."

* * * * *

It had been raining hard all day, and there was nothing for Marriott to do. Arthur was trying to make something that obviously couldn't be made, and Parkin was messing about with the ultra-violet microscope, and Lucy was solemnly cutting and staining very easy tissue sections like a first-year medico at a practical histology class. None of it mattered and nobody even thought it mattered. It was raining and they were all busily waiting for something. Usually when this happened Marriott took a lot of paper, a slide rule and Kendal's *Advanced Statistics* and settled down quite happily. But this afternoon he wanted employment, or at least company. He went and watched Parkin, but all that happened was that Parkin stopped messing with the microscope, and sat and smiled at him, and looked inquiring.

Marriott said, " What's wrong with Lulu now ? " And Parkin said, " Oh, there's nothing *wrong* with her. Just giving her the once over," and waited for him to go away. Arthur didn't stop. He just said, " Hullo," and went on working as though Marriott wasn't there. Nobody else was even in, so that left Lucy and he didn't want to talk to her.

He wandered back to their lab. She was still working very intently and didn't look up. Her white coat was unbuttoned at the top so that he could see the tight green jersey.

Marriott said, " The section is first floated on a little warm water so that the wax flattens out. It is then carefully drained and blotted as a preliminary to the extraction of the wax with xylol. . . ."

She took no notice. Her hair was done differently so that it was much smoother at the back.

A Sort of Traitors

Marriott leaned on the bench and said casually, "You never really told me how you got on with Prof. the other night."

Lucy still didn't look up. "What d'you mean—really told you? I've told you twice that it was rather fun. D'you want to know what we had for dinner?"

He said, "If you're going to do first M.B. sections you might as well do them properly. Some of these look as though you used a bread knife in the microtome. Make Arthur sharpen it for you."

He turned away satisfied. She didn't know anything. She was angry with him and a long way away, but it wasn't because of that.

Silkin was on leave, and he went into Silkin's room and stood looking out at the rain. It was here at the Haughton that the glass bubble of loneliness was somehow most uncomfortable and most frightening. He had always liked to talk to people about everything—to hear his own voice working out the answer, and to see the rightness of the answer reflected in other faces. This solitary wrestling with the quadratic equation was almost physically painful.

He had hoped that it would be different to-day—different in daylight, without Ivor's face, away from an evening when one had drunk too much and talked too much, and been generally excited. It *was* different, and a lot of the things that he had thought about on the walk to Victoria seemed far away and melodramatic. But it wasn't as different as it should have been—not a thing you could laugh about and forget. The question was still there and that meant that the loneliness was still there. And it was the loneliness that was intolerable—that crisped his fingers and made the palms of his hands sweat. He stood there looking out and wiped the palms of his hands on his white coat. Apart from the silly sweating and the loneliness he was quite calm. A messenger girl in old blue overall trousers came out of a doorway opposite and ran down the street in the rain, jumping over the puddles. She ran awkwardly as girls do.

It was about four o'clock when Shole sent for him. He had known that Shole had somebody there, but not that it was Brewer. Brewer didn't get up or shake hands but he smiled very cordially and said, " Hallo, Marriott," as though they had known one another for years. As though he had been one's boss for years.

Shole said, " Sir Guthrie wanted to have a word with you, Bob," and made for the door, but Brewer said, " Oh, don't go, Shole please," and he came back and stood by the window looking rather uneasy.

Brewer smiled at Marriott and said, " Well, now, Marriott —d'you know Yorkshire ? "

" No, Sir Guthrie."

" Lovely country—in places. How would you like a six months' holiday there ? "

It was irritating. He obviously thought he was good at this sort of thing.

Marriott said, " Doing what ? " shortly and almost rudely.

" Giving us a bit of help. Teaching us a bit of biology." Brewer glanced at Shole with a grin as though to make sure that he was enjoying the joke.

Shole said briefly, " Sir Guthrie's got a job to offer you."

He not only thought he was good at this, he thought he was wonderful. He switched the smile on and off like a traffic light, and he wrapped it all up in a nice parcel with pretty ribbons so that baby would like it. But he made it quite clear that it was damned nice of him to be so nice. He said, " After all, it isn't everybody aged twenty-four who's asked to come and advise some of the best scientists in the country, is it ? "

Marriott said slowly, " Why are the super-virulents so important ? "

Brewer smiled because baby was so precocious, and said,

" Oh, well—you'll have to talk to Dr. Shole and Dr. Childs about that. I mustn't try to be professional. I'm only a poor physicist myself."

" But I don't know what the job amounts to, sir. And not knowing that . . ."

" It amounts," said Brewer, with obvious patience, " to coming and giving us the advantages of your experience. Giving it to the country instead of—of just to your own group here."

Marriott glanced at Shole. " I'm not quite sure that military work's much in my——"

" Military work ? " said Brewer. " Who said anything about ' military work ' ? What a lot of you younger people have got that bee in your bonnets. It's all science, isn't it ? Surely there's nothing wrong in a scientist thinking about the defence of his own country ? "

Marriott looked at Shole again, but Shole was looking out of the window. He stood there in his white coat, like a short, dumpy grocer's assistant, looking out of the window because he wouldn't look at what was inside. Marriott's palms were sweating again. He wiped them secretly on the side of his coat and said slowly, " Is it really—defence work on the super-virulents ? "

" Exactly," said Brewer, smiling. But he didn't smile because he saw the joke. " For about six months probably. And of course your post here would remain open."

" And Professor Sewell—— ? "

Baby being precocious again. " You don't have to worry about that. That's all been settled between the Professor and me." Everything was settled. Baby would do what he was told. " I'm hoping Dr. Shole will be coming and probably Parkin, so you won't be among strangers."

Marriott said to Shole, " You're going ? "

Shole turned his head and said, " It's not settled yet."

There was a silence and then Brewer smiled very brightly and said, " Well, Marriott—what d'you say ? "

To gain time he said, " I should like to think it over, sir, if I may."

Brewer's smile flicked off and on again. " I see. Well, that's quite reasonable. You'll have to be fairly quick, though, because we want to get on."

Marriott said fatuously, " It would mean giving up my digs of course, and——"

" Yes. Still, we might be able to help you. . . ." Brewer suddenly cocked a roguish eye at Shole. " By the way, Shole—one thing we haven't said anything about is salaries."

Shole turned quickly. " No," he said uneasily. " But presumably . . ."

Brewer's eyes had come back to Marriott. " Well, of course I can't *promise* anything. You know how bound up in red tape we are. But if our friend here was going to be more or less teaching our people I should have thought it would be only right to grade him as a—a Senior Scientific Officer or something like that." He winked at Marriott. " Which would be—all right, you know."

He never had any money. He ought to have been able to manage on what the Haughton paid, but somehow it always went, and now, on the twenty-seventh of the month, he was hanging on desperately for the next pay cheque. Perhaps if he had had ten pounds in his pocket it wouldn't have mattered, but as it was, the wink and the confidential smile were conclusive. He suddenly knew so clearly what he must do that he was afraid it would show in his face, so he bent his head and muttered something about that being very nice.

" Don't take that as a promise," Brewer was saying. " There may be a snag about your age or something. But I'll speak to Dr. Childs and I expect we can fix something."

They could fix it. One had only to teach them how to produce the super-virulents and they would pay one another ten pounds a week. He raised his head, and was about to say, " Thank you, sir, for your generosity." But Shole was looking at him, and though Shole was a fool, it wouldn't do to take any risk. So he merely nodded.

Brewer said, " Well, *I* think it's a great chance for you, Marriott. I tell you so frankly."

He went back to Silkin's room and shut the door. He was trembling all over, so that his knees felt weak and he had to sit down at the desk. His mind went back to a time when he had seen a man in an East End street stoop down and smile in a ten-year-old child's face and then suddenly hit it hard with his doubled fist. There had been the same nausea of anger and fear at the monstrousness of the thing. He picked up the telephone directory, and his hands were shaking so that he fumbled with the leaves. But the number was there all right, and he had heard Lucy ring up and knew what to do. You asked for L Department, and when you got that you asked for Captain Gates.

Squinting down at the mouthpiece of the telephone he could see his breath condensing in beads of moisture. That was very unhygienic, and some people advertised a service for disinfecting telephones. He found himself wondering how they managed when they got Ivor to the telephone. Did somebody hold it for him or was the whole thing on one of those extending arms ? There was a long wait while they found Ivor, and when the voice suddenly said, " Hullo. This is Gates speaking," it startled him, so that for a moment he was confused and couldn't remember what to say. But it was only for a moment and then he said quite calmly, " Ivor —this is Bob. Do you happen to know the number of our friend last night ? "

There was a long pause. Then Ivor said, " No. But I can find it out . . . if you're sure you want it."

He said, " I'm sure I want his number. I'm not sure of anything else yet."

He went back to Lucy and leaned against the bench. She

203

was still staining section. He said, " You know I'm very jealous of Prof. over this. If you wanted to be taken out to dinner, what's wrong with me ? " She didn't say anything so he had to go on, " As it was, I spent a very lonely evening." But she just went on looking at her work and said, " Never mind. Perhaps he'll take you next time."

That was all right and he went away and sat down, and opened Kendal at random and stared at the page.

✳   ✳   ✳   ✳   ✳

Shole was in the lavatory, washing up with great deliberation. He saw Sewell coming in the mirror and said without introduction, " I've been talking to Brewer. He said you knew all about it."

Sewell shook some liquid soap on to his hands, and said, " I loathe this stuff. You mean about your going to him ? " He didn't look at Shole.

" Yes. He's seen Marriott and Parkin too." Shole's eyes went instinctively to the lavatory doors. They were all open.

Sewell said, " That's right. He did mention it."

" What d'you think ? "

" It's not a question of what I think," said Sewell carefully. " It's what *you* think."

Shole scrubbed at his wrists in silence. For a moment Sewell had a foolish hope that he was thinking up some ultimate comment on Brewer and the whole idea. But Shole's face in the mirror was thoughtful and worried. Sewell stared blindly at his own hands in the water and said, " I've no right to stop you, and no desire to, if you want to do it. It's entirely a matter for you."

" I can guess what you said to him," said Shole. " I nearly said it myself. But it isn't really any good just disliking Brewer. He's beside the point."

" Then what *is* the point ? "

Shole started to dry his hands, wiping each finger

separately. " Whether what he wants done is a—a good thing to do. And whether it's more urgent than what I'm doing here."

Sewell had placed his hands flat on the bottom of the wash-bowl. The ring on his left hand glinted as the water moved. " Oh, there's no doubt that what he wants done is desirable enough. He wants to be able to protect people against attack by pepped-up bugs. There's nothing wrong with that in itself. Whether any such attack's at all likely is another matter."

" I wasn't really thinking of that side of it," said Shole. He was looking slightly puzzled. " *That's* all right, of course."

" What other side is there ? "

Shole hesitated. " Well . . . surely the snag about all defence work is that before you know where you are the best defence is attack ? "

Sewell turned quickly and said, " You mean that he really wants this stuff as—as a weapon ? "

" I don't suppose he does—primarily. Whatever else you can say about us, we never *do* start the really nasty ideas in war. We leave that to the more logical races. But you know how it is. If an aggressor uses something against you, you use it back at him and that's just self-defence. It's one of the places where everybody reckons that two wrongs make a right." He threw his used towel into the basket. " I tackled Brewer about it point blank. Of course he swore that they were only interested in our stuff from the defensive side, and I think he meant it. But that doesn't mean anything. It wouldn't be in his hands."

Sewell's face had gone a dirty grey colour. He said, " I never thought of that."

" Well, I'm probably quite wrong. But after all, it's even been plastered over the newspapers—that we're preparing . . ."

" I know it has. But it just never occurred to me over

205

this stuff. . . ." Sewell pressed his hands over his eyes and said savagely, " I'm getting old and slow. That's what it is." After a moment he added, " And thinking of *that* was what made you hesitate ? "

" Yes. Mainly." Shole stood with his short legs planted slightly apart, looking at Sewell with his mild, worried eyes. " I don't think very clearly about things like this," he said simply. " And I can never see how far one ought to stick to —to principles and how far one ought to accept things as they are and—and make the best of them. I'm all against war—any sort of war. But if for some reason a war crops up, I'm all in favour of winning it. I'm a pacifist until it comes to the point, and then I don't go through with it. I suppose most people are like that. Probably that's why wars happen." He paused and then said politely, " I'd welcome your advice about the whole thing, if . . ."

" I've got no advice to give you," said Sewell roughly. " It's up to you to work it out." He turned away and said over his shoulder, " I gather that at the moment you think you'll probably go ? "

Shole hesitated. " Well—no. At the moment I can't imagine going. It just seems damned silly to spend time playing around with those super-virulent things which don't exist unless we make them, when we could be tackling the natural ones and doing some good. It's like digging a hole in the ground for practice in filling it up again, when there are plenty of natural holes that want filling already. That was my reaction. But one doesn't want to be just—selfish."

Sewell said, " Selfish ! . . ."

" I mean one doesn't want to duck something unpleasant just to salve one's conscience. If this stuff of ours were going to be published it would be different. But if we're not going to be allowed to help in one way, it's a bit difficult to refuse to help altogether."

" All help being just—help ? " said Sewell. " Including, if necessary, giving the military boys a new weapon ? "

" That's the trouble," said Shole restlessly. " One doesn't really trust these people. But, damn it all, one must trust *somebody*. Otherwise we must just fold our hands and sit and do nothing in case it's the wrong thing."

" How about trusting ourselves ? "

Shole smiled. " We can do that. But it doesn't help because we can't—can't alter things. We haven't any power. If we've got to go on living in society we've got to take its orders."

There was a moment's silence. Sewell was staring fixedly at the towel basket. Suddenly he gave a quick nod. " That's right," he said. " That's the point. As long as we've got to go on living in society . . . That's it entirely. How about the others ? Bob and Parkin ? "

" I think Parkin would quite like it. I'm not sure about Bob." Shole hesitated. " As a matter of fact I thought he'd say ' No ' at once. But he was quite calm about it. Of course, I doubt if either of them realise quite what it might imply. . . ."

Sewell went and sat down at his desk and lit his pipe slowly and deliberately. There was a curious feeling which was almost happiness. Ideally, the letter should go to the Minister with a carbon copy to Brewer simply marked " for your information." But if it was to be typed, he would have to type it himself, and he typed very badly and inaccurately. Besides, scoring off Brewer was not important and perhaps a trifle cheap. The essential thing was Gatling. Gatling would understand, and in a way, approve.

He picked up a pencil and began to scribble rapidly and without hesitation.

" Dear Minister,

" During our recent conversation it was clear that whilst we both sought the same end—i.e. the common good—we differed as to how it would best be served. You were not slow to point out that you, representing, however indirectly, the will of the nation, were in a position to impose your view on me, representing nobody but myself. We were arguing in fact, not in terms of wisdom, but in terms of power.

" Since then, however, I have been reminded of something which I think we both forgot—that I am an elderly man, who can only expect a very limited number of years more of active life ; and since the power of society over the individual depends entirely on the individual's need to go on living, it follows that society's power over me is now small. I am therefore in a position to consult my own wisdom, such as it is.

" I have never accepted your view that the world is full of mad dogs against whom we must defend ourselves. I believe that the level of society and good will in all countries is much the same. If the world acts insanely it is because sane men will give no lead against the growing paranoid tendency. Those who could won't, and those who would daren't."

Sewell paused and read it through. It was a statement of opinion. One man's opinion against another's. . . . He hesitated for a moment and then wrote :

" I make this assumption, not because I can prove it, but because it is the only *useful* assumption. To work from any other hypothesis is to despair, and despair is a useless thing."

His secretary came in and said, " Have you any files, Professor Sewell ? "

Sewell looked up and smiled at her. She was a pretty child with bright red hair and a solemn freckled face. " Why ? " he said in a hushed voice. " D'you want to put them in the safe ? "

" Yes, Professor Sewell."

" Well, I haven't got any, Claire. Not one."

She looked suspiciously round the office, but it was quite
true. For once he had none of Shole's precious files. She
said, " Thank you," primly and went out. Sewell grinned
happily to himself and went back to his letter. " Despair
is a useless thing. . . ." He hesitated for a moment and then
wrote rapidly.

" I know no other use for a conviction than to act on it.
Accordingly, I have despatched copies of the report to
the heads of appropriate scientific bodies in most civilised
countries, including the following . . ."

He seized a piece of paper and started to jot down names.
There were a surprising number of them and he would need
fifty copies at the very least. It was going to be difficult to
get out fifty copies without giving the show away.

*   *   *   *   *

When Marriott left that evening at six-fifteen it was still
raining as hard as ever. He had no coat, and he stood for
some time in the doorway waiting for the rain to slacken.
But it went on pouring down out of a solid, dun-coloured
sky, and in the end he turned up his collar and ran the
quarter of a mile to the tube station.

Running in the rain was always exhausting. He was still
panting as he scrambled on to the crowded train. It was
warm and dank, with a smell of wet clothes, and Marriott
stood pressed against an old woman in a soaking mackintosh,
feeling his wet trousers clinging uncomfortably to his thighs.
He tried to get his arm up to look at his watch, but the arm
was tightly wedged against his side, and it was easier to see
the time by the watch of a man who was sitting reading the
evening paper.

The train began to rock violently. The old lady lost her

balance and swayed back against him. He could not move, and it forced him back against the man behind him so that a whole file of people tottered, and the last man fell awkwardly on to the top of a soldier in one of the seats. Marriott grabbed the overhead rail to steady himself, and shut his eyes. The clattering and roaring and swaying made it impossible to think. And yet the train was tearing along towards something and it was not necessary to go on clinging and be carried with it. In a moment it would stop at a station, and it was perfectly possible to get out. He was free. He was uncommitted. The boats lay unburned behind him, and this feeling of plunging forward with his head down and his eyes shut was only there because there might be danger ahead and he knew no other way of facing danger. One fastened the fly-cage on one's arm and let the flies bite. Certainly, or almost certainly, nothing would happen. But one could not be sure without trying, and to try was the essence of the experimental method. There were the Brewers, and the Sholes, and he had looked at them and knew that whatever was right, that must be wrong. The answer must be elsewhere and one must look for it ; and this feeling now was just the price one paid.

He told himself that whatever the answer—even if it was the police—it was essential to talk to Brown—to get Brown to commit himself. For a moment this cheered and even excited him. " Suspecting that Brown might be an agent I arranged to see him again. . . ." But it was only for a moment and he knew that if Brown wasn't the answer he was nothing. Of no interest. Just a dull part of the whole heartbreaking stupidity of it all.

The rain had stopped, but a cold wind was blowing. His clothes were damp and as he came out of the warm, muggy air of the tube he shivered violently. It was five minutes past seven already and he still had to find the place, but he walked slowly in the crowded street. His glasses were misty, and he stopped and took them off and wiped them very slowly and deliberately. There was a blind man playing the violin in the gutter. The closed eyes reminded him of Ivor and that contorted face and the strangled cry, " If only it had been me ! . . ." But Ivor had given all he had already, and now it was his turn to look on.

He remembered the last sentences of Havelock Ellis. They had always impressed him, and he had learnt them by heart. " For a brief space it is granted to us, if we will, to enlighten the darkness that surrounds our path. . . . We press forward, torch in hand along the path. Soon from behind comes the runner who will outpace us. All our skill lies in giving into his hand the living torch, bright and unflickering, as we ourselves disappear in the darkness." If we will. To enlighten if we will. . . .

It had sounded difficult to find the pub, but he walked straight to it. It was a dreary Victorian place and it looked very full. As Marriott came to it he suddenly increased his pace and walked straight past the door without looking at it, and on down the street. It was the last lighted place, and after it there were only slummy houses and the dim street lights. He stopped in the shadows between two of the lights and looked back at its doorway. He was still shivering but it was only because his clothes were wet and clammy, and he didn't in the least mind meeting Brown or anybody else. It was only going in at the doorway into a bar that had a lot of people in it, and standing there for the second until he saw Brown. Standing in the doorway and looking round, and that would only be for a moment.

A man and a woman passed him, going towards the pub, and he fell in behind them. He meant to go with them to the door and then quietly turn aside and go in. But they turned in at the lighted door themselves and he followed close behind, so that one opening of the inner glass door was enough for all three of them.

The place was crowded and very noisy and smoky, and there was no sign of Brown, though it was nearly quarter-past seven. He felt that he had never been anywhere so intolerably public, and half-turned towards the door. But there was a corner with an upturned cask as a table, and nobody at it, and he went and sat down and decided to give it five minutes. As soon as he had done so he realised that the backs of the crowd standing at the bar and the roar of talk, shut everything in with a kind of perverse privacy, like the roaring of a mill wheel.

He saw Brown come in and look quickly round, and he half-raised a hand in greeting. Brown saw him, but he did not come straight over. Instead he jerked his head slightly towards the bar and went up to it and gave an order. The barman started to pour whisky, and all the time that he was pouring it, Brown's eyes were flickering about the bar as though he was looking for somebody. Even when he had the whisky and had paid for it he seemed to hesitate for a moment before he came across.

Marriott said, " You're late," and he said, " Yes. I'm sorry," and put the drinks down on the table. As Marriott looked up he saw that Brown's face was a dirty yellow, and that his hands were shaking, and realised that the man was frightened. There was something at once utterly disgusting and reassuring about his fear.

Marriott said contemptuously, " I won't keep you long. I only wanted to ask you about something you said last night."

Brown's eyes were still roving round the bar. He sat down and said vaguely, " Last night ? "

" Yes. About—what was it—the International Scientific Exchange." When one came to say it, the title had an absurdly improbable sound.

Brown said shortly, " Oh, that ? " He seemed to make an effort, and for the first time turned the bulging eyes on Marriott's face. " What did you want to know about it ? "

Marriott lit a cigarette. " Supposing I wanted to make use of it," he said thoughtfully. " What should I have to do ? "

" I don't know," said Brown. " I told you—I don't really know anything about it." He spoke with a sort of querulous irritation.

There was a pause and then Marriott said, " You offered to introduce me to somebody who knew all about it."

" Did I ? Well, I suppose . . ." Brown hesitated. " I don't guarantee that I've got it right, you know. It was just something mentioned casually."

" Well—*can* you introduce me ? "

Brown took an audible breath. He said. " I suppose I could. Of course, I imagine they're pretty sticky about who they take on, you know. . . ."

In a way that was a relief—the moment when the flies settled down into that obscene position. Marriott looked at the end of his cigarette and said, " You wouldn't have been willing to take the stuff and show it to them, and see what they said ? "

There was a long pause, but he deliberately didn't look up. At last Brown's voice said, " Well—I don't know. It's nothing to do with me, of course. But I might possibly be able to—to arrange for somebody to look at it for you."

Marriott had meant to go on longer, but the crudity of it turned him suddenly sick. He said, " Jesus Christ, what d'you think I am ? " He looked up. Brown was looking carefully puzzled.

Marriott said, " I know what the game is. I knew last night. All I don't know is who you're working for, and I can have a pretty good guess at that."

Brown's face was yellower than ever, but he still looked puzzled and only said slowly, " I don't understand you."

Marriott had expected him to show more fright. He said roughly, " Well, I understand *you*. As it happens I haven't

213

brought the police with me, but I don't doubt they'd be very interested in the International Scientific Exchange."

Surprisingly, Brown smiled. " Of course they would," he said calmly. " I always told you the whole thing was illegal." He picked up his beer, and his hand was quite steady now. " But I assumed you were a person who could be trusted."

" You assumed that I was a bloody fool."

" I really don't see what you mean, Marriott."

" Are you sticking to it that the International Scientific Exchange exists ? "

" Presumably. Unless the man who told me about it was lying."

" Well, I'll suggest something else—that he wanted to get hold of this information for—for a foreign power."

" But of course. For all foreign powers. Surely that was what we were talking about ? You said . . ."

" I know. It's all beautifully international, isn't it ? Grossman of Harvard is a member."

" I told you I didn't know any of the members."

" Anyhow, the idea is that the stuff goes everywhere, eh ? America, Russia, France, China, everywhere ? "

" So I understand."

Marriott shook his head. " I don't see what you gain by this," he said, frowning. " If I was going to turn nasty I could put the police on you for what you've said already. I don't care who you work for. They're all just human beings to me. Why should I care which lot pay you ? Why not put your cards on the table ? "

" Pay me ? " said Brown indignantly. " What d'you mean ? Nobody pays me. I tell you it's nothing to do with me." His voice took on a note of injury. " You're being rather unreasonable, aren't you ? You tell me that you desperately want some stuff published. I tell you about something I happen to have heard about. And the next thing is that you bring me here and talk about putting the police on to me and ask who's paying me and God knows what. I wish I'd never mentioned the whole thing."

"But all the same, you'd take the stuff if I'd hand it over to you?"

Brown hesitated. "I'm not at all sure that I would after the way you've talked."

"You would," said Marriott bitterly. "You'd find you would. Just because you feel so strongly about science and humanity and—and so on." He suddenly felt oddly limp and tired.

He said, "Look—you think I'm a fool. Maybe I am. But I'm not the sort of fool you think. I know exactly what I'm doing and all this is just a waste of time. I want to be put in touch with—with whoever you work for. That's all. I'm not making any promises. I haven't made my mind up yet, and it's most improbable that I—that I should give anybody anything. But I'm willing to meet them and—and see what I think." It was essential to remember that it was nothing to do with Brown at all—that Brown was quite irrevelant. It was easier to do that if one kept one's eyes shut.

Brown said gently, "Well, of course the only person I could put you in touch with would be the man who told me about the Exchange."

The obscene attitude. Fastened there, sucking with the infected mouth. The price one paid. But one could pay it.

Marriott said, "All right. I dare say he'll do." He opened his eyes and with an effort smiled at the yellow face that goggled at him across the cask. "I know you've got to be careful," he said. "After all, you don't know me very well. I can quite see that."

Brown said, "It's a thing where we've all got to be careful. I told you from the start . . ."

"But you needn't think," said Marriott suddenly, "that it's anything to do with you—that you've been clever or—or charming or . . . You wouldn't have taken in a child of three, and what I'd really like to do is to kick your backside."

The monstrous obscenity of it rose up and blurred his eyes and filled his throat. " You dirty skunk," he said hoarsely. " If anybody could have stopped me doing it, it's you. Putting dirt on everything. . . ." His voice cracked and he turned aside with a sudden retching cough.

Brown was staring thoughtfully at his glass. After a moment he said curtly, " Well—d'you want to meet—this man ? "

Marriott shut his eyes. " I've already told you I do," he said with dreary obstinacy. One would not be sick really. One never was. It was all a part of the price one paid ; and when one's eyes were shut, there was no Brown, no cheap pub, and no cheap whisky, but just a huge multitude stretching out of sight. They were vaguely Asiatic. He didn't knows what race they belonged to, and didn't care. But he knew that they were people, and that they needed help, and that they had never patronised him or tried to bribe him.

XII

Lucy said, "We'll just pop down the alley and straighten you up."

"You say that every morning, as though you'd just thought of it," said Ivor. He grinned down at her. "New every morning is the love . . ." As they went into the alley he sniffed and said, "It's just the same as in a garden. The rain brings out all the smells."

"Prop yourself up against that wall, darling, being *very* careful to Commit No Nuisance." Lucy fumbled in her bag for a comb.

"Use mine," said Ivor. "Breast pocket."

As she was combing his hair he said, "I wish I'd learnt to write with my toes. They offered to teach me and I wouldn't let them. There are times when it's a nuisance not to be able to write."

"What d'you want to be able to write?"

"A letter. To you."

She stopped combing and said, "To me? What about?"

"This and that."

"Why not just say it?"

Ivor smiled. "I can't do that. It wouldn't come right."

"Is it a nice letter? I mean the sort of letter I should like to get?"

"Mixed. You wouldn't like some of it but I think . . ." He suddenly frowned. "I don't know."

Lucy said, "There," and put the comb back in his pocket and stood waiting, but Ivor still leaned against the wall. He said, "There's no hurry. We're early. I don't think that you've ever really understood our relationship, you know."

217

" Is that what you'd like to write me a letter about ? "

" Partly." He opened his lips and said, " Cigarette."

" Have you got time ? "

" Yes." He waited while she lit the cigarette and put it between his lips. " Thank you. You see, your trouble has always been that you think I'm either too sorry for myself or not sorry enough—depending on how I'm feeling. You think the right amount to be sorry for me is the amount you are. Natural, but quite wrong." He smiled and said, " You can look at your watch if you want to. It'll tell you that you'll be five minutes late getting to the lab., which will be a tragedy. And then again you're wrong about my feelings towards you. You think I'm grateful for all you've done for me, but that I don't love you. Both wrong, as it happens. I'm not grateful and I do love you."

Lucy said, " You're making me out a bit dumb, darling."

" All that sort of thing," said Ivor. " Perfectly easy to set out on paper, but difficult to explain clearly in words. Anyhow, kiss me. No. Not like that. Properly, with your arms round my neck."

After a moment Lucy said, " Look—I think this is probably committing a nuisance, you know . . ." and took her arms away. He was leaning against the wall with his eyes shut. He said, " Thank you," in a low voice. Lucy stood looking at him with a slight frown. She was holding the burning cigarette that she had taken from his mouth. He opened his eyes and looked at her in silence for a moment. Then he pulled himself upright and started towards the mouth of the alley.

Lucy said, " Want your cigarette ? "

" No," he said wearily. " Chuck it away."

" Going in now ? "

" Why not ? It's time, isn't it ? " He lifted his head and looked at the big square building. " My God," he said with sudden bitterness, " when they do spoil things for you, they spoil them good and proper. It's not fair, not being able

218

to write you that letter. It's a thing they've no right to stop anybody from doing."

Lucy said, " You must just have a shot at saying it some time. I can probably sort it out."

He gave a sudden laugh and said, " All right. I will say it. All you hear you have, and the rest you'll have to guess. You'll get it pretty wrong, but what the hell does it matter ? "

They were near the entrance now. Ivor said, " By the way—no need to fetch me to-night. Somebody's coming my way."

" Sure ? "

" Yes. Just come straight home. I'll be there before you." He turned and looked at her for a moment. His face was twitching and there was that queer look of fear and entreaty in his eyes. She had seen that look so often as they stood there in front of the big building. She said gently, " It's all right, darling. It'll be all right once you're inside."

" That's right," he said slowly. " It'll be all right once I'm inside."

* * * * *

It was striking five o'clock when Jumbo took Peach up in the rope lift. Shole had just arrived and was hanging up his raincoat. Mr. Prince said, " Ah, here you are, Mr.— Mr.—— Let's see—you don't know Dr. Shole, do you ? "

Peach said, " Yes. It's Dr. Shole I d-*do* know." He shook hands with Shole.

" Well, if you *know* one another," said Mr. Prince in surprise, " that's fine. It makes it easier. At least, it doesn't make it any harder ; which is something."

He sat down, wriggled himself deeply into his tub-chair, grunting gently as he did so, and said, " Cigarettes in that box. Or if there aren't I'll skin that girl of mine." He closed his eyes and sat for a moment as though in prayer. Shole took out his pipe and blew through it very gently, as though not to disturb him.

After a few moments Mr. Prince opened his watery blue eyes and stared at Peach. His face looked even more cyanosed than usual in the hard, bluish, artificial light.

" Well, now," he said, " I don't know how far you're concerned in this, Mr.—Mr.——"

" Peach."

" That's right. Mr. Peach. I don't know who *is* concerned. I wish I did. But I was told to keep you in touch, and here I am, keeping you in touch." He turned to Shole. " Dr. Shole's a different thing. He *is* concerned." Mr. Prince paused and turned his head sharply from one to the other and back again for several moments, like a man watching a tennis match.

" Now, as you both know, some time back we were told to keep an eye on the Haughton Laboratory. It was one of these ' no trouble ' jobs. We weren't to *do* anything, of course. We were just to see that nothing leaked from a place which wasn't under proper security control, which was part of another building, which might be open all hours of the day and night—and so on. Just one of those little jobs that make us go away and shoot ourselves." Mr. Prince sighed. " Anyhow, we did our best. And with Dr. Shole's kind help I think we got the inside part of it into some sort of shape. But of course we've never had any control over the tongues of the people who worked there, and as Mr. Peach knows, that's given us all a lot of anxiety."

Mr. Prince had stopped watching his tennis match and was staring dreamily at the ceiling. " Now, one of the first things we did, of course, was to have a little check up on those people who worked in the place, just to make sure they were all right, you know. Well—they *were* all right. In fact, there was nothing there at all—except one small point."

Without moving his head, Mr. Prince lowered his eyes to Shole. " You've got a girl in your department named Byrne."

" Yes. Lucy Byrne."

" That's right. Well, Lucy Byrne's got a boy friend named Gates. Rather rum sort of boy friend, because he's got no arms. Lost both his arms in the war. She lives with him. You may know about it, Dr. Shole ? "

Shole shook his head. " No. I thought there was probably somebody, but . . ."

" Yes. Well—no reason why you should know or why you shouldn't. No reason why she shouldn't live with him if she wants to. There's nothing against Gates personally, except that he's an Irishman and he can't help that. But it *did* come up—and I don't mind telling you it came up more or less by chance—that Gates has got one or two friends that— that are friends of ours, if you follow me. I don't know how well he knows them. Quite probably not well at all. May be just casual acquaintances. But, anyhow, Gates was certainly on some sort of terms with a fellow named Evans— sometimes he's Evans and sometimes he's Brown, and I think his name's really Parsons. But he's most often Evans, so we call him Evans. Well, now, we don't care for Evans."

Shole said, " Does *Lucy* know him ? "

" I don't know. Maybe yes or maybe no. Anyhow, that was the starting point." Mr. Prince shook his head at the ceiling and sighed. " Now look what happens," he said sorrowfully. " You've got a man named Marriott. He knows Byrne."

" They work together."

" Yes. Well, Byrne takes Marriott to a pub and they meet Gates, and then who should come in but Evans. Now, let's be fair. That may just be chance. Easily."

Shole was sitting right forward in his chair with his head slightly on one side like an anxious Alsatian's. " I think it quite probably was, you know," he said. " After all, there's nothing odd in . . ."

" Nothing odd at all," said Mr. Prince, waving it away. " But *now* what happens ? Just after this Marriott goes along again and meets Gates, and again Evans shows up. And this time they go to Evans' house—or the house he uses."

" Marriott and Lucy as well ? "

" No. That's where it gets a bit involved. *She* isn't there —because she's spending the evening with . . ." He cocked a watery eye at Peach. " With your father-in-law."

Peach's hand went to his Imperial. He said, " Oh ! " rather blankly.

" Now, let's be fair," said Mr. Prince. " Let's *still* be fair. There's no reason that I know why your father-in-law shouldn't take one of his staff to dinner, even if she is pretty. There's no reason why this should have anything to do with her boy friend meeting Marriott and Evans. But, as you know, he's been a bit naughty over this whole business and —well, there you are."

" You've no reason to s-suppose that he's m-met Evans ? "

" I don't know. You never know anything on these jobs. There may be nothing to any of it. In fact I thought there probably *wasn't* anything to it till this morning. But now I get this. . . ." He picked up a piece of paper from his desk. " This is from a different angle altogether—right outside the Haughton job. It just tells me that some of the people we're interested in are expecting some information— *scientific* information—within twenty-four hours. Now, let's be fair. I always like to be fair. This may not have anything to do with the Haughton job. But it *has* got something to do with Evans." He turned to Shole and said anxiously, " You're a scientist, Dr. Shole, and I wouldn't like to go jumping to conclusions in front of you and have you laughing at me. But here it is—we don't like Evans. Evans reckons he's going to get some scientific information. He's recently been in direct touch with two members of the staff of the Haughton and maybe directly or indirectly with Mr. Peach's father-in-law." He shook his head. " Well, you see, my instructions are that there isn't to be any trouble. . . . This Marriott. What sort of fellow's he ? "

Shole hesitated. " Well, he's rather young and—immature for his age. But I should have said he was as straight as a line."

" Honest, eh ? "

" Absolutely."

Mr. Prince shook his head. " I don't like the sound of that," he said gloomily. " I don't mind a slippery one, but these honest chaps turn you grey. How well's he know Sewell ? "

" Well—he's one of his young men."

" They get on together, eh ? "

" Moderately. He irritates the Professor rather. He's an irritating boy in some ways. But the Professor's had him since he was a student and I think he's fond of him."

" And he works with the girl ? "

" Yes." Shole hesitated. " I think . . . I think he may be—rather smitten."

" That's right," said Mr. Prince. He looked at the ceiling for a moment and then sighed. " Well, I think we must start asking some questions. I don't *like* asking questions, but I don't see what else we can do. Start with the girl, eh ? "

Peach said tentatively, " It's nothing to do with me, but from what you've told us isn't *Marriott* the—the point ? "

" I don't know," said Mr. Prince. " That's the devil of these jobs. You never know anything." He turned to Shole. " Byrne'll be at the lab ? "

The man with the blue face said, " Now, Miss Byrne, if you'd sit there . . ." and put her in the chair immediately facing the desk. Lucy smiled nervously at Shole in the corner, and he smiled back and nodded reassuringly.

Mr. Prince said, " All right. Going to ask you some questions and I know you'll give us all the help you can. How old are you, Miss Byrne ? "

" Twenty-four."

" How long have you been at the Haughton ? "

" Just over three years."

" Went there straight from the University ? "

" Yes."

" And all the time you've been there you've been working on—on this stuff with Dr. Shole ? "

" Yes."

" Who d'you work with chiefly ? "

Lucy hesitated and glanced at Shole. " Well—I work under Dr. Shole, and chiefly with a man named Marriott."

" That's right." Mr. Prince nodded and glanced at his fingernails.

" You've got a friend named Mr. Gates ? "

" Yes."

" You see a—a lot—— ? "

" I live with him."

" *That's* right. How long have you known him ? "

" Since . . . I think it was 1943. We were engaged and then . . ."

" Yes. I see. How long have you lived with him ? "

" Since I—got a job. About three years."

" Sure." Mr. Prince blinked at her for a moment. " Look," he said hopefully, " do you know a man named Evans ? "

Lucy hesitated. " Yes. The doorkeeper at the Haughton?"

" No. 'Nother one ? Friend of Mr. Gates ? "

She frowned and shook her head. " Evans ? No. Is he somebody at the Centre ? "

" No. All right. Forget it. Know a man named Brown ? "

" Bill Brown ? Yes."

" Friend of Mr. Gates ? "

" Yes."

" You know him ? "

" I've met him. I don't know him well."

" How long have you known him ? "

" I'm not really sure when I met him first. I think about

224

a year ago. Then I saw him again about three weeks ago in a pub. Those are the only times I've met him."

" He's never been to your house ? "

" Not when I was there."

" When you weren't ? "

" Yes. I think once. When I went out and somebody had to come in and sit with Ivor."

" Anyhow, Mr. Gates knows him well ? "

" I wouldn't say *very* well. He knows him better than I do. But he hasn't seen him very often."

" You're sure of that ? "

" Yes. You see—I have to be with Ivor practically all the time when he's not at the Centre."

" Yes," said Mr. Prince thoughtfully. " Yes. I see." He studied his nails. " You work chiefly with Marriott ? "

" Yes."

" Has he ever met Mr. Gates ? "

" Yes. Two or three times."

" Has he ever met Evans ? I mean Brown ? "

" Yes. He has met Brown. In the pub when I did."

" Any other time ? "

" Not as far as I know."

" Can you answer me this . . . is there any time that you can think of, apart from the pub, when Marriott and Gates and Brown could have met ? "

There was a moment's pause. Then Lucy said slowly, " I don't know of any time when they *did*. But I can think of one when they might have. About a week ago . . ." She turned to Shole. " It was the night I went out to dinner with Professor Sewell. Bob dined with Ivor to keep him company. They might have seen Brown."

" But you weren't told they had ? "

" No." She smiled slightly. " I wasn't told anything about it."

" Why ? " said Mr. Prince quickly.

" Well . . . I didn't want Bob to go in the first place."

" Why ? "

There was a long silence. " I don't really know," said Lucy slowly. " It was a—a purely personal thing. I just didn't think they were—very good for each other." She hesitated. " It's a bit difficult to explain. . . ." She looked up suddenly. " Can I ask a question ? Did—did something funny happen when Bob went to dinner ? "

" Why should it ? " said Mr. Prince gently.

" No particular reason."

" But what makes you think it might have ? "

" I don't know," said Lucy helplessly. " I just wondered. It's the only time I haven't been with Ivor for . . ."

Mr. Prince was looking at her with the mild, watery blue eyes. " Well, look," he said. " They went to see Brown that night. Does that mean anything to you ? "

" No. Except that I don't like him."

Mr. Prince said, " We'll come back to that later. Just before we do—you went out to dinner that night with Professor Sewell ? "

" Yes."

" Why ? "

" Well—because he asked me."

" Has he ever done that before ? "

" No."

" Did he want anything in particular or was it just—just social ? Did he want to talk about—work or anything ? "

" I don't think so. As far as I remember he didn't talk about work all the evening."

" I see. Has he ever met Gates ? "

" No."

" Or Brown ? "

" Not as far as I know."

" All right. Now about this evening. How was it fixed up ? You went out with the Professor and Marriott went to Gates. Which was fixed first ? "

" My going out with Professor Sewell. I told Ivor I was

going and asked him if he'd like somebody in, and he said
Bob Marriott."

" And you say you were against that ? "

" Yes. Ivor wanted me to ask Bob and I wouldn't, so he
asked him himself."

" And you were never told they saw Brown ? "

" Bob never told me he'd been at all. He may still think
I don't know. Ivor told me Bob had been but he never
said anything about Brown."

" So far as you were concerned, Miss Byrne, there was
no connection at all between your going out with the
Professor and Marriott going to see Gates and meeting
Brown ? "

Lucy shook her head. " No . . . except that I was out
and so Ivor was—was by himself."

Mr. Prince sat back in his chair and looked from Shole to
Peach and back again. " That's right," he said. " That's
quite right." He turned back to Lucy and said gently,
" Miss Byrne—I'm going to have to ask you some questions
about Mr. Gates. I've got to ask these things. Do your
best for me."

Her lips said " Yes " soundlessly. Then, as Prince was
beginning, she said, " Before you do—can you just tell me
—what it's all about ? What you want to know ? "

There was a moment's silence. Shole said, " Can I—— ? "

Mr. Prince hesitated and then nodded curtly. " O.K.,
doctor. Go ahead."

Shole said, " There's some question of a—a security leak,
Lucy."

" On the work ? "

" Yes."

" I see," she said very quietly. " All right."

" Well, now you know that," said Mr. Prince, " you'll
see what I want to ask you. First of all—is there anything
that you've done or said that—that could lead to a leak ? "

" No." Instinctively. And then, " I don't think so."

" Have you talked to Gates about it ? "

" He knew the sort of work we were doing. He knew that before there was any question of—of its being secret. But I've never told him any details. He wasn't interested."

" He's never asked you about it ? "

" No. It's—it's not the sort of thing he would ask."

" Have you ever heard him ask Marriott about it ? "

She had picked the pub cat up, and it had clung on to her skirt with its claws. Bob's face had been flushed and his voice loud. We mustn't talk about it in pubs. She raised the calm brown eyes to Mr. Prince's face.

" No. I don't think so."

" Just be sure about that," said Mr. Prince unexpectedly. She thought for a proper length of time and shook her head. " No."

" Is there anything you know about Gates—anything in —in his attitude or his politics or what have you—that might lead you to think he'd be interested to—to get this information ? What are his politics, anyhow ? "

" I don't think he's got any." She frowned slightly. Mr. Prince was waiting. " You see," she said, " Ivor's not—not like an ordinary person. He hardly sees anybody except me and the people at the Centre. I don't think he could have a —a thing like this without my knowing. . . ." Her voice faded away.

Shole had been scribbling on a piece of paper. He passed it to Mr. Prince, who read it and nodded.

Shole leant forward and said, " Lucy—I think there's a thing here that you may have got wrong. This leak hasn't *happened* yet. At least—we don't think so. But it may be going to and what we're trying to do is to stop it."

She was sitting up very straight now. She said, " It *hasn't* happened ? " in a queer, strained voice.

" Probably not. And if we know where to look we can probably stop it altogether, with—with no bones broken. Now—can you help us ? "

She sat and stared at Shole. Her eyes were slowly filling with tears. She bit at her lip and shook her head silently.

Mr. Prince said, " You've no idea *why* Gates took Marriott to see Brown ? "

She shook her head again and then lowered it quickly. The only defence now. No. No. I don't know.

Shole said quickly, " She doesn't know. I'm sure she . . ."

" That's right," said Mr. Prince. He got up and just brushed Lucy's shoulder with his hand in passing. " That's all right, Miss Byrne. Don't worry. You've done fine."

Lucy blinked quickly and looked up. Her face was pale but quite calm again.

" Now, look," said Mr. Prince, standing looking down at her. " We shall have to go out and see Gates. Must, you see. You'd better stay here. . . ."

Lucy said calmly, " No. If you're going to see Ivor I'd better come."

" Why ? "

" Well—he may be frightened and—and so on. I'd better really. You see, I—I'm used to handling him."

Mr. Prince pursed his lips. " May not be very pleasant for you."

Peach said, " Less unpleasant, perhaps, than s-staying here."

Lucy turned and looked at Peach as though she was noticing him for the first time. She said, " Yes," and smiled at him gratefully.

" All right," said Mr. Prince. " As you like. Then suppose you come through here and sit down and talk to Miss Berry until we're ready to go."

There was a telephone in Miss Berry's office. And this time he wouldn't smile patronisingly. But they never left her alone for a moment.

*   *   *   *   *

The young soldier fumbled with the key. His hands were large and red, with ginger hair on their backs.

Ivor said, " It goes in upside down. That's it."

The door swung open. The soldier grunted and started to try clumsily to get the key out again.

" No—turn it back straight and it'll come out. Thank you very much. Now, if you could slip it back in my top waistcoat pocket . . ."

The boy was shy about putting it back in his pocket. People were always shy about that.

Ivor said, " Thank you very much indeed. Very kind of you."

" That's all right," said the soldier gruffly. " You O.K. now ? "

" Yes, thanks. I can manage now." Ivor smiled. " I'm sorry I can't offer you a drink but . . ."

" I don't want any drink," said the boy almost angrily. He nodded and said, " Well, so long," and turning abruptly, went clattering off down the stairs.

As the front door banged behind him Ivor suddenly realised that he was the last one, and went to the window. The soldier was just crossing the street, walking with a plodding slouch, as though his boots were too heavy for him. He stopped on the other pavement, as though not sure where to go, and then went slouching away towards Victoria. It wouldn't have mattered if he had gone the other way. There would have been a pub and a girl there too.

Ivor went back to the door and closed it with a gentle kick. The room was cold and though it was only just after five the light was going. He went across to the gas fire and pushed the tap on with his foot. Then, balancing carefully, he put the toe of his shoe on one side of the self-lighter tap and let it go sharply. It missed the first time but the second time it snapped properly, and the fire lit with a pop. He stood and looked at it until the radiants began to glow, and then went and sat down in his straight-backed fireside chair. His reading-table was beside the chair with a book open on it, and he looked to see if it was open at anything appropriate. But it was only Pepys, open at one of his duller days, with a lot of going to the office and talking to Sir W. Batten, and it was too much effort to arrange everything so that he could turn over. He wished dully that he had a drink, and there was some whisky somewhere. But for that matter there was golf and painting and duck shooting and women and steeplechasing and piano playing, if you could reach out your hand and take them. That had always been the most difficult part—to realise that though the things were there, they weren't yours any more. However close they were, they weren't yours.

He sat for a while just looking at the fire and then shook his head sharply and heaved himself out of his chair and went over to the window. That was all right. There was the chimney, but it had three-ply across it with the gas fire let into it. The door was bad. There was a space of half an inch between the bottom of it and the floor. But there was nothing to be done, except to ruckle up the carpet against it with his foot as best he could. He went back to his chair and sat down and closed his eyes and said, " Dear Lucy. Not ' *My* dear Lucy ' or ' Lucy Dear ' or ' Darling ' or ' Bitch.' Dear Lucy. I said I would try to say this sometime. They say sounds go on, and maybe you'll catch some of this hanging about the place. If not, it doesn't matter. You'll draw your own conclusions and they'll be wrong as usual, but why shouldn't you have it your own way ? " He stopped for a moment with puckered brow. " First I want to thank you for having looked after me. I always say thank you to people who open doors for me and buy me tickets and so on, though, really, they ought to say thank you to me for giving them a chance to be such grand chaps without its costing anything. I only ever met one chap who said he couldn't buy me a ticket because he was in a hurry. I could have kissed him and I hope his soul will burn in hell for it.

Anyhow, you've always bought my ticket, and I hope you've made a profit out of it. But at least you've been the right sort that just goes away when it's done something for you and doesn't stay to be worshipped. Thank you. You can go now. I hope you'll be happy, though I don't think you will because you're not the happy sort and now you won't have me as an excuse."

He stopped and sat for a long time with his eyes shut, breathing heavily.

" You'll see what happened about your pink and white boy unless you're being even denser than usual. I can't think what you were doing to put him in my mouth—unless you *wanted* him scuppered. If not, you're just mad. My only regret is that you couldn't have found somebody more worth while. He can't ever have been more than a hand up your skirt, and though in your position that may have been important, I wish he'd been a tougher proposition. I'm good, and it was a waste to use it on him. Incidentally, I gave him every chance. If he'd been a bit brighter I should have had to tip the police off about him *au moment critique*. But I haven't because I can't believe it's necessary. He *must* give himself away. In a way it'll be better fun if he doesn't. Because sooner or later he'll tell you, because he's the sort that always tells people, and that'll teach you to go whoring. At least it'll teach you to go whoring with a proper man and not with . . ." He was breathing very quickly now. He stopped and stretched himself with a slight groan, his eyes still closed. After a while he smiled slightly and said, " Your bloody England with its bloody sanctimoniousness and all its people with arms and no heads. Don't you know an Irishman when you see one ? "

" It wasn't possible and it wasn't decent, and if you'd cared about the truth you would have known it. You did know it, anyhow. If you want pets keep a dog and slobber over him. He's a dog anyhow and he can cock his own leg up against a lamp-post and tell you to go to hell. But you took this on and couldn't go through with it. I'm not blaming you for not going through with it but for taking it on. You bloody little fool with a lot of phrases in your head. There'll be nothing to boast about now. You'll have to face things and stop acting, now there's no dolly."

He said, " No dolly " again. " No dolly." The tears oozed out from his closed eyes and ran down his cheeks. He shook his head sharply, and bending down, rubbed his face on the arm of the chair.

" You'd better get on and get married," he said hoarsely. " You want it, you bitch, and I could tell him. . . . I always knew. Before I came back. You ought to have looked at me and said you couldn't buy me a ticket because you were in a hurry. But you hadn't got the nerve."

He suddenly opened his eyes and cowered down in his chair and started to whimper. He said, " It's bloody unfair. I can't write to you. I wanted to write to you and I can't. They oughtn't to stop that. You think I'm grateful and I'm not. I scuppered your boy. Why haven't you come back early ? You're never here when you're wanted."

The fire was glowing almost white hot. He could feel the heat of it on his legs. He shut his eyes again and put out his feet to the warmth. He said, " You thought I was grateful and that I didn't love you. Both wrong as usual. I suppose I ought to have licked your hand. But if you don't know now you never will so what's the use ? "

When he had sat for about five minutes he opened his eyes and smiled across the room and said, " Dictated, but not signed, by Mr. Gates." He heaved himself up out of the chair and pushed the gas tap so that the fire went out. After a moment, he pushed the tap on again, but the radiants were still hot and the gas caught again with a bang. He cursed vaguely and put it out again and turned slowly away. His eye fell on the book, and he stood for a moment straining his eyes to read it in the failing light. He couldn't remember what a Theorbo was, though he had known at one time. It had a neck, so presumably it was some sort of lute.

The radiants weren't glowing now. He went back to the fire and pushed the tap over and stood for a moment listening to the gas hissing. Then he pushed the leather hassock into position with his foot, close to the fire, and went down on one knee and edged himself round so that he could lie with his head on it. The leather was warm from the fire, but the hassock was rather low for comfort. As his cheek touched it he remembered that the Theorbo was the big bass lute.

He had meant to make a last statement, but nothing came to his mind but " Thank you, darling," because that was connected with lying down and being put to bed. So he said, " Thank you, darling," and glanced up with the smile with an edge on it. The room looked very strange from that angle, but soon he got tired of looking at it and closed his eyes, and knew, as he had known every night for years now, the tremendous relief of not seeing.

XIII

EVERYBODY went home promptly at six nowadays. There had been a time when people stayed on till eight and nine at night to finish things. But that was in the days when there was something worth while to do. Just before six Marriott went round and carefully said good night to anybody he could find. There was no sign of Sewell, and Shole and Lucy had both gone early.

When he had said good night he slipped into the lavatories and stayed there until just after six, and when he came out the place was silent and deserted. He went into the main office and stood there for a moment in the dark, hesitating about switching on a light. But it only faced on to the light well, and nobody could see into it, so he put the light on and sat down on one of the typists' desks and looked at the green steel cabinet. It suddenly occurred to him that Mary might have taken the key home with her, and he got off the desk in a panic of undefined excitement to look. But it was there all right. He didn't take it out, but went and sat on the desk again and looked at the steel cabinet, standing there smooth and dark green in the yellow light.

Ever since he had left Ivor's flat and seen Root in the bus he had been promising himself that at sometime he would think properly. But somehow there had never been a chance to think ; and now, when it was quiet and he was alone, he could hear and see with unusual and almost startling clarity, but he could not think. He could hear the roar of traffic in the distance, and he distinctly heard, amongst it, the sound of a bus accelerating. The cabinet was a nice colour but there was something unpleasant about its shape. It was too tall for its breadth. Tall and narrow-shouldered like a grandfather clock. Tall and narrow-shouldered like Ivor.

He grasped at that and tried to start from Ivor. But somehow Ivor got him nowhere. It wasn't anything to do with Ivor any more than it was anything to do with Brown or Brewer. One didn't do things like that because somebody else thought it was right, even if somebody else was a man with no arms. He tried conjuring up the vision of Ivor with his eyes closed and the tears oozing out from under his shut lids. But though that had always worked before it didn't work now, and it only reminded him of the blind man who had been playing the violin. Pathetic, but not touching. Ivor cried very easily and he suddenly hated Ivor. The feeling startled him and he would have pursued it further, but his eye fell on his watch, and he realised that there was no time for it. He closed his eyes and put his hands over them and made a terrific effort to formulate the question. He tried saying words under his breath. " Human beings." " Responsibility for human beings." There was just a flicker of something there and he tried again. " The scientific responsibility for human beings." If you wanted a smear of your own blood the only way was to take the lancet and jab below your nail, not once but a dozen times, till your finger was sore. " Knowing exactly what I am doing, to assume the scientific responsibility for human beings. . . ." But they were just words, without meaning, and he found himself turning them round and muttering, " human responsibility for scientific beings." A sudden fear came over him—that he never would be able to think, and that he would be carried on, as the tube train had carried him, into some almost mechanical, uncalculated action— that the action might even have happened. But he opened his eyes, and the green cabinet was standing there still locked, and the silence was still questioning but uncommitted.

* * * * *

A Sort of Traitors

Mr. Prince's car was big and very old, with a glass division between the front and back seats, of the type used as a taxi at country stations. He drove himself, with Peach sitting beside him, and Shole and Lucy and Iverson in the back. Iverson was a small thin man in a shiny blue serge suit and a hard collar. He had a faint cockney accent and a face the colour of old brick. He was very polite and tried hard to sit on one of the occasional seats. When Shole insisted that he should sit on the back seat he perched on the extreme edge of it so as to take up as little room as possible.

Mr. Prince drove with great care and concentration, as though he had only just learned, grunting a good deal and muttering under his breath at the traffic.

As they crossed Kingsway, Peach said, " I think this l-lets me out, doesn't it ? "

Mr. Prince said, " No, you don't, guv'nor," very firmly as a taxi tried to edge out in front of him and added, " How d'you mean, lets you out ? You weren't ever in."

" I mean about my father-in-law. There's nothing to s-suggest that he knows Evans or—or anything about it."

" He wrote that letter," said Mr. Prince doubtfully.

" What letter ? "

" To Sir What's-his-name Pelly. That was naughty."

" But that was a l-long time ago. And, anyhow, it's nothing to do with this."

Mr. Prince said, " It's no good standing there looking like that, madam. You'll have to wait till the lights go." He changed down with a loud grunt. " I should think you're all right," he said. " I shouldn't think he'd do anything. He's too old."

" If what she says is true, going out with him that night was a pure coincidence."

" Well, a *coincidence*, anyhow. Mr. Prince smiled slightly and shook a good deal. " She's telling the truth," he added. " Except every now and again, and then she sends you a post-card about it. Nice girl. Think she'd have chosen a chap who could put his arm round her, wouldn't you? I'd rather drive anywhere than in Oxford Street."

At Oxford Circus Peach said, "What'll you do when you get hold of G-Gates?"

"Just talk to him," said Mr. Prince briefly.

Peach hesitated. "It's nothing to do with m-me, but I should have thought the obvious key to the whole thing was this m-man Marriott. Or else Evans. Gates may have been the go-between but if there is a leak, surely M-Marriott——?"

"Marriott?" said Mr. Prince. He hauled laboriously out of the line of traffic, flapping a hand violently out of the window. "Yes. He might quite well be in it."

"*She* thinks so, anyhow."

"You think she does? Well, she's telling the truth. Most of the time. Yes. I think we shall have to see about Marriott."

"I thought you'd go straight for him."

"We could have done that. Never mind, we can't be everywhere at once. Perhaps we shall get something out of Gates."

They smelt the gas as soon as they opened the front door. Nobody said anything, but Lucy went racing up the stairs, and Mr. Prince was close behind her. She tore the key out of her bag but Mr. Prince seized it and pushed her roughly aside and said, "Keep out," as he plunged into the flat. She tried to follow but Shole grabbed her arm, and then Mr. Prince came out at a sort of shambling run with Ivor in his arms and said breathlessly to Iverson, "Open the window, Pete. It's pretty thick in there." Then he put Ivor down on the floor gently and started to examine him, his thick hands moving very quickly.

Lucy said, "I always knew that would happen." Shole had jumped forward. He said, "Get him over on his face." Lucy said again, "I always knew that would happen. He could turn it on with his foot." She dropped down on her knees beside Ivor's head. Shole and Mr. Prince were turning him on to his face. Peach and Iverson had disappeared, and nobody was listening to what she said. " I've thought of it half a dozen times but what was the good ? There were other things he could do if he wanted to." Shole was kneeling astride Ivor's back, and now he would press and release and press and release and it was worth going on for a long time. She knelt there watching Shole and breathing deeply in time with his movements. He looked up and caught her eyes, but his own were intent and unseeing. It was necessary to say something, so she said, " I always knew that would happen. He could turn it on with his foot." This time Mr. Prince heard. He said, " With his foot, eh ? " Lucy said, " Yes," and started to cry. It was an immense relief to cry. Mr. Prince said gently, " Look, you can't do anything. You go down with Pete and sit in the car. We'll look after him." She said, " No, thank you. I'd rather stay here," politely.

Mr. Prince hesitated and then said, " Tell me when you want a spell, Doc. Tiring job."

Shole said, " It's all right." There was sweat on his forehead.

Lucy fumbled in her bag and found her handkerchief. She wiped the tears off her cheeks and then held it to her mouth. She was still kneeling by Ivor's head. She put her hand under it so that his cheek was on her hand instead of on the floor, and knelt there watching Shole pressing and releasing. It suddenly occurred to her that if you went on doing that the person might begin to breathe again. She said, " He is dead, isn't he ? " almost anxiously. Shole shook his head, which might have meant that he was or wasn't or that Shole wasn't certain. But she knew that Ivor was dead because it wasn't conceivable that he should be brought to life again now.

Ivor's cheek was on her hand. She could feel the hard

projecting bone pressed into her palm. But he was dead, and nothing they could do would pump life back into him. He had done his part of it and gone. She accepted that, as she had accepted him alive, patiently, without hate, almost without comment. But the living had claims and the dead had none, and when Shole said, " Get some brandy, Peach," she slipped her handkerchief under the cheekbone, and got up quickly and said, " I'll go. I know where," and went racing downstairs.

The telephone was in the entrance hall, and they were three flights up, but she dared not risk it. You could always hear people talking in the hall. She ran along the street to the bar. There were only a few people in it. She was quite calm, and remembered that she mustn't go back without the brandy. Phil grinned and nodded when she asked if she could use the telephone, and she went into the little side room while he got the brandy. It was only then that she realised that she didn't know Marriott's number, or even the address of his rooms. It was a hundred to one against his being at the Haughton still, and when she heard the buzz-buzz of the ringing tone, she could almost hear the loudness of the bell in that empty darkness and silence. But there was no other chance.

* * * * *

It was nearly seven o'clock when Sewell stopped. He had been writing almost without a break for eight hours—writing, and throwing it away, and rewriting, and altering and starting again. He stopped now, not because he was satisfied, but because it was getting so dark that he couldn't see ; and because he was tired and empty, and knew now that he never could be satisfied. He sat back in his chair, and when he did so the paper on his desk was just a grey glimmer in the dusk. He could hardly see that there was writing on it, let alone read it. There was nothing to prevent him from getting up and switching on the light, and then he would be able to read the writing. But he knew that would make no real difference. The argument was there, cut to show a dozen different facets, and polished till it shone, bright and unanswerable. But however much he polished it, there was always the opposite argument that had been with him all day, unspoken and unwritten ; and he realised, dully and wearily, that that was unanswerable too. He looked at the sheets of paper with sudden disgust. They were just skill—just point-making and phrase-making ; good debating, designed to show what a clever fellow he was. And there was no need for skill or cleverness. It was all quite simple. One either believed that men were creatures of good-will, and came towards them with hands outstretched ; or else one didn't believe it and kept a loaded gun in one's hand. When all the pretty phrases were left out, it boiled down to this, " I believe in man. I believe in him so strongly that I'm going to cock a snook at you and trust him. And as I've nothing to lose, it's a safe bet—for me." And yet despair was a useless thing and a pretty phrase wasn't untrue just because it was pretty.

Sewell gathered up the sheets of paper. There were a lot of them—the letter to Gatling, the letters to go to those who would receive the paper, and the third thing—the manifesto which was to go somewhere, he didn't know where, as the final, public, considered self-justification. He sat for a moment with it all in his hand and there was the waste-paper basket which was the proper and comfortable end of failure. But it was getting dark and he was cold, and if he tore it all up and forgot it there was no next move— nothing to warm or brighten, or even to lift him from his chair.

He pushed the sheets into the drawer of his desk unsorted, locked it, and put the key in his pocket. The essential was action. In sixty-four years, his only regrets were things he had not done ; never things that he had. He reflected with artificial briskness that the next item was a thorough revision of the paper. There might be two opinions on the ethics of publishing it, but there must be no room for two on its facts or its claims.

The door of his office had been locked all day. He unlocked it now and came out with his key-ring still in his hand. He had never seen the paper since Shole's last revise. It had been locked away there, and he had been content to let it be locked away.

It was dark in the corridor and very silent. Sewell suddenly realised that he was walking very silently and that his heart was beating quickly as he went through his own laboratory to fetch and revise his own work. That was what it did for you. A man could be a thief of his own effort, and steal from his own safe with his own key, in the darkness and silence. Every man his own burglar.

He switched on the corridor light, and noticed with surprise that it was only just on seven o'clock. The place had seemed so dead and silent that he had thought of it as midnight. In normal times, he thought bitterly, there would have been somebody working still. But not now.

He was inside the general office and feeling for the switch when the telephone rang. The sudden urgent sound in the darkness startled him, and even when he had found the light and switched it on he stood for a moment looking at the telephone almost in fear. Then, with a little grunt of self-derision, he picked up the receiver and said irritably, " Haughton Laboratory. Sewell speaking." After a moment he said, " Hullo, Lucy. No. He's gone. Everybody's gone but me. No. Sorry. No idea." He was impatient, and eager to ring off, but she was saying something else and he caught enough of it to make him pause. He said, " *What?* I didn't get that. Try and go a bit slower, my dear. . . ."

She spoke quietly, but her voice was breathless as though she had been running. Sewell did not interrupt her again. When she paused he said quietly, " Look—can you hold the line for twenty seconds ? . . . All right then—don't bother. You just go back to them and leave it to me. I don't suppose for a moment there's anything to worry about but I'll get hold of Bob and just make sure."

He still had the key ring in his hand, and almost before the telephone was in place he was unlocking the door of the safe. For a moment he thought it was all right. The other copy was there. But Shole's last revise in the blue cover was not with it, and though he stood stupidly turning over papers for some moments he knew instinctively that it was gone, and began to swear viciously and childishly because he was startled and shaken.

* * * * *

Mr. Prince suddenly looked at his watch and said, " My word, the time's getting *on*," in a surprised voice as though he had been expecting it to be going back. He put the watch back in his pocket and said, " Well, Miss Byrne, I'm afraid we shall have to have another talk later on. But there's just one question I'd like to put to you again. You say he seemed a bit odd this morning but you've no idea *why* ? "

Lucy said, " No."

" There'd been no dispute with you or anything like that ? "

" No."

" What I'm trying to get at is the motive, you see."

" He had plenty of motives," said Lucy. " Every day. It—it wasn't any fun for him."

" Quite. I see that. But there's usually something, you know, that—that tips a man over." Mr. Prince thought for a moment. " You don't reckon that it was anything to do with this business of Brown and Marriott ? "

She lifted the calm dark eyes. " What business ? " she said.

" I see," said Mr. Prince irrelevantly. " You used to go out with Marriott, didn't you ? "

" We had lunch together occasionally or—or a drink. And I went out in the evening with him once."

" Did—*he* know about that ? "

" Ivor ? Oh, yes."

" Didn't mind ? "

" No. He was always saying I didn't go out enough and trying to make me go more."

" But you didn't like *him* spending an evening with Marriott ? Why was that, Miss Byrne ? "

The one slip. It came back every time. " It was just that Ivor was very easily upset by—by people. There were very few people I really liked leaving him with."

" Anyhow, to you Marriott was just a friend ? . . ."

She said carefully, " He was just a man I work with."

Mr. Prince nodded in silence. After a moment he got up. " Well, now, you don't want to stay here by yourself. You'd better let my people take you back and look after you, and then we'll have another talk." As Lucy rose he said, " And he's still just a man you work with ? "

" Marriott ? "

" Yes. You don't feel any differently about him after— what's happened ? "

Ivor's face had been on the floor. She had put her hand under his cheek. Her eyes were filling with tears, but she said stonily, " I don't quite understand ? . . ."

" You don't feel that he's responsible in any way for— what's happened to Gates ? "

I know he is. Right way up and upside down. I am. Thou art. He is. But if you said things they always came back later. She said, " I don't see how—— ? "

" That's right," said Mr. Prince. He just touched her shoulder with his hand and said, " Well, now, you go along and they'll look after you."

When the other car had driven off Mr. Prince climbed laboriously into his driving seat, grunting loudly. He said, " Get in, gentlemen."

Peach got in beside him and Shole and Iverson waved one

another courteously into the back. They were both rather over-polite and had a lot of difficulty over doorways.

Peach said, " Where now ? "

Mr. Prince turned and looked at him abstractedly for a moment and then came to life with a startled grunt and took out a small diary. He thumbed through it for a moment and then said, " 49 Etheridge Street, Pimlico," rather doubtfully.

Peach said, " But that's where we are n-now."

" Well, I thought that was what you were asking," said Mr. Prince irritably. " Anyhow, it's a lousy place. Let's go somewhere else." He thumbed some more and then grunted and put the diary away and started the engine. " D'you know the way to Denmark Hill ? "

" I'm not absolutely sure of it."

" That's all right," said Mr. Prince reassuringly. " I do. Leave it to me. Pity that chap hadn't got any arms."

" Why ? "

" Because if he had had he would have left a letter for her. Didn't you hear her say he wanted to write to her ? Suicides always want to write to people. Now he's gone and she won't talk, so we have to guess. That's the trouble about this job. You never know anything."

" You think G-Gates knew you were on his track and killed himself because of that ? "

" Maybe. But if that was it we're out of luck."

" Why ? "

" Because if he knows they probably all know."

" Evans and Marriott ? "

" Or whoever." Mr. Prince frowned. " The girl's in *something*," he said irritably. " But we don't know what. May not be this at all. That's the snag with people. They've always got something to hide. You're after opium running and people won't talk because their Uncle Joe was a deserter from the army in 1916. Maybe she went to bed with a man named Parkinson and feels bad about it."

" Why Parkinson ? "

" Why not ? It's a good name." The lights went to amber just as the car was passing them. Mr. Prince braked hard and stopped exactly in the fairway of the cross traffic. " It's all right," he called out of the window. " Plenty of room to drive round me, isn't there ? "

Peach said, " What are we going to do at Denmark Hill ? "

" Oh, that ? Well, I'm told that Evans and some of his friends are out there expecting some information. So if we go out there and see who brings it we might get somewhere. That is, if anybody does, which they probably won't."

" That's why you haven't tackled Marriott ? "

" That's right. Don't care about Marriott. It's Evans I want. Don't like Evans." Mr. Prince let in the clutch with a shattering jerk and said, " Damn the thing. Sorry, all. It's all right as far as it goes. Girl takes Marriott to Gates query on purpose. Gates takes him to Evans query on purpose. Evans fixes it. Gates knocks himself off query motive. Knows we're on to him, remorse, or having no arms, or *x*. I don't really mind which so long as nobody's tipped Evans off. I don't care for Evans."

Peach said, " I don't think the g-girl knows about it."

" That's right," said Mr. Prince. " Nor do I. Pretty girl. I never believe pretty girls know about anything. It's no good tormenting yourself."

In Denmark Hill Mr. Prince drove about a good deal in side roads, peering anxiously at the curbs. After a while he said doubtfully, " I should think this would do," and slowed up and then changed his mind and grunted, and drove on again.

Peach said, " You don't know which house it is ? "

" House ? Oh, yes. I know *that*. I'm looking for somewhere to park the car."

The road was quite empty and about thirty feet wide. Peach said, " I should have thought anywhere here was all r-right."

" Maybe," said Mr. Prince gloomily. " But the police are very hot round here. *Very* hot. We don't want any trouble. Ah—now *this* looks all right." The road was now much narrower, but there was another car parked in it already. Mr. Prince pulled in behind it with a sigh of relief. He got out and said resentfully, " Now we shall have to walk."

There was somebody in the driver's seat of the other car and Iverson went and spoke to him. But Mr. Prince waddled straight away up the road. Iverson ran after him and said something and Mr. Prince grunted and turned round and started to waddle in the opposite direction with equal decision.

The houses were all big nineteenth-century places standing back from the road with drives leading in to them. Mr. Prince said to Iverson, " Let me get this straight. It's Brinslow House and Prospect Lodge. Now *we're* going to Prospect Lodge ? "

Iverson said, " No. We're *going* to Brinslow House."

" Brinslow House ? " said Mr. Prince. " Good job I asked you or I should have gone to the other." He paused for a moment, struck by a good idea. " I tell you what," he said. " You know the way. You just take us there."

Brinslow House was at the end of a long drive of chestnut trees. It appeared to be a private hotel, and through one of the big bay windows in front one could see a lighted room with a lot of small tables set for dinner. Iverson paused and said, " Want to go in ? "

" Have they got a licence ? " said Mr. Prince doubtfully.

" No. But we could get a cup of coffee, I expect."

Mr. Prince shook his head. " I don't think we've got time for coffee," he said. " If they'd got a licence we might have fitted it in. We'd better go straight down." He looked round and said peevishly, " Hell of a lot of us, aren't there ? Which side of us is it anyhow ? "

Iverson pointed to the left. " Over there."

" All right," said Mr. Prince, as though he would have preferred it to be the other side. " Let's go along."

Iverson said apologetically, " I think we'd better keep fairly quiet now. We're only about thirty yards from it at the edge of the garden."

" That's right." Mr. Prince turned to Peach and Shole, and said politely, " If you gentlemen could manage to keep fairly quiet it would help us."

Peach said, " We're going to get where we can see the— the other p-place ? "

" That's right," said Mr. Prince. " Brinslow House. No. Prospect Lodge. Anyhow, we want to keep fairly quiet." As they started he said to Iverson, " How are you going to see anything at thirty yards in this ? "

" *I* don't know," said Iverson in an undertone. " You suggested it."

" Well, they'll have to open the door, won't they ? " said Mr. Prince irritably. " There's no point in *making* difficulties."

There was a beech hedge about six feet high and through it some lights were showing. Iverson whispered to Mr. Prince, " There's a nice row of peas coming up here. Don't tread on them." Mr. Prince whispered to Peach, " Don't tread on the peas. Pass it back." Peach said to Shole, " They want us to av-void the peas."

When they had moved up to the hedge the front door of the next house was very close. Iverson whispered, " I think this is the best we can do." Mr. Prince gave a loud grunt, and suddenly and surprisingly began to sink to the ground, like a horse lying down. From a sitting position he beckoned to Peach. Peach bent down and Mr. Prince hissed in his ear, " It's too damp to sit down. Very damp. Dew."

" Do you want to get up again ? "

Mr. Prince shook his head. " No," he whispered. " God knows how long we shall be here."

A man appeared out of the darkness farther down the hedge and said in a low voice, " Three of them so far. Gelderose and Steiner and another. Didn't get him."

" Evans," said Mr. Prince hopefully.

" No. Not Evans. Tall and bald."

" No Evans ? "

" No, sir."

Mr. Prince said, " Damn it. I was afraid of that," and sighed. After a moment he said, " Still, it's nice to have Gelderose. I wonder they need Gelderose on a thing like this."

He drew up his knees and bent his head forward as though to rest it on them. His head came nowhere near his knees but he seemed quite comfortable and appeared to sleep.

XIV

SEWELL said, " Well, thank you very much. I'm sorry to have bothered you. If he does turn up soon, will you ask him to ring me ? It's rather urgent."

The thin, very ladylike woman who let rooms to single gentlemen said, " You wish him to ring you at your private residence ? "

Sewell hesitated. " No. At the laboratory. He knows the number."

When the door had closed he went and sat in the waiting cab for a moment in silence. The only chance now was to ring round to other members of the staff on the off-chance that Marriott might be with one of them. For a moment he thought of going to the door again and asking the woman if he might use her telephone. But most of them lived in lodgings, and without the staff address list he had no idea of their numbers. He leaned forward and said, " I think we'd better go back to the Haughton Laboratory."

There were only seven names on the list, apart from his own and Marriott's own and Lucy's, and from four of them there was no reply. Levers was in and knew nothing ; and nor did Drake. That left Parkin, and he knew that there was no real chance that Marriott would be with Parkin. But he had to ring Parkin for completeness, and because he couldn't, for the moment, think of anything else to do. He dialled the number and heard the bell at the other end begin to ring. But he never knew whether Parkin was in or out because at that moment he heard the sound—slight, but quite different from the distant noise of the traffic—that sent him quickly across to the light switch to plunge his room in darkness. Sewell opened his door very quietly. The corridor light was out but there was a glow in the cross passage. He went silently towards it, but before he reached the general office Marriott heard something, and when Sewell came in he was standing there with the despatch case in his hand close to the door.

Sewell said, " What the devil are you up to, Bob ? " and Marriott said, " I came back for something."

He held up the despatch case and when Sewell took it out of his hand and opened it he did not resist. There was nothing in it but a few sheets of pencil notes. Marriott picked the case up and tried to smile and said, " Why, sir ? What's up ? " But Sewell was unlocking the safe. He saw the blue cover and turned and said, " What have you been doing with this ? It wasn't here a minute ago."

There was a moment's pause and then Marriott said, " I took it home. I wanted to go through it."

" In your digs ? "

" Yes."

Sewell said, " You haven't been in your digs all the evening. I've just been there. Come on. Out with it."

Marriott stood for a moment in silence. His lips were trembling. Then he drew himself up and said defiantly, " All right then. Perhaps you'd better know that I have recently been approached. . . ." His face crumpled up suddenly and he began to cry in loud choking sobs, standing there quite stiff and straight with the despatch case in his hand.

* * * * *

The moon had risen and was shining brilliantly, so that the gravel outside Prospect Lodge was a glimmering silver in the darkness. There were still chinks of light at the same windows, but no other sign of life. Peach was very cold and he had turned up his coat collar and kept his hands in his pockets. Nobody had spoken for a long time. Every now and again Iverson melted silently into the darkness and recrystallised again equally silently a few minutes later. Mr. Prince was still sitting as though he thought he was resting his head on his knees, breathing like a man asleep.

Shole whispered, " What's the time ? "

Peach took his hand out of his pocket and showed him his watch. The illuminated hands stood at nine o'clock. They had been waiting just over an hour and a half. Shole spoke and Peach moved very quietly, but it seemed to wake Mr. Prince. He sat upright very slowly, looked at his own watch, and grunted softly two or three times. Tipping back his head till it looked as though his neck was broken, he stared straight up at the stars for some moments. Then he grunted again and made a wide gathering movement with his arms. As they all bent over him as though about to form a scrum he said, " Who brought the brandy ? " There was a moment's pause. Shole whispered foolishly, " Well, *I* haven't. I wish I had. It's damned cold."

Mr. Prince slowly shook his head. " No. The brandy for him. What's-his-name. Gates. Who went and got it ? "

They straightened up for a moment and looked at each other. Then Shole said, " Lucy did. I remember seeing her come upstairs with it."

Iverson said, " Mr. Peach and I were inside. I didn't know where you got it."

Mr. Prince looked up at the stars again for a moment and heaved a deep sigh. Then he suddenly scrambled to his feet with surprising agility and said, " Well, come on, gentlemen, it's no good staying here getting pneumonia," and started back towards the house. As they went he said over his shoulder, " Mind the peas. Mind the bloody peas. I shouldn't like anything to happen to them." Nothing else was said until they were close to Brinslow House and then Mr. Prince said to Iverson, " Go and get the bloody car if the bloody police haven't taken the bloody thing." As Iverson vanished into the darkness he sat down heavily on a stone mushroom and looked up at the stars again and said very bitterly, " The little bitch. I ought to be in a home. We all ought to be in homes."

As they were getting into the car Peach said, " You're just going to leave them there ? "

Mr. Prince said, " Leave who where ? "

" G-Gelderose and these other people ? "

" Why not ? They're not doing any harm. Probably playing solo. For matches."

" I thought you might be g-going to arrest them."

" Arrest them ? " said Mr. Prince, startled. " You can't go round just arresting people. It's an interference with the liberty of the subject. They could sue you and get a packet."

Peach considered. " Of course I suppose if Evans isn't there there's nothing to p-prove that they're anything to do with it."

Mr. Prince started the engine. " I wouldn't be surprised," he said, " if they'd thought of that, and if that's why Evans *isn't* there." He let the clutch in with a spine-breaking jerk and said, " Damn. Sorry, all."

Passing through Camberwell, Mr. Prince suddenly said, " There's no reason why we shouldn't smoke or talk or sing songs *now* if you like. They won't hear anything."

" What happens if any one does turn up now we're gone ? "

" That's all right, sir. Anyhow, they won't." He shifted slightly and said, " The seat of my trousers is wet. That ground was too damp to sit on really. Dew."

" Are you going to pick up Evans ? I should have thought you'd got enough on him ? . . ."

Mr. Prince shook his head. " Maybe," he said. " But where does it get us ? They'd only get somebody better. Besides, Evans is very valuable. You've only got to keep an eye on him and you get on to quite a lot. I don't see how we'd manage without Evans sometimes." He rumbled slowly and carefully past a traffic signal that was at red.

" I reckon," he said thoughtfully, " that we shall have to
wait till there's a war to fix up Evans. It's different during a
war. You can get something done about a chap like that
then—something that *stays* done. I wouldn't care for Evans
to be bound over or put under the probation officer."

At the Elephant Peach said, " Are we going back to the
office ? "

Mr. Prince said, " No. Jumbo goes home at seven. Don't
want to walk all up those stairs. Don't ever do it. They
kill you."

" Then where——? "

" We'd better go and have a look at the laboratory. After
all, that's what we were told to keep an eye on. Somebody
might have stolen it."

* * * * *

Marriott was quite calm again now. He sat and stared
defiantly at the corner of the room, and his voice was rather
loud, with a trace of West Country burr in it, as it usually
had when he was being emphatic. He looked sulky, rather
injured, and about seventeen. There were times when
Sewell had had a wild desire to slap or shake that sulky
expression off his face. But they were not times like this.
He smiled and said warningly, " Well, don't shout it around
the town, old chap."

Marriott took no notice. He said again, " I never believed
it for a moment. It was childish. Anybody'd know where
stuff of that kind came from, whether it was signed or not."

Sewell said, " What you *haven't* told me is how Brown
came to know there was any such information about. How
did you ever get on the subject ? " He didn't ask because he
wanted an answer. It was there before him in the big,
rather loose-lipped mouth. Anybody could have guessed
what had happened, even if they hadn't known Marriott
since he was eighteen. But there must be time to think.
He said gently, " You say you met him in a pub, Bob ? "

" Yes." Marriott hesitated and then said, " He was with
—some people I knew and they told him I was a scientist."

" And then you ran into him again ? . . ."

" Yes. In the same pub."

". . . and then he spun you this yarn ? "

" Yes."

" Why didn't you report it then ? I mean, why did you
meet him again after that ? "

Marriott defied the corner again. " I—I wanted to be
sure of my ground."

It was clear enough, but somehow he must be made to
say it. Sewell said, " I don't quite see what you mean by
that. Whether his yarn was true or not he was preparing
something illegal, wasn't he ? "

Marriott swung round and faced him. " Yes," he said
breathlessly. " He was. But if it had been true about the—
the Exchange . . ." He stopped and gulped.

" Well ? "

Marriott's eyes went drearily away to the corner again.
He said nothing.

" You mean," said Sewell gently, " that if his yarn had
been true you would have felt differently about it ? "

Marriott's voice was barely audible. " You said it was
wrong. You kept saying it. That it wasn't right for work
like that not to be published. But you didn't do anything
about it." His voice began to rise. " It wasn't my job. I
was only a junior. It ought to have been Shole or—or . . ."

" Or me ? "

Marriott said, " Nobody'll take any—any responsibility.
Everybody's afraid. People like Shole . . . They work and
then they let it be taken away and used to kill people and
don't—don't say a word. They even go and work for people
like Brewer. They sell out for—for five pounds a week. . . ."

Sewell said, " There's one thing I want to get clear. You
say you started to go and then changed your mind and
brought it back. Why did you change your mind ? "

" I don't know," said Marriott wearily.

" Try and think."

Marriott pushed his glasses more firmly on his nose. He was frowning effortfully. " Partly because I was afraid, I suppose. But that wasn't it altogether. . . ." He paused and shook his head. " I never had made my mind up," he said restlessly. " That was the trouble from the start. I couldn't see any logical reason why I shouldn't do it. I didn't want to, but I thought that was probably just emotional thinking. Not liking Brown and its all being rather messy. In a pub and so on."

" And you thought of that somewhere on the way ? "

" I didn't think at all," said Marriott contemptuously. " It was just emotional. I saw something. You know how it is. Nobody's reasonable, really." He had gone very pink. He took his glasses off and began to wipe them with great care.

" What did you see ? "

Marriott hesitated. " Well, the bus stopped facing the Houses of Parliament. There was a bobby with his hand up. He grinned at the driver of my bus. . . ." He turned aside restlessly. " It was nothing whatever to do with it really," he said angrily. " I'd never wanted to go, but I couldn't think of any good reason not to, so I suppose I made one up. That's what it comes to. If I'd been logical I should have gone."

Sewell smiled and said, " You're talking like a dud statistician."

Marriott flushed. " What d'you mean ? " he said indignantly.

" When you get an answer that makes plain nonsense you check your figures over and if you can't see an actual slip in them you say the answer must be right because you can't see where it's wrong."

" Well, so it is if the figures are right."

" Of course. But you don't know that they are. All you

know is that you can't *see* what's wrong with them for a moment. You can only feel it."

" Feel . . . ! " said Marriott contemptuously.

" Well, even feeling is a fact, isn't it ? It's evidence of something. Hell, Bob, if you're going to leave feelings out you'd better go and play with the physicists. Well, now— about these people. You don't know who any of them are except Brown ? "

" No."

" But you were going to meet them to-night ? "

" Yes. If I'd gone."

" Where ? "

Marriott hesitated. " I can't tell you that."

" Why not ? "

" I had to promise not to put the police on them or else they—Brown wouldn't talk at all."

Sewell had a sudden vision of Marriott solemnly wetting a finger, drying it and drawing it across his throat. " You won't sneak on me ? Honest Injun, I won't." It was all like that. And if you were found out, you might get six from the headmaster. But you weren't expelled. They only expelled you for serious things.

His eyes went from Marriott's white face to his own hand lying on the desk. It was a long, fine hand, old but experienced and firm. Sewell suddenly realised that he was immensely happy. He smiled and said, " Now listen, Bob. You're in a considerable mess. From what Lucy said the police may turn up at any moment. They may or may not believe your story, but they'll certainly want to know what you were doing making this appointment with Brown. And you'd better not tell *them* about any promises."

Marriott was looking startled. He said, " But I haven't done anything."

" Maybe not, you fathead. But you've gone damn near to committing treason and they may think that's quite a lot."

Marriott said in a low voice, " I'm not ashamed of anything I've done. In fact I'm not at all sure . . ."

Six from the headmaster. That was the size of it. And you took it bravely and that was the end.

Sewell said, " Never mind about that. What matters is what you're going to say to the police." He put the firm hands palm downwards on the top of the desk and stared steadily into Marriott's face. " Now listen carefully. You met Brown. You saw through him at once. You met him again because you wanted to confirm your suspicions. You only got the address out of him this evening. You then came and reported the matter to me. See ? There was never any doubt that you intended to report it. None of your philosophical doubts or promises to Brown, mind you."

Marriott hesitated. Then his lips framed " Yes."

" Now then," said Sewell rapidly. " What did I do ? Of course I wanted to report it at once. To the police." He closed his eyes and frowned. " What police ? No good just going out and finding a bobby on point duty. Shole's security boys. Don't know where they live. But Shole does. So of course I rang up Shole. Well, I've already rung up Shole and left a message for him to ring me, so that's fair." He smiled happily. " Now the next thing is to take a note of your story. Paper."

He unlocked and opened the top drawer of his desk and stopped short. He sat and looked into the drawer for a moment and then carefully pushed the papers in it aside and took out an address book. " Now then," he said briskly. " Whose number is it ? Oh, yes. Shole's."

*　　*　　*　　*　　*

The car stopped just before the turning to Haughton Street, and Iverson got out and disappeared. After a few moments he came back, muttered a few words to Mr. Prince, and got in again. Mr. Prince grunted and dislocated every-

body's spine again, this time without apology. He said to
Peach, " Well, they're both inside still."

" Who ? "

" Marriott and your pa-in-law. Been out, severally, and
came back. Lucky thing. Saves us having to drive all
round London."

Peach said, " There's nothing in Lucas being here. He
often works very late."

" Been home at six every night for the last fortnight,"
said Mr. Prince briefly. " But why shouldn't he work late
to-night ? Maybe he's got interested in something and hasn't
noticed the time. We all do it."

Peach said, " Look here, you don't s-*still* think he's mixed
up in this ? Because surely—— ? "

" There isn't any surely. That's the trouble about these
jobs. You never know anything."

" Well, I can tell you d-definitely that he won't have had
anything to do with men in pubs or going to Denmark Hill.
He's a very clever man but he's a bit of a s-snob, if you see
what I mean. . . ."

Mr. Prince had stopped the car at the laboratory entrance.
He turned and looked at Peach for a moment in silence.
" You know, there could be something in that," he said
unexpectedly. " Anyhow let's go and see."

* * * * *

Sewell sat at his desk, and the fat, red-faced man with
the watery blue eyes sat opposite him. It was queer to sit
at his desk and be interviewed by a man sitting on a hard
chair. He had tried to make Mr. Prince sit at the desk,
but Mr. Prince was very polite and wouldn't hear of it.
Sewell was a little worried by his own voice. It sounded a
trifle glib and ingratiating and nothing he could do would
roughen the edge of it.

Sewell said, " My own guess is that he probably was
mildly indiscreet in the first place. He's young for his age

and tact was never his strong suit. Anyhow, when this man Brown pitched him this yarn about an International Scientific Exchange he had enough sense to see that there was something wrong, and quite rightly came and reported the whole thing to me."

" Fair enough," said Mr. Prince briefly. " What time was that ? "

" This evening."

" What time this evening, sir ? "

" Don't know exactly. Just as I was going." He waited for the obvious—the unanswerable question. But Mr. Prince merely nodded in silence and he had to ask it himself. " Of course I told him that he ought to have reported it before, but . . ."

" Well, the main thing is that he *did* report it," said Mr. Prince reasonably. " And then you did what, sir ? "

" I wanted to contact you—or whoever was our security contact. I didn't know your number or where you were but I knew Shole did. So I rang up Shole's number and left a message asking him to ring me."

" And you were hanging on here waiting for him to ring ? "

" Yes."

" That's right," said Mr. Prince. " That's clear enough." He reflected for a moment. " You didn't know Gates, did you, Professor ? "

" Gates ? Lucy Byrne's young man ? No, I don't know him. I know of him."

" You've no ideas about why he did it ? "

Childish. " Did what ? " blankly.

Mr. Prince sighed. " That's right," he said. " He's committed suicide. But why should you know why he did it ? *I* don't know and she doesn't know."

" When was that ? "

" This evening."

" You think it had—some connection with this business ? "

" I don't know, Professor. Your guess is as good as mine. You never know anything on these jobs." Mr. Prince sighed. His eyes were very watery and vague. " Well, I suppose there isn't anything else you can tell me, sir, before I have a word with Marriott ? Anything else you can think of that I ought to know ? "

Sewell hesitated. If the man had been keen-eyed and hatchet-faced and sharp-spoken it would have been different. But this bleary acceptance of everything—this refusal to ask the awkward question—this thing that made you sound so smooth—was something unexpected and dangerous. He thought of Marriott's white, sullen, injured face and knew that Marriott could never get away with it. There was only one other way and he had to make up his mind quickly. He made it up and said, " Yes. There is one thing. I hope you won't misunderstand it. . . ."

Mr. Prince said, " I'll try not to, sir."

" This prohibition—this clamping down on our work so that we can't publish it—has been a big blow to us here. . . ."

" Sure."

" And it's left some of the younger people—and some of the older ones if it comes to that—feeling very—very sore and fed up. Young Bob Marriott's as straight as a line. But he believes in internationalism and co-operation and universal brotherhood and all the other things we all believe in when we're young. He'd never do a thing like this— commit treason and so on. But he—his *attitude* about the whole thing is likely to be different from yours or mine." The letter to Gatling, the letters to the people abroad and the manifesto were in the top drawer of the desk, about equidistant between their waistcoats. Sewell said, " I'd like you to bear that in mind when you're talking to him. He's frightened now, of course. He knows he's been a bit of a fool and he'll say whatever he thinks you want him to say. Which of course won't deceive you for a moment and may even make you suspicious. All I ask you is to take my word for it that he neither has done anything nor *would* do anything. . . ."

" That's right," said Mr. Prince slowly. " Thought about it and thought not, eh ? "

" I should think that's about it."

There was a long pause. Mr. Prince was staring at the ceiling. After a while he said, " Dangerous thoughts. The old Jap had got something there. . . ." He shook his head sombrely. " You see, it's all very well, Professor, and I don't say you're not right. But what I've got to think of is if they'd used somebody who stank a bit less than Evans—that's your Brown—anything might have happened."

Sewell said, " No. It wouldn't. I've known Marriott since he was eighteen."

There was another pause. Then Mr. Prince sighed. " All right," he said resignedly. " Anyhow, we were told there wasn't to be any trouble. Let's take it that way. Then there's only one other thing. What time did Miss Byrne ring up ? "

It came suddenly and he had not expected it, but Sewell raised his head and said, " Just after seven o'clock." His voice was working now. He had meant it to be matter-of-fact and it sounded matter-of-fact. He looked down at his hand on the desk, and it was old and firm and experienced, and he knew instinctively that it was not going to fail him.

Mr. Prince grunted. " That's right. She slipped us when we were looking at Gates. Rang here and got you ? "

" Yes."

" And in fact that was really the first you'd heard of it, sir ? "

" Yes." Once started, one must go all the way.

" That's right. And then you went to look for him ? "
Sewell smiled ruefully. " Yes."

" And didn't find him and came back here. And then he came here ? "

" Yes."

" And reported it all to you ? "

" Yes."

Mr. Prince nodded. " You didn't happen to ask him where he'd been this evening, sir ? "

" From what you've said you probably know that better than I do. But I gather he'd been riding about on buses worrying about it all."

" That's right," said Mr. Prince gently. He reflected for a moment. " 'Course at one time he chose the wrong bus if you see my meaning. Still, that could happen to anybody."

There was a long pause. Sewell said, " I've put myself in your hands. And him."

" That's quite true, sir," said Mr. Prince. " And that helps. Anyhow, you've known him since he was eighteen and you don't reckon he's more than a young silly ? "

" He's a damn young fool and no more."

" All right," said Mr. Prince rather vaguely. " It *could* be like that." He suddenly turned his watery eyes on Sewell with deep indignation. " That girl," he said. " Now what can you make of that ? With the other one lying dead there she skips off and does that."

Sewell said, " Well, of course women have no principles. At least no masculine principles."

" You don't reckon they have ? " said Mr. Prince with deep interest.

" No. None at all."

Mr. Prince nodded emphatically. " That's my experience too, Professor. Now with a *man* you know where you are."

*　　*　　*　　*　　*

Marriott was very tired, and as he sat at the desk in Silkin's room waiting for them to send for him he could not keep his eyes open. Every time his head dropped forward and roused him he sat up and told himself that it was ridiculous and dangerous to be so sleepy and tried to concentrate on what they were to be told. But it was no good, and in the end he gave it up and put his head down on his arms and let his eyes close. He could only have dozed for a few moments, because he glanced at his watch when Iverson came for him, and it was still only half-past nine.

He had expected to be questioned alone. But Sewell was there and Shole, as well as the detective and the bald man with the beard. It confused him that there should be so many of them. Sewell smiled and said, " Ah, hullo, Bob, here you are," and the sight of Sewell's smile and the pipe made it better. But just as he was sitting down Iverson brought in Lucy, and he had not known Lucy was there. He hadn't reckoned on Lucy, and for a moment he almost panicked. But Sewell was still smiling and said, "Hullo, Lucy," and he forced himself to look at her and grin, and she smiled back at him quite calmly and as though it was a departmental meeting.

Mr. Prince looked at Sewell and said, " Shall I go ahead then, sir ? "

Sewell nodded, and Mr. Prince grunted and, instead of going ahead, sat and looked for a long time at some notes in front of him as though he wasn't seeing them. Then he said suddenly, " Well, gentlemen—I mean Miss Byrne and gentlemen. I've had a talk to the Professor and what with that and the talk you and I had this afternoon, Miss Byrne, I think I've got the gist of this business." He turned the watery blue eyes on Marriott for a moment. " There's only one or two points I'd like to check with Mr. Marriott. But we don't want to spend a lot of time, so perhaps the quickest way would be for me to read this and any of you tell me where it's wrong or where there's something missing."

He looked down at his notes and started to read rapidly and monotonously, without punctuation. " On the evening of the third March Miss Byrne and Mr. Marriott went to the Leyden Arms public house in Etheridge Street Pimlico with Mr. Gates." He looked up inquiringly. Lucy said, " Yes," quietly. Marriott nodded.

" While they were there a man came in who was introduced to them by Mr. Gates as a Mr. Brown in the course of conversation Mr. Gates mentioned that Mr. Marriott was a scientist."

Marriott said, " I may have mentioned it myself." His voice came out rather loud.

" Thank you, Mr. Marriott. Anyhow, it was mentioned. There was talk about this and that not important and then Miss Byrne, Mr. Marriott and Mr. Gates left." Mr. Prince turned over a page. " March tenth Miss Byrne dined with Professor Sewell, so it was arranged that Mr. Marriott should go in to sit with Mr. Gates it being necessary that somebody should be with him. . . ." Mr. Prince did not look up and Marriott risked a quick glance at Lucy. She was looking at Mr. Prince with an odd, puzzled expression. Mr. Prince read on in his quick, monotonous voice. " Mr. Marriott and Mr. Gates met in the Leyden Arms and whilst there the man Brown again appeared there was some talk and Brown then invited them to his house in Preynor Mews for a meal during the course of which Brown asked Mr. Marriott various questions about his work discovering that Mr. Marriott was involved in work of which publication had been forbidden he spoke of an International Scientific Exchange which would arrange publication if Mr. Marriott liked to put the material in his, Brown's, hands, Mr. Marriott was at once suspicious." Mr. Prince looked up again with raised eyebrows. " You *were* suspicious then, sir ? "

" Yes. I knew it couldn't be true because . . ."

" I know," said Mr. Prince. " The Professor's told me. Mr. Marriott therefore arranged to see Brown again suspecting his *bona fides* and wishing to confirm his suspicions March thirteen they met at the Paternoster Notting Hill Gate Mr. Marriott asked for further details but Brown refused to give them." Again the eyebrows.

Marriott said, " He just stuck to the story he'd told before. About the Exchange. I couldn't pin him down to . . ."

" No," said Mr. Prince. " March fourteenth about six p.m. Brown rang up and suggested that if Mr. Marriott wanted to use the Exchange he should bring the material to Prospect Lodge Leaf Road Denmark Hill the following evening." Mr. Prince paused for a moment and then, without lifting his eyes, added briefly, " Mr. Marriott then reported the matter to his superior, Professor Sewell."

He had been puzzled before but he saw it now—what they were doing to him. His eyes met Lucy's and she had seen it too. He looked at Sewell, but Sewell was squinting at the bowl of his pipe. Mr. Prince was droning on, but he did not hear the words. He looked round at them and they all knew, and he flushed scarlet with the humiliation of it, and maddeningly, felt his eyes blurring with tears. He had been afraid—afraid they might question him, and trip him up and tear it out of him and prove him a liar and worse. But they had been principalities and powers, and there had been some pride left in fighting them. Now a fat, bored-looking man was tearing the last shred of self-respect off him, and they were all looking kindly and tolerantly down their noses, and not seeing his nakedness. For a moment he saw nothing but the bitter unfairness and stupidity of it, and knew that they could do anything to him, but he would not just be excused. Mr. Prince's voice had stopped and he said loudly and huskily, " There's just something that I should like to add to that . . ."

He could feel Sewell's eyes on him in the silence. Mr. Prince said quietly, " Yes, Mr. Marriott ? " as though he had been expecting it.

He said, " I'd like to make my—my attitude clear. I thought it was wrong to stop that paper. I still do. I think they must have been crazy to do it. A thing that might have saved a lot of lives. . . ." It wasn't what he wanted to say

and he began again. " I don't believe in nationalism and—
and preparing for war and . . ." But his voice trailed away
and he gulped and sat there in silence, with trembling lips.
For a moment nobody spoke.

" Don't believe in war ? " said Mr. Prince vaguely. " Who
does ? I've been in two and I got trench feet in one and
bronchitis in the other. If you ask me, nobody believes in
it. There isn't anything in it you *can* believe in." He waited
a moment and then said, " Anyhow, that doesn't alter this,
does it ? " He flicked the papers with his finger.

Marriott looked at the watery eyes. They were bloodshot
and infinitely weary, like a depressed mastiff's. He thought
he could see contempt in them, and for a moment he
hesitated. But he was too tired, and there were too many
guns on the other side, and when he had tried to say it the
words wouldn't come. It was all a mile away from the real
question—the question he had never solved, and was too
tired to solve now. He dropped his eyes and said, " No,"
almost inaudibly.

" In fact that statement's O.K. with you, Mr. Marriott ? "

" Yes." It was O.K. with him. Anything was O.K. with
him.

* * * * *

As they went out through the animal room Phillips came
hopefully to the bars of his cage and put an arm out. Mr.
Prince jumped and said, " Crikey ! That gave me a turn.
Didn't know it was there." He skirted the cage carefully
and said, " You keep some queer things about here,
Professor."

Sewell smiled and said, " Only one of our ancestors. I
wonder sometimes how much better we are than our fathers."

" Well, you keep him in a cage, don't you ? He doesn't
keep *you* in a cage."

" What does that prove, except that I'm stronger than
he is ? "

" Prove ? " said Mr. Prince irritably. " You can prove

black's white if you know the trick. I used to know a man who could prove two equalled one by proper mathematics."

The big old car was waiting at the door. Iverson and Peach were already in it. Mr. Prince stood on the steps for a moment in silence, as though some idea was struggling for expression. After a while he turned and shook his head and said gravely, " It's all very *well*, you know, Professor. . . ."

Sewell said, " I know. I'll talk to him. It's my fault really."

" See, it's all right you having known him since he was eighteen and so on. But there's other people to think about. If we hadn't been told particularly that there wasn't to be any trouble. . . . So I'd talk to him. And the girl. It's no good talking to women. But I'd do that." Mr. Prince closed his eyes and his face wrinkled into an expression of agonised concentration. " See, if people start going away by themselves, and reckoning they can prove two equals one by proper mathematics, and there's nobody to check it through and say it doesn't. . . . Wants a person who understands it, see. So I'd talk to them."

" I will."

" That's right," said Mr. Prince rather dubiously. He waddled heavily down the steps to the car.

Sewell said, " And I'm infinitely obliged to you."

" That's all right, Professor. We were told there wasn't to be any trouble." He climbed into the car and started the engine. " Tell him you'll smack his behind if there's any more of it," he said through the window. " And hers. Not that it's really any good talking to women." He let the clutch in. The car jerked forward and Sewell heard him say, " Damn it. Sorry, all."

Shole and Marriott and Lucy were standing in a group, talking in low voices. They stopped as he came in. The group was familiar enough, but there was something not quite right about it, and he realised with an inward smile that it was because they weren't wearing white coats. Their faces were worried, and he knew that they were stuck on some point, and that only he could come in and solve it for them and get them going again. There was happiness in that, and he knew then that it was the source of happiness. He said, " Well, I think we're well out of that."

Shole gave a little grunt of agreement.

" The question is," said Sewell slowly, " how we ever got into it. Probably it was because I didn't give a clear lead. For which I apologise."

There was Shole, and for him there was no problem. And Lucy, and for her there were plenty, but this wasn't one of them. But Marriott's face was sullen and frozen and lost, and he spoke to Marriott.

" We aren't alone on a desert island. We've got to live with people, and that means that sometimes we've got to accept what they think and act by it even if we don't agree. . . ." He saw the slight flicker of contempt on the frozen face and smiled. " But the snag is—how big's the group we've got to live with ? It ought to be everybody of course. But people haven't been living in big groups very long yet and they haven't got used to the idea that there should be just one very big one. It's irritating of them, but it isn't any good being irritated and trying to make people go faster than they can. We've got to have patience. Because if we don't we shall find ourselves fighting the very people we want to help. . . ."

The face was sulky but it was very young, and that was as it should be and as it had always been. He said, " It's all right, Bob. You don't believe me. I never thought you would. You're twenty-four and you don't see why you shouldn't put it right before you die, and leave it all neat and tidy. There's nothing wrong in thinking that. Just use your brains about it, that's all. . . ." He suddenly smiled. " Short-cuts and starting too quickly. It's the old trouble. And I let you down by not coming along and making you think it all through again. Nobody can do these things alone. . . ."

He had wanted to make Marriott say something—to break that frozen silence. But though he thought he could see the ice melting, no words came and he saw that they couldn't yet. It was nearly ten o'clock and he glanced at Lucy, and noticed for the first time the deathly tiredness in her face. She saw his gaze on her. Her eyes flickered significantly towards Marriott and back and she gave a tiny nod towards him. Sewell understood and said abruptly, " We must think about it some more sometime. But for now, I think the best place for all of us is home."

" I agree," said Shole promptly. " Sooner the better. Lucy's coming back to our place for the night, so we can all go in one cab and drop Bob."

" Cab," said Lucy briskly. " I'll go and forage for one."

As she turned to go Marriott pulled himself upright. He glanced quickly at Sewell and Shole and said vaguely, " No—I'll go, Lucy." They were the first words he had spoken since it had been O.K. with him.

Lucy said, " All right, you go to one end of Haughton Street and I'll go to the other. Then we shall probably get two each."

Sewell looked after them and said, " The King is dead. Long live the King. What extraordinary creatures women are."

Shole said rather stiffly, " I don't think Lucy . . ."

" I meant that as a compliment. They must look after somebody. The good ones, that is. I'm glad she's coming back with you." After a moment he said, " Did that do any good ? What I said to him ? "

Shole hesitated and said, " I think it may have. It's a difficult thing to be altogether convincing about."

Sewell said, " Convincing ? It's the easiest thing in the world to be convincing about—both ways. Come along to my office. I've got something to show you."

The letter to Gatling was still in the drawer. He pitched it across to Shole without looking at it and said, " That's very convincing indeed, isn't it ? "

Shole seemed to read the letter very slowly. When he looked up at last Sewell said, " I nearly showed it to Prince. Should I have done ? "

Shole said, " What for ? His job's difficult enough already." After a while he said, " Are you going to send it ? Because, of course, I'll make one. . . ."

Sewell took the papers and tore them in half and threw them into the waste-paper basket.

Shole said, " Here—half a minute. That won't do." He picked the papers out and lit a match and burned them one by one until they were within an inch of his fingers. Then, holding the ash, he burnt the remaining inch. He dropped the last ashes into the fireplace and frowned and said, " I hope you're—happy about it. I don't think I ever felt as strongly about all this as you or Marriott. But, frankly, I can't really see that anything that's happened alters the— the main problem."

Sewell laughed. " It doesn't alter it for you, because to you it was always the main problem that mattered, with nothing for Fred Shole in it either way. What are you ? Forty-five ? But Marriott's twenty-four and I'm sixty-four ; when you're young you're in a hurry and silly, and when you're old you're in a hurry and selfish. In that letter, every time there's anything about ' the interests of humanity ' you want to read ' the interests of Lucas Sewell.' "

" I don't believe that," said Shole mildly.

" Oh, not entirely. It's all mixed up together, of course. But it isn't really the loss to the human race that hurts us when you come down to it. It's the loss to *us*. The stuff's there when people want it, and one day they will. If they don't use it or misuse it for a few years—well, that's very deplorable. But what hurts is that we shan't live to see it used properly. ' Oh, God, it makes me mad to see what men

271

shall do, and we in our graves.' ' And we in our graves.' That's the rub."

" And don't you still feel that ? "

" Of course I do. But does it matter, if that's all we're fussing about ? After all, it's fair enough. There were a lot of things here for us when we came that had been made by the people before. It's our turn to leave something behind. . . ." He suddenly smiled and said, " I remember old Phillip Lowes. Forty years ago. I was just young Marriott's age. He said, ' Always remember, Sewell, that though Prometheus brought the fire, it is highly improbable that he ever had an opportunity to sit by the hearth and smell the supper cooking. Science matters, but scientists don't. Sometimes scientists forget that ! ' He had a deep voice and a big beard. It was just through there, forty years ago. He was very old then. But of course he was a great man."